·INDUSTRIAL DIVINITY·

·INDUSTRIAL DIVINITY·

REGINA WATTS

Text: Regina Watts
Editing: Michelle Hope
Cover & Typesetting: Nuno Moreira, NMDESIGN

www.hrhdegenetrix.com
www.paintedblindpublishing.com
publicity@paintedblindpublishing.com

PAINTED BLIND PUBLISHING
PO BOX 35 ASHLAND, OR 97520

MITCH: Didn't you stay at a hotel called The Flamingo?

BLANCHE: Flamingo? No!
Tarantula was the name of it!
I stayed at a hotel called The Tarantula Arms!

MITCH [stupidly]: Tarantula?

BLANCHE: Yes, a big spider!
That's where I brought my victims.
[She pours herself another drink]
Yes, I had many intimacies with strangers.

—*Tennessee Williams, A Streetcar Named Desire*

· GERMAINE KRULL ·

1

ONCE UPON A TIME lived a woman who was immortal but not invulnerable. She noticed this gift a few months before her twenty-ninth birthday: The diner where she worked made famous fruit pies, and every morning, she prepped apples. Her boss, a fat control freak who liked to look down her blouse, would drop off the morning's load of fruit, touch her back, then make himself scarce in his office. Her lip curled while she tried not to think about what happened behind the shut door. What a rancid human being!

Human beings were the dominant species of the planet Earth, and the only confirmed one with the capacity for communicable consciousness. Some human beings were good. Many were not. The woman's boss was one of the latter. Because her beloved had not yet been lured into the web of her love, she feared the world had more bad people than good ones, and she hated venturing into it to make a living. Someday the woman wouldn't need the diner. She wouldn't need any job. Her art would carry her. Someday. Maybe. For now, the diner's pay was reasonable, and its location was near her apartment, and apple peeling was a task that stole no creative energy.

A long task, though. The apples were infinite until the second she reduced them to a single-digit number, five or three or four. She never understood that magic trick any more than she understood their starting volume. Where did all this fruit come from? The country where the woman lived, called "the United States of America" but shortened to "America," was a big country—it got its name from the continent it spanned. It seemed impossible there should be so many apples every day just for the diner where the woman worked.

Did all diners across the sprawling city have as many apples? The wider country? All the apples in grocery stores, farmers' markets, bakeries. New ones growing in orchards—rotting there, too. Quick: apples collapsing into themselves, skin oozing putrefied innards across the counters of negligent housewives. Elsewhere, starvation. Famine in other poorer countries—the bloated stomachs of African and Indian children packed together in the street like slices of fruit in the crust of a pie. And how many types of fruit were in the world! The whole world. Starvation everywhere. Such a shame. Don't think about it much. Think about your fellow Americans. People starved in America, too. The patriotic thing to do was to think about America and its Americans rather than about anybody else. The more patriotic thing to think about was American success, the American dream. Not American failure. Optimism: American as apple pie. She was lucky to work in an American diner, a slave to such plentiful apples!

Her paring knife slipped. Boss's fault: one week prior, the peeler with the plastic guard had broken in her hand, and he had yet to provide a replacement. The molecule-severing sensation of the blade was so sharp, so intense, that she did not even react on being drawn from free-flow thought and into the structured matter of space-time. While her delayed nerve jolted with pain, a thick dot of blood— blacker than crimson—bloomed from the wound. Its redness only became apparent when, beneath its own weight, the bead gave way, rolled down her thumb, and streaked across the surface of the apple in perfect invisibility. The woman set the fruit down to study the well of her palm, the pretty pool within. Too bad she didn't bring her camera to work.

By the time the woman found a bandage, she expected her hand to be a gory mess. By rights, it should have been. Imagine her surprise to find her steel grip had prevented the loss of any more blood drops after that first. Quick as she could, she tore the adhesive of the bandage away from its protective lining.

Where exactly was the cut? The frowning woman lifted her thumb nearer her face: the digit was as it had been that morning when she had gotten up, come to work, put on her apron, and pulled her long black hair beneath the matching hairnet. The sting lingered, its voice insistent that injury had occurred. What was there to do? Not wanting to delay further, she picked a likely place, applied the bandage, and returned to the cutting board with its bloody apple.

This one could not be used for pie: her blood had spoiled it. She set it aside for her lunch break and later realized she had forgotten to wash the camouflaged droplet from its surface.

At home, poised on the edge of her bed, the woman removed the bandage to study her thumb with fresh eyes. Not a scratch. Had she dreamt the whole thing? The pain was so vivid at the time, but hours removed, the sting had faded into memory, and memory could not convince her of anything. Memory lied more than fiction. Pain, a streak of red fluid despoiling the skin of an apple: Were these images hers? Perhaps she had seen them in a movie. Perhaps she was mad. Yikes, not that.

Being mad was not good. Being mad meant you couldn't work. Not working meant you couldn't take care of yourself; and if you couldn't take care of yourself, you couldn't be free. Americans were strongly encouraged to believe freedom was the single most important thing—even more important than their own lives, which the country sometimes spent for the sake of others' freedom. Those whose lives had paid for liberty could not enjoy anything, because they had died, and the dead had no rights: not to the pursuit of happiness, not to liberty. Certainly not to life.

And, just like the mad, the dead could not take care of themselves. In Western countries such as America, being mad was like being dead. Afraid in those days of death, therefore also afraid of madness, the woman decided it was better to avoid thinking about the whole thing. Tomorrow's apples needed peeling. Who had time to be mad? Who had time to be dead? There was little enough time to sleep!

2

THE WOMAN LIVED in a big city, and was one of about 8.4 million people living in that city. Because it was expensive to live in a place so important—a big apple that everybody wanted to bite—her apartment was petite. One room: a matchbox with a counter to divide it into kitchen and not-kitchen, not-kitchen being where the woman kept her bed, her books, her television, her clothes.

The apartment had three doors: the hall, the bathroom, and the closet. She ought to have kept her clothes in her closet, but she had not used a closet for clothes since she was a small child discovering a passion for photography. Photographs were to her like dreams perceptible in waking life. During the day, she was just another woman. A cook at a diner. A body filling a social need. At night, she was a goddess. A divine creatrix reproducing in film the visions of her eye: able to take a thought from her head and say, "Look, look at it with me."

Perhaps the woman wanted someone to look with her because she was so lonely in her tiny apartment. She often found a guest to keep her company, but hardly anyone stayed more than a night—and most weren't welcome to. After three decades of life, half of which had been spent dating, a pattern had entrapped her. Work would end; she'd change at home; she would take the subway to a bar or someplace else and meet someone to bring to her apartment. People who came back to her apartment wanted to get laid right away, and she obliged, anticipating the real thrill, the later thrill. After things were finished, she would keep them awake by pulling a fat leather-bound album from beneath her bed.

Page after page, she would show her new friend photographs with the zeal of a small child showing off the proudest toys of her collection. Many things she loved lay in that book. The first good photographs she took, ones of her mother and father. Friends, dogs, cats, horses, increasingly artistically rendered and better framed, pieces amputated by these more audacious framings. Architecture only rarely, and only buildings under construction: she enjoyed the modesty of a facade dressed in the peekaboo steel of scaffolding. The one time a static building could be said to be in motion—that grave fourth-dimensional march visible within a metal veil.

She wanted from photography what it couldn't give: motion. Photographs so often implied only the possibility of change—the history of change. The two-dimensional depiction of the act of change seemed impossible. War photography: now that, the woman admired! A career she wished she'd been disciplined enough to pursue. Protestors standing in front of tanks, prisoners of war about to be shot in the head. That kind of potential energy was the moment of change on display forever. That was what she admired. But instead of a frontline photojournalist, the woman had dropped out of college and was a line cook who took lovers home to show them her hobby.

Some were not interested. There were women who barely looked from their phones or men who fell asleep between pages or nonbinary people who had appointments in the morning and had to hurry home. But there were those who were interested: who would lean in with a greater intimacy than that shown in their anonymous liaison. These would watch as time, page by page, developed the woman's skills with the photographer's lens. "Did you go to school for this," some would ask, while others demanded, "Why are you cooking breakfast for a living? You could be on the cover of *TIME, Vogue, National Geographic*."

The lovers who were interested in her work were sometimes invited back. Not always, but sometimes. Of these lucky guests, a few became the subjects of her photographs. After their coming and going grew regular, she would ask them if she could take their picture, and by then, they would be ecstatic. Many asked, "How should I pose?"

She did not like that question. The verb "to pose" implied a pretense at work. Photography was truth. So, once she had asked if she could take someone's picture, she wouldn't follow up on it for days—weeks. Then, when the subject least suspected, half asleep or looking out her window across the city lights: *click!* Her shutter's victory cry as it stole them away forever.

They would laugh, her lovers—always laugh to be crept up on. Those whom she had chosen were not liable to take offense at her sneak attacks. They would laugh, and she would smile, and once they left her alone in her apartment, she would shut herself in her closet, pull closed the curtain, and develop the image in all the space of an upright casket. No movement was wasted. Every tiniest twitch of muscle was devoted to the progress of the work, to evoking image from chemical mists. Witchcraft.

Perhaps she should not have been surprised when she discovered her gift. Was it not normal by the standards of a witch to have uncanny power? Blessings that to others seemed curses? Was it not normal for the witch to wrestle with her nature?

Of course, that presupposed it was normal to be a witch.

3

THE WOMAN TRIED to go on with her life after cutting herself at work. The day of the strange happening faded into the same memory that consumed the moment, and the week of the event faded, too, and with the dangerous ease of a fractal's inward zoom, the woman found herself two weeks from the strange cut.

She had just finished with her favorite lover: her girlfriend, an art student attending the same school from which the woman had dropped out. Knowing this person had not eaten, the woman volunteered to make food. Nothing elaborate. Toasted sandwiches courtesy a small panini press. Half naked, the sleeves of her robe rolled up to her elbows, the woman waited for the sandwiches to toast, staring into space, until her friend called from the not-kitchen to ask if she had any wine. She turned to get a glass without lifting her arm enough to avoid branding it against the hot metal edge of the press.

Pain surged down the nerves in the left side of her body. The woman jerked her wrist away and observed the immediate development of a cruel pink streak whose deepening to angry burgundy recalled the blood of the mystery cut. After running her new burn beneath the tepid water of the kitchen tap and shaking off her grimace, she finished acquiring the wineglasses, filled them with wine, and presented her friend with a late, simple, but kind substitute for dinner.

"I hope you're happy," she teased while they ate, perched together upon the hamper that served as window bench, couch, chaise longue. "I burned myself while making this—injured in the line of duty. Where's my purple heart?"

"Where'd you hurt yourself? I don't have a medal for you, but I'll kiss it."

The woman lifted her arm, pushing back her sleeve to demonstrate the evident burn whose spectral pain still plagued her. After taking her hand and turning it toward the light, her friend's cupid mouth slanted down at the edges. "I don't see it—where?"

The woman slipped her hand away and bent her arm back, head twisting to investigate. The uninterrupted flesh of her forearm was so pale that it glowed in her apartment's artificial light.

She couldn't understand. The pain had been real. She knew it was real. How did proof of these injuries keep vanishing? The possibility of rapid healing did not occur to her in those first weeks. More likely, she misplaced her own injuries. Misunderstanding where she had been hurt, she was therefore unable to locate her wounds a second time. Such things happened. How many paper cuts were only rediscovered when somebody cut a lemon or tried to salt a dish? She tried salting her arm to see what would happen: by the time she was through, she felt silly. Maybe the burn hadn't been that bad.

But the woman was haunted. Her thoughts were her ghosts, and she wanted less than ever to be alone. Every single night, she hunted for a friend. Human beings, who were by then several decades past the stage of computers in terms of technological development, had created mobile devices called "cell phones," which were far more than ordinary phones. Humankind had then produced later versions called "smartphones," which were far more than ordinary cell phones. These were palm-size computers of glass and metal that permitted one person to communicate with another over a vast distance, and in a wide variety of styles. Many computer programs, called for smartphones "applications" or "apps" in the English language, had been created to help people. Humans then enjoyed convenient smartphone applications permitting them to, say, read the news or talk to friends—better still, to order food or household supplies or books or movies or clothes or animals or many, many other absurd things—without having to leave their domiciles. Mankind once lived in caves and cowered for fear of saber-toothed tigers every night; now impatient people everywhere sat on the edge of aneurism when a pizza delivery driver arrived five minutes later than the app had estimated.

Sex was among the list of things one could acquire through one's smartphone. The woman didn't enjoy this method of meeting people because it made her feel like a robot, but after the burn, she didn't want to feel anything. Feeling inspired thinking, and once her thinking started, well—better not to think. Better to fill time, make love, take photographs. Not think.

There is a problem, though, with anonymous lovers. Anonymous people can be anyone. "Anyone" includes dangerous people as well as pleasant people—bad people, just like good ones. One night, the woman used her cell phone to exchange messages with a man who was charming, who had more than a few commendable physical assets, and whom, on waking from her postgame doze, was discovered in the act of removing money from the purse on her nightstand. Incensed, the woman attempted to wrestle her billfold back and was not prepared for the stranger to snatch up her ceramic bedside lamp. By the time she comprehended his instinct, it was too late.

The first unyielding impact resonated so sharply through her skeleton that the pain settled not in her head but her stomach, where it took the form of vicious nausea. "Please," she said as the second impact fell upon her. Ceramic flew in all directions, the blood spurting in her mouth like a special-effects squib on a movie set as her jaw clamped on her tongue. Then: waking up alone in a bed of wire and broken lightbulb and cold shards, wallet empty in her purse, body aching, mouth still iron with blood. A lesson on anonymous sex. Embrace the alone time. Got it.

4

THE MIRROR TOLD a less comprehensible story than the dust disarraying her bed. When awakening after a surreal event, whether a great accomplishment or deep trauma, one tended to find oneself displaced. After realizing her hands and sheets were covered not just in ceramic debris but a great deal of dried blood, the woman stumbled from her not-kitchen and into her cramped washroom, then squinted as the light flickered on.

The woman looked like she'd been in a building collapse: pieces of the lamp clung in her hair, tangled into a black nest matted by the flow of blood from her broken scalp. Was she still bleeding? No: All of it was dried. Caked in against her scalp, roughly marking the structure of what she assumed was a split trailing from the temple of her forehead and up to the crown of her skull. Panic bloomed as she leaned toward the mirror's glass. Her eye was caught by the glistening maroon of a ceramic chunk, a triangle of ruby in her hair—the woman carefully extricated the piece, held it to her eye, and a few seconds later, identified it as a bone fragment.

Okay. Stay calm. Okay. Did she need to go to the emergency room? Nobody had money for that. City life was impossibly expensive. She worked at the diner so she could live off the scraps and save on food, and although the insurance program through her work was fair, American people with fair insurance were frequently bankrupted by the ER. For a split skull? She couldn't imagine the cost. Yet—

Yet, if her skull were split, would she have regained consciousness? Let alone gotten up, let alone asked herself these questions? Frowning, the woman lowered the bone chip upon the edge of the sink and, like an ape picking lice from her own fur, set about plucking pieces of lamp and bone from the bloody mats of her hair. She set lamp pieces on the left side of the sink—the bone chunks, on the right.

Were they bone chunks? Really? They certainly felt that way, were covered in blood as if they were—the lamp pieces were not near so coated. But when the many shards were out of her hair, she ran the water of her sink and, with a warm washcloth, gingerly wiped at the blood that had dried on her forehead. Layer by layer, she buffed the scarlet stain away without the least discomfort, and when it was gone, she leaned back, astonished to find her face bore not the slightest abrasion. No hint of physical trauma.

The woman's mute reflection, baffled in its own right, was unable to offer an explanation. Her neighbor's toilet flushed, and the sound brought into relief other sounds from the always-noisy city: honking cars, an air-conditioner vent puttering along, the rapid timpani of her heart. Unhealthy beats per minute. Minutes. Time? Almost late for work. Yes, yes: go to work.

Moving in numb haste, the woman showered the blood from her hair, plunging her fingers against her scalp in a futile effort to uncover any injury. Where was the gash, the source of bones and blood? Why wasn't she dead—at least, waking up in the hospital? The water at her feet swirled pink into the drain. Once it disappeared and she stepped out to comb her hair, the only pieces of evidence testifying to her ordeal were the bone fragments and lamp chunks, the sorry state of the bed in her not-kitchen, and the money missing from her wallet.

She was so shocked that it was almost like she forgot to be traumatized by the assault. Dazed (shock, a latent concussion?), the woman pulled up her still-wet hair, dressed, and went to work. She said nothing of what had happened. She ate an apple for lunch and did not explain to her coworkers what had made her quieter than usual, saying only, "I'm thinking about a collage project."

At the end of her shift, she stuck around for a cup of coffee, small in the great fire-engine cushion of the diner's window booth. After thinking it could do no harm, she pulled out her smartphone and sent an instant message to the stranger from the night before.

Hey—if I let you keep the money, will you answer some questions?

She wasn't sure what she expected. Certainly she shouldn't have been surprised or disappointed when the stranger not only failed to respond but blocked her account on receipt of the message. He was frightened, she supposed. She would have been frightened if she were him. Why—she was frightened, herself.

At home, she cleaned her bed and tried to make sense of the facts. What had happened to her? The cut, the burn, the altercation. Three times, she had been injured; three times, she had discernably felt injury occur. Three times, she had found no evidence of suffering upon her person. Was she losing her mind? Maybe she didn't need to check into the ER—maybe she needed the mental hospital. Oh, she wished that guy hadn't blocked her! Not that it would have helped her to talk to him…what was he able to add to the conversation that she didn't already know? What was there even to know?

The issue preoccupied her. America was soon planning to elect a president: this was a big deal because the current one was controversial yet still entitled to try for another term. He had managed to weasel into the highest office in the land by throwing a lot of money at a base of people who were very afraid, and because they were afraid, they needed things to hate. Mostly, this base of individuals hated Black people and other minorities. The woman was a minority, technically, but she was also Asian, which made her a secret majority. It also made her less frightening to the base of red-hatted people in love with their orange president who were more upset by colors like black or brown. Politics was all ugly in those days—all about hate and fearing what was different. The woman hated politics and had made up her mind that she would vote for any candidate who was not the sitting president. Whoever came into the role of consul after Caligula's horse could have murdered a child on the senate floor and looked like a political genius—anything was better than the horse.

Yet even a depressing subject like politics was favorable beneath the pressing issue of her condition. She tried to watch the news. Mass protests in Asian countries: better to think about. More Americans all the time shot dead in the streets by uneducated police officers, these vulgar domestic terrorists: better to think about. A third dead woman found in the city's park in the course of a year: better to think about. The virus that had been spreading, country by country, across the planet since December and was now being propagated on globe-trotting cruise ships filled with American citizens: better to think about. Anything was better to think about. But no matter how she tried, filling her senses with news and film and art and books and pornography and music and food and alcohol and sex, her mind always circled back to the same problem. Was she being injured, or going mad? If she was being injured, where were her injuries going? How was she supposed to prove the truth?

Oh, that answer was obvious enough. That was why she had trouble focusing on anything else. Her hypothesis, the unspeakable theory lurking in her brain, was so easy to test—so dangerously easy that she couldn't stand to answer her own question. What if she was wrong? She would have hurt herself for nothing.

But what if she was right and only found out when she was rushed to the ER in the aftermath of some incident? Subsequently made a science experiment for somebody else? What if her hypothesis was right and the morgue didn't realize? What if she made it to a mortuary? What if she was right and discovered it when she awoke in a casket?

The pressure was too much. The mystery of her vanishing injuries plagued her. Endless testing methods presented themselves all day, every day, from morning until night. These ideas flowed like words from an intrusive voice, a new stream of consciousness that sat in the back of her skull and urged her to settle her mind on the matter. It was a persistent voice. A hijacker, at first indistinct from her own internal monologue. Look at that, the razor sitting like a little pink sex toy in the damp shower: break open the head and run one of the blades over your arms a few times. Or get exotic with it! Take that fork and stick it in the electrical socket over there—or, no! Try the garbage disposal. You could stick your hand in the garbage disposal and hit the switch.

Happens all the time in horror movies.

Curling her hair before she went out: push the iron against your cheek and see what happens after. Putting on makeup before work: slip that pencil in your eye, find out if it grows back. Walking down the steps of her apartment building; hailing a taxi; God forbid, riding the subway. The voice was constant, compulsive, louder than her own and infinitely more creative. Whose thoughts were these? Not hers. They didn't feel like hers, but they were in her head—stowaway thoughts trying to prove a point. A simple point.

But…if she was wrong. If she was wrong, it was not injury she feared. It was her mind. Maybe these delusions were what living in her studio in the big city, in her cold and divided country, had done to her.

And worse than all that—worse by far, infinitely worse, worse beyond any human reckoning—was the possibility that her hypothesis was right. That she was not mad.

That was the most terrifying possibility of all.

5

THE WOMAN STOPPED having guests after the incident with the stranger, and a few of them noticed. Her art student girlfriend, that strange and funny waif who changed hair colors by the term, came over one afternoon to make love and talk about the virus gaining media attention.

"I heard all those bodies showing up in the park are from a serial killer, but nobody's paying attention because they're all prostitutes, and everybody's all worried about that virus." As if to prove nobody cared about sex workers near half as much as the encroaching disease, the student asked in a nervous tone, "Do you think it'll come here?"

"Oh, probably," said the woman without thinking. "Where are those people on the cruise ships going to go? Home. America. Of course it'll come here: it's supposed to be more contagious than the flu, two or three times."

"They say it's six times deadlier, too. What do you think will happen if it comes here?"

"I guess lots of people will die."

"Doesn't that bother you? You don't sound scared."

What was a virus? What was anything? Dreaming all the time, the woman. Completely disconnected from consequence—from any potential for consequence. She had not yet even proven whether she'd lost her mind. The compulsive thoughts were so intense that she couldn't even enjoy her friend's company. "Can I ask you to do me a favor," she began, studying the belt abandoned on the floor.

This solution wasn't a good one. The woman's history of anonymous and pseudo-anonymous sex involved all manner of sadomasochistic additions, so she knew that welts tended to quickly disappear from her flesh in the first place. Her belt whipping at the hands of her friend only confirmed she still felt pain: each lash of leather snapping across her nates, her thighs, her feet, was most certainly real. The impacts happened. That was not in dispute. Also not in dispute was the electric charge of pleasure surging after each stroke. One after another after another, they came, each harder than the last, until the woman buried her face in her pillow and plunged her hand between her legs. Her girlfriend tried to stop.

"No, please—I need it harder, give it to me harder. Bruise me, break my skin."

"You don't want that!"

"Just tonight. Do me a favor, please. I need it."

Sadomasochists said that kind of thing a lot when trying to be sexy with each other: "Yeah, Daddy, whip me, I deserve it, I'm a bad girl." All that. But the woman might have been the first person on earth who psychologically required a beating. She needed to settle her mind. Needed evidence.

Yet the evidence was not enough. Two minutes after the beating ended, she frowned at the mirror's reproduction of her ass. Not a mark. Her girlfriend, thinking nothing of it, lamented, "I went to town on you, but you heal so quickly. Sorry…I'll give you a nice souvenir or two next time."

She could try. This beating had already gone well beyond the point of the woman's endurance, and to take a harder one required practice. In arranging this session, she had hoped to put herself in a situation where her body would at least bruise, yet no blemish interrupted the hill of her rear. No welt lasted on her thighs. Even her feet told no tales of what they had endured once the residual sting faded. To prove what she'd been through, all she had was the feeling of pain: mere memory of feeling pain, at that. Much of wound pain was not in the wound's receipt but in the aftermath. Its exposure to air, its infection, its healing. Without an actual injury of which to speak, corresponding pain lessened. Nothing but the moment of impact, of slicing, of burning, of shattering. The explosion of pain, then great silence. Nothing. Only her, the witness, all subjective observation useless without corroboration.

Imagine her relief when she bumped into the stranger again.

6

SHE RECOGNIZED HIM—headphones in ears, eyes glued to his phone—as soon as she stepped into the subway car. Her heart sped: seeing this man who had beaten and robbed her was like seeing an old friend. Everything about him inspired an unyielding torrent of hate (the way he scowled at his smartphone, how he slumped in the handicapped seat, his absolute lack of spatial awareness while splaying across the aisle), but all the same, her sense of relief surged. She stood out of his field of vision until the doors closed. Only when the subway lurched into motion did the woman sit in the seat nearest his, listing toward him as a natural result of the train's motion. When that failed to capture his attention, she touched his arm.

How quickly his expression changed from dumb dreaming into his phone to unbridled, animal terror! She had barely opened her mouth when, recoiling, he leapt from the seat and jerked open the door to the next subway car.

She couldn't lose him. In the middle of Friday morning commute and tourist traffic, the woman plunged through the adjoining doors, pushed, tripped, apologized her way through scores of angry people. By the third such car, she was close enough to touch the man's coat before the train stopped; he slipped out under the pressure of the bodies shielding him from his pursuer. His foot touched the platform, he tore off at a sprint, and she, gritting her teeth, dashed after him.

Oh, he was quick. Like all criminals used to running from police, security, and figures of authority as far back as parents in the nursery, the stranger was quick. He bounced off pillars, bolted through groups of idling travelers, took stairs two at a time and used the handrail to vault past the top three and onto the concrete streets of the city above while impatient citizens cursed him. The woman, her muscles burning, could not clear the stairs with nearly such speed, and by the time she emerged at street level, he was already on the other side of the nearest crosswalk. City traffic rolled on at the behest of a green light in the same second the woman reached the curb. Desperate, sprinting as fast as her body would permit, she darted into the packed lanes, dodged the angry honking hornet of a great yellow taxi, let a sleek black Bentley sweep in front of her, and, seconds before managing to remount the sidewalk opposite, was blindsided by a red Nissan making a right-hand turn.

The woman felt her pelvis jerk out of alignment, felt her leg come out of joint with her hip amid an almost satisfying *pop* that resembled in some ways the cracking of a knuckle but in other ways the tearing of muscle and vein and nerve. That was before her face hit the glass, which shattered against her and spiderwebbed a sequence of cuts across her cheek. Her ringing head muted the people around her screaming, gasping: the shock of the injury clutched her body so intensely that she was likewise only half aware at best of the car's driver stumbling out to see the woman who had run in front of him.

A crowd gathered. The taste of the blood brought her back to awakening in her apartment, and there she was again, sitting bolt upright, all at once present while people around her gasped to see her move. Someone put a hand on her shoulder to lay her down again— she pushed it away, recognizing in the back of the crowd the familiar, truly terrified face of the stranger. He was quick to disappear, and she was likewise quick to spring from the hood of the car upon which her body had come to rest. People gasped: she ignored them and, grimacing as her thighbone popped back up into place on her effort to stand (yes, that was all it was—a realignment of the angle that permitted the bone to replace itself), the woman plowed through the crowd and after, after, onward after the miserable thief of a stranger. Her speed was not good: her thigh was not quite right, her limp pronounced and painful. Each step produced a bone-on-bone *click* that only she could hear. But there he was, running out of breath, visibly slowing as he cut down an alley and, emerging on the other side, darted down another subway entrance. It occurred to the woman that, if her theory was correct, perhaps the limits of her natural human endurance were nonexistent. Could she still fatigue?

Running down to this new subway platform and vaulting the turnstile in the fashion the stranger surely had, the woman's attention was faltered by disappointment. The sound of the train pulling off— had she missed him? At the bottom of the stairs, she braced for an empty platform: instead, she discovered the stranger running a hand over his forehead, looking as if he weighed whether to cross the tracks to the platform's other side. Anything to get away from her.

"Hey." She extended and quickly retracted a hand she realized to be blood covered. "Excuse me—"

"Get away from me!" The stranger stumbled back a step, arm extended before him. "I didn't mean to kill you. Please—"

The stranger, on the verge of tears, made as though to leap upon the subway tracks. She caught his wrist before he did and drew him back, amazed by the vigor and violence of his thrashing efforts to extricate himself.

Voice edged with panic, he cried, "I thought ghosts weren't physical, man!"

"You think I'm a ghost!" On seeing a couple descend the platform stairs, she pushed the stranger behind the nearest pillar and tightened her bloody fists around his jacket. "Okay, so maybe I'm a ghost. That would make as much sense as anything. Are you sure you killed me?"

"Sure! Sure, I'm sure. I don't understand."

"I don't, either. How do you know I was dead?"

"Brain," he stuttered, his wild eyes trailing over her face, into her hair, down her cheek again. "I saw brain under your hair. I panicked—I ran home. Thought the cops were going to come get me."

"You left out the part where you took my money."

"I'll give it back to you! Do you want it back? I'll do it, I swear, I'll give you anything. Please, don't hurt me."

"I'm not going to hurt you." The woman licked her lips and lowered her voice with respect to the couple, who had taken notice of the whisper-shouted quarrel. "In fact, maybe you could do me a favor."

Still perplexed—and, to her satisfaction, visibly frightened even on realizing the ghost that chased him was not going to take revenge—the stranger's hands lowered from their defensive posture. His voice remained unsteady. "What kind of a favor?"

7

"SURE YOU WANT ME to do this?"

The stranger had asked this no fewer than five times since following her back to her apartment. She continued adjusting the lamps lighting her kitchen counter. He was not content with her silence and, from where he hovered in the not-kitchen, continued, "Because—I don't know, man. Seems like you already have your answer."

"I don't. I have your opinion. I have memories of people staring at me before my leg popped back into place. I have a lot of hearsay. Nothing empirical."

"Maybe you should go to a doctor."

"Do you want the money or not?" When, in the subway, the stranger's reluctance had proven almost insurmountable, the woman promised him another hundred dollars. Standing there, however—obviously his first experience in the apartment left him with second thoughts about what he'd do for cash. A criminal but not a psychopath. Cute in a way. Maybe the stranger had gotten into the wrong line of work, a kid swept up in a game so intense it had at some point become too real a career to escape.

But that was the thing: too-real careers were just too lucrative. At the mention of money, the stranger's pupils dilated. His arms crossed, chin jerking toward her camera. "You a photographer? My ex is a model."

"No kidding. Magazines? Runways?"

"Porn," he answered. "I used to help her take pictures and put them up on the web sometimes. Videos, too. Made good money. Our camera wasn't an SLR like yours, though."

"Sounds like you were living the dream… What happened?"

"She made enough money to hire a professional videographer and started banging him."

"We artists are an untrustworthy lot." Satisfied with the lighting, the woman turned away, washed her hands, dried them, inspected her knuckles for debris, then took a knife from the block in her kitchen. When set upon the counter, the blade shone in the light: the stranger stared as if hypnotized. She took the camera in her right hand, switched on its auto-focus feature, rested her finger beside the trigger, and lay her nondominant left hand into the center of her intended frame. As her fingers unfurled beside the waiting knife, the stranger returned to Earth, lips set in a firm frown.

"So…you want me to…" He picked up the knife with a helpless expression, a boy terrified of making a mistake while helping his father fix a car engine.

"Cut me. Here." She flipped her palm upright. "It's like a blood-brother ritual or something. Think of it like that. Totally harmless. Remember, you're getting paid."

The stranger tightened his grip on the knife, let his lips peel back from his teeth with the force of his sigh, then took her hand in his free one. Given his stunt on the first night they met, the gentleness of his touch was somehow surprising. As, with one more reluctant glance to her face, he drew the knife across the well of her palm, she thought of all the time-filling Internet videos she'd seen—films of people consoling animals while freeing them from thorns or untangling them from the barbed wire of a fence. Maybe the better metaphor was veterinarians comforting animals they simultaneously vaccinated.

Click, click. Blood flowed in time with the fiery pain streaking her hand: the woman's trigger finger twitched. *Click, click, click*—the shutter was the only sound once the hiss of her lips faded into the crackling afterglow. Pain submitted to endorphin-delirium. When she remembered to breathe, her soft gasps of astonishment at the sensation were a second sound; third was the sound of the stranger remembering himself, jolting into motion, grabbing the prearranged tea towel from the edge of the counter to wipe away the blood. While the white fabric absorbed its new crimson stain and the blood was transferred from surface to surface, the shutter clicked, clicked, clicked.

And with the blood gone, and the shutter clicking, the woman and the stranger stood in mutual astonishment: the deep gap in her hand self-sealed. The shutter had time to take maybe four more reasonable pictures before the cleaned wound shut like a prude's pursing lips into a scar that subsequently faded until it was as if it had never been there. All this healing occurred in the space of thirty seconds after the blood was wiped away.

"What is up with you?" The alarm in the stranger's voice exceeded that exhibited in the subway station.

Saying nothing, the woman set down her camera and lifted her hand closer to the light. No—nothing. Only a faint bloodstain. No explanation: no other possible excuse or cause or source of misunderstanding. And there were photos, but…

But she wanted even more proof. It was the way she had felt after her first psychedelic trip: mushrooms, way back in high school. To experience subjective, personal transcendence like that—it was like being abducted by an alien craft, taken to another planet, returned to Earth unharmed and not being permitted to retain any tangible memento of the experience. The only way to prove a psychedelic experience was to have another and watch as, once more, said experience slipped through the fingertips of the experiencer. There went the state of confidence, of oneness, of enlightenment; there went the state of injury.

The woman gazed at the stranger with girlish hope, hand extended. "Please—do it again?"

Consulting her palm yielded some ill omen. He shook his head and, remembering the bloody knife in his grip, lowered the blade to the counter. "Nah, man…I—nah. Sorry."

Disappointing. People didn't often reject her requests when it came to sex or sadomasochism. But, well—like she'd thought of the stranger before. A kid, in over his head. "Okay," she said. "Will you hand me my wallet, then? You know where I keep it."

In the end, she gave him an extra twenty dollars while citing his obvious mental trauma. He didn't refuse it and didn't even try to act like he wasn't affected, which was sort of refreshing. After a brief conversation by her front door, she convinced him to add her as his friend in another social media app so they could keep in touch. "I need somebody to talk to about this…condition. I feel alone. Nobody else in the world knows."

"I don't think it can stay that way. Do you?"

She sort of hoped as much, but she knew he was right. This was the modern world. Every human had a smartphone; every smartphone had a camera. Like in photography, exposure was a matter of time.

This only impressed upon her the importance of understanding herself before somebody else did. Alone in her apartment, the woman shut down her lighting equipment in a haze of automation. The flash of a bulb's reflection in the corner of her eye drew her attention back to the knife: there again was that voice in her head. Clear, persistent, more persuasive than ever. Before, she'd been able to provide any number of arguments against the compulsions. The uncertainty, the consequences—all that disappeared. The woman was defenseless against the voice's persuasive talents while isolated in her matchbox apartment.

Go on, the voice urged her. *Nothing's going to happen. You don't have a reason to resist.*

She didn't. It was true: she was all out of reasons to disobey the constant litany of suggestions, methods by which to experiment with the limits of her body. There were still questions. Unproven factors. What if she injured herself past the point of return? The question stalked her to the bathroom where she set the knife on the sink's edge to undress herself.

That wasn't how she should have asked the question. The question should have been: How far could she go? Or: Was it possible to go too far? Cuts, burns, concussions, dislocations, skull fractures: these had all healed. Where, then, was the limit? What would it take to kill her? She sat naked on the floor of her glass-doored shower and studied the stained knife. Vampires required a stake in the heart. Decapitation. Would these methods work on her? Was there a way to know without dying, thus rendering the point moot?

Was there anybody like her, anywhere?

Maybe not. She unfurled her pale arm and, with her elbow braced against her knees, drew the knife across her flesh for the first violin-shriek of electric agony. Her mouth made noises as if of its own volition, closing again into clenched teeth. Her hiss echoed the one elicited by the stranger's cut. But she was determined: she dragged the knife again, a few centimeters away from the first mark—then again, then again, striping her white flesh with red blood until a scarlet curtain poured down her limbs to splatter upon the shower floor. Like a small child discovering her body, she continued her assault against herself and felt her own descent into a curious state of trance. The pain was high definition, but what did pain mean when, within a minute, all marks were gone and only blood remained? Pain was intended as a signal. A sign something was wrong—an emergency alert broadcast, a tornado siren, a fire alarm. When a person's fire alarm rang and there was no fire, two options existed. Shut off the alarm or adapt to the sound.

Slice by slice, cut by cut, the woman adapted to the sound of her own internal alarm until it meant nothing. Even then, she continued. On and on, the feeling was so dreamlike that she might not have stopped if blood loss hadn't soothed her to a dreamless sleep in the corner of the shower stall.

8

IF THE WOMAN had been thinking about it, she might have been surprised to awaken a mere nine hours later. One would suppose that for the blood loss she'd endured, her body would need time to recover: evidently this was not the case. She had the feeling that if she'd gone slower on the cuts—made one at a time, waited for each to close—she could have sat there playing with herself for eternity without consequence. This was why children needed parents, she guessed. Somebody to discourage navel-gazing. Granted, the average parent had to tell their kid, "Don't touch yourself there," rather than, "Don't cut yourself there," but the principle was the same.

Consequently, after showering the dried blood from her immaculate body, wrapping herself in her robe, and belatedly finishing the process of putting away the lighting equipment from the night prior, the woman arranged her phone on her nightstand to call her mother. Back when phones were things that stayed at home, they could only provide audio conversations; the cameras attached to them now meant people could have video conversations the way characters used to communicate in old science-fiction stories. On one side of the country, the woman sat in front of her smartphone; on the other side of the country, another phone rang. Back in the city, the woman's glass screen filled with her mother's soothing face.

"I was just thinking about you," her mother began. "Are you staying safe? I keep hearing about this virus—you're not going out, are you?"

"I haven't been partying lately, no."

"Good, that's good. Stay in more. I don't even like the thought of you *working*."

"I don't, either." She felt that way because of her boss, not the virus, but went on without elaborating. "Can I ask you a weird question? Have you ever had an experience where, like—say you, uh, cut yourself while cooking, or trip and scrape yourself, and it… heals right away?"

"Are you talking about that video on the news?"

The woman sat up a few inches. "What?"

"Oh, I thought that was what you meant—I don't know, there's some silly video somebody doctored. It's all over the Internet! Actually it's funny, the girl looks like you—"

While her mother described the video that had rushed across several social media platforms (that was to say, programs people used to communicate, share pictures, and hook up), the woman hit the power button on a nearby remote control. The wall-mounted television across from her bed came to life, and while she muted it to flip through the channels, her mother was busy laughing. "I watch your news stations more than I watch my own! It makes me feel close to you—oh, I miss you, honey."

"Miss you, too, Mom." The woman lowered the remote as one of several twenty-four-hour news stations conveniently provided what her mother described. "I know I called you, but I just remembered something I have to do. Can I call you back?"

After hanging up, the woman sat entranced by the silent footage of her chase. She lifted the remote to rewind a few seconds and eventually hit "Play" to watch herself appear in the background of some tourists' video. Here was the beguiling city, among the most famous in the world; here was one of its most famous streets, and the tourist family smiling on the famous street; and here was a random woman in the background being hit by a car, a fatal consequence of that famous traffic. The pictured family whipped around on the cameraman's scream; the footage blurred. When the commotion settled, the woman realized the cameraman must have been in the crowd around her—the wild tangle of black hair hid her bloodied face, but she had to be damn sure never to wear that outfit again. No wonder people were so freaked out: even she had to admit the uncanniness of seeing somebody covered in blood leap from the crunched windshield of a car, rearrange their broken limbs, and spring off in pursuit of some goal.

The news segment wrapped with a few bystander interviews, including one with the cameraman who had uploaded his footage to a popular online video-hosting service. Neither witness had anything interesting to say beyond a rehashing of the filmed events and the addendum that it was "totally crazy," as the younger of the two put it. Once the witness interviews ended, the camera cut back to the news studio and the desk-bound reporter who encouraged viewers at home to send information to local police.

Absorbed, the woman picked up her phone in search of articles about the video. Most Internet websites made money on advertising: the more pages a website had, the more advertisements it could run. Most websites—especially ones that claimed to be sources of information on current events—had to pump perpetual content out into the already impossibly cluttered assortment of data available in servers across the globe. The woman was therefore not surprised when she found several articles regarding the video, though she was provided with a definite sense of relief to read the speculative discussions. Readers were invited to comment on website news articles; throughout these comments were proposed any number of mundane explanations. The most popular suggestions were drugs or injurious shock that prevented the woman from realizing she was in pain.

The wave of relaxation that rushed along her muscles to discover nobody thought the video was real— Ah! It was almost orgasmic. Shutting off both phone and television, the woman lay back among her pillows, shut her eyes, and spent Saturday in bed loving life.

· FLORENCE HENRI ·

1

KNOWING AT FIRST proved as difficult as not knowing. More difficult, even. Maybe that increase in the burden's weight came from the notion that before, with everything unconfirmed and her as ignorant as anybody else, she had a kind of ready-made excuse should anyone discover her condition. When she herself was ignorant of anything that needed to be hidden, how could she be responsible for hiding anything?

Well…she was certainly responsible now. After seeing that shaky camera footage broadcast across the country and almost certainly the world, she couldn't help but think it more important than ever to take control of the narrative. What was the solution, though? By God, the only thing she could see was a cross-country move—and even that wasn't guaranteed to ensure privacy. Although the blurry camera footage did a poor job showing her face, it was still possible somebody somewhere would recognize her.

The stranger certainly did. He messaged her that same Saturday afternoon to ask if she had seen the news. With some coaxing, she soon had him in her apartment for a third time, where he became committed to a task he appreciated much more than cutting her with knives. The woman liked the way he felt inside of her and even let him orgasm without pulling out: though she was on birth control, she was finicky about the men she let release in her, but he had done a good thing by confirming her condition. That merited reward. Anyway, she liked it: liked the thought of the semen, physical evidence of the man's pleasure the way the blood still staining her shower grout was evidence of her pain. Women's pleasure never left real evidence. Pussies got wet, but the fluid produced by a woman's anticipation of desire was less tangible than that produced by a man's fulfillment of desire; and a woman's fulfillment of desire yielded no evidence distinct from her anticipation, rendering impossible any objective confirmation of the woman's internal, subjectively experienced orgasm. Not unless you were a doctor with a photographic dildo, and that merely recorded the physical convulsions of muscle. A camera could penetrate the cunt but not the mind—the seeing, discerning, experiencing mind that turned the twitches of flesh and flows of blood into starbursts of relief, ecstasy, nonexistence. That inner universe of pleasure: that truer universe that women held within and men clamored to experience.

After, the stranger asked, "What'll you do?" She knew what he meant. What would she do about her condition, the video, her future? It all fused into a single subject.

"I'm going to have to keep my head down. You won't tell anybody, will you?"

"Who'd believe me if I did?" Scratching the close-cropped hair of his shaking head, the stranger clicked his tongue. "There's nothing to tell."

She supposed not. No, nothing to tell. No evidence except the video—except the photographs she developed once the stranger left. Gradation by gradation, the specter of her white hand was distinguished by the gray counter fading in around it. The edge of her nail; the handle of the knife; the blood, the blood tarry black in the final glossy prints hung to drip over her makeshift sink as she studied the sequence. Pride filled her. After all these years of trying to find that special element to her artwork! This was a turning point. This was a creative evolution.

This was her very soul.

2

THIS DISCOVERY should have been enough. Yes: this first emergence of the theme at the heart of her artistic journey, it should have been the key to a kingdom unfurling before her on the instant of her understanding. All the galleries in town should have been knocking at her front door, all the models lining up to fight for her time, all the magazines calling to beg for first rights to print her pictures no matter what she charged.

None of that happened. The woman stepped out of her darkroom, back into her quiet apartment, and ate an anticlimactic dinner before going to bed. But she certainly enjoyed an angelic night's sleep, and awoke with a smile in her heart if not on her face. It was not wise to smile too widely in the world, because those who lacked in smiles hated seeing someone with an abundance of them—and, at any rate, to be happy with an accomplishment before it was accomplished was a sure way to accomplish nothing. She was still a slave, the woman reminded herself: still a slave to her country and its economy, to the apartment that cost most of her monthly wages. A slave who looked too happy was liable to be beaten by the master who thought his slave had something undeserved. As she dressed for work, she tried to look normal—even unhappy, which was, in truth, normal for her.

Not a hard emotion to emulate. While bringing over the morning supply of apples, her boss frowned at the conservative neckline of her turtleneck. In a tone that declared he thought it a perfectly normal thing to ask, he demanded, "Why don't you wear something more flattering once in a while? You'd be prettier if you took time to think about your sense of style."

The interaction was so baffling that, instead of replying, she laughed in his face. While she selected an apple ready to fall from the sagging lip of the sack, he grabbed her wrist. "Maybe it's a wardrobe problem? I've helped one or two employees subsidize clothes and rent before."

"I'm not that sort of person," she said, disgust oozing from her voice as she jerked her wrist from his fat fingers. "Frankly, I'd rather die alone."

Anger tightened the tiny, piggy features already forced out of proportion by the fat padding his cheeks. "At this rate, you might. You're almost thirty—you think men like me are going to come around forever?"

"I hope not."

At a formal loss for words, red from the tips of his ears to the stubble of his chins, the woman's boss opened and closed his mouth a few times before warning, "You'd better watch how you speak to your manager," and then wheeling about-face to storm into the safety of his office. She waited until the door was shut before entering the walk-in freezer to scream awhile.

The woman needed to get that parade of well-wishers started as soon as possible. It had always been infuriating to be beholden to such a walking garbage bag, but given this intense discovery of her new artwork, she wanted to quit right then. It was as if she discovered that for all her life she'd been a princess, lost among the rabble, raised to believe herself just another peasant. Didn't he know? Didn't he know whom he addressed? The woman was an *artist*. An artist, a real artist, whose art was worth infinitely more than the thirteen dollars an hour she made cooking at the diner for forty hours a week, every week. Yes: in the eternal view, fifteen minutes of the woman's time was worth more than her boss's entire life.

Maybe her ego was out of control, but it was difficult to know what she knew about herself and not feel a surge of self-confidence. No matter what happened, she would survive. Yes, she would survive. For all she cared, she could have quit her job there on the spot, been evicted, been made homeless—and she would survive. Not comfortably, but she could do it.

Her girlfriend came over a few nights later. "Watch this," she said, pulling up a video on her phone. A musical remix of the hit-and-run that, for a backbeat, utilized a sample of the woman's bones crunching against the car. The girlfriend laughed. The woman did not.

"I think it's messed up to laugh at something like that."

"Oh, whatever…I don't think it's even real."

"How could you fake that?"

The art student put her phone away. "They do all kinds of things now. Have you heard of 'deepfake' technology? They can take one person's face and put it on another's but make the whole thing look so seamless that you can't tell what's real. Like, they'll put Jim Carrey into *The Shining* instead of Jack Nicholson, or Jayne Mansfield into *Breakfast at Tiffany's* instead of Audrey Hepburn—if you hadn't seen the movie, you'd think it was real."

"Okay, but there were witnesses. Did you see them on the news? This was a real event, it actually happened."

"Maybe they're actors—or! No, maybe she's an actor."

"Like a performance artist?"

"More like she's doing a publicity stunt for a movie."

"What kind of movie?"

"I don't know! It's kind of an action hero thing to do. Running into traffic, getting hit, getting right back up and plunging off into danger. A superhero sort of thing."

A superhero sort of thing. She didn't feel like a superhero—not by any means—although she supposed she could have done some good with her abilities. Maybe someone could have studied her and created cures for all the world's ailments. Cancer, aging, even that novel virus with its treacherous two-week incubation period. It was possible her blood could have fixed it all.

But could her gift be replicated? It could have made her a good cop or soldier, but the human being was inclined to study what it couldn't achieve. That was why mankind worshipped gods of all stripes, all infinitely better than the worshippers themselves. If she were discovered, they would study her: and if it were determined that she was a threat to mankind because mankind could not learn from her, well…

What could you do with—to—an immortal woman? You could torture her, but the pain was a memory from the second it began. Further, if she was truly immortal, she could not be destroyed. She did not know the limits of her abilities, assuming there were any, and although she carried around a tumor of questions, she also felt absolute confidence: nothing could touch her, nothing would ever stick. Even if her abilities were discovered, who would believe them? Being absurd, the narrative was easy to control. Cartoonish, unreal. Superheroes needed to hide their identities because they lived in worlds where such things as superpowered humans were possible, part of the culture— therefore, in these fictional worlds, post-human vigilantes running around in masks needed to be taken seriously.

But nothing like what unfolded for the woman had unfolded for anyone in the history of the real planet Earth. The reality paradigm shared by the billions of human beings did not leave room for the concept of bodily immortality, with the distinct exception of a controversial carpenter who was crucified about two thousand years before the woman was born: and enough time had passed that nobody could agree whether or not he had actually existed. Hers was a planet ruled by the forces of time, and time's child, entropy—both of which were cosmic laws flowing in one direction.

Neither of which applied to her. After the conversation with her boss and the subsequent one with her girlfriend, it occurred to the woman that her body might have changed so radically that her aging process had ceased. Forever almost twenty-nine didn't sound bad. Relieving to know there might be fringe benefits beyond this constant compulsion to test her limits.

She needed to put this stream of inspiration to positive use.

3

HER BOSS WAS SLOW when it came to most things, so the woman wasn't surprised he didn't see the video until it had floated around for a few weeks. Damned if he didn't surprise her with his observational skills, however…she guessed he did have sort of that "fat gumshoe cop" look about him.

"It's the ass," he explained once she stood behind the shut door of his office. Astonishing how quickly he could make her regret consenting to a private meeting. The woman folded her arms.

"Excuse me?"

"I recognized it as soon as I saw it." He turned the monitor of his computer toward her; she tried to feel nothing upon seeing the frozen frame of her body twisted across the hood of the car. "That's you, isn't it?"

"Don't be ridiculous."

"How'd you do it? I want to know."

"I don't know what you're talking about."

His eyes narrowed. "This something you're trying to keep quiet? Why? What's going on in this video?"

"You're wasting my time," she began, turning toward the door until he said, "The police—"

Exhaling, she faced him. He resumed, "The police are looking for this woman. Not, uh, a manhunt…but they're open to tips, given the nature of the public disturbance. Not every day the running party of a hit-and-run is the pedestrian." Leaning back in a chair that pitifully protested the imposition, her boss folded his round hands over his rounder gut. "Probably want to see if she was on drugs, or if she's dead in the gutter…what was it? Crystal? PCP? Come on, you can tell me. I could get it for you, whatever it is."

"I think I'm going to find a new job."

"You quit and I'll tell the cops I know the woman in this video."

She gritted her teeth. "I have no idea what you're talking about. Are you accusing me of something?"

"No—I don't know."

"You don't know."

"I mean…it's up to the police to accuse you. It's up to me, as your employer, to look out for you." He leaned forward while she imagined smashing the monitor of his decrepit personal computer over his fat head. "You ought to let me look out for you, baby."

Skin crawling, fists trembling, the woman could only turn on her heel and slam his office door behind her. Feeling as if she were an observer outside her own body, the woman put on her apron, netted her hair, and worked in stony silence.

It wasn't that she was worried about him telling the police. The whole thing was too absurd. They would make her take a drug test, maybe cite her for jaywalking. At that point, cops were not her problem. Her problem was her boss. He made her skin crawl—made her every cell burn with rage. Who the hell did he think he was, trying to push her around? Did he think she was stupid? Naïve? That she had no other choice? She was an artist, damn it. More than that, she was untouchable. She didn't need him, his job; she didn't need anything. The average human being lived around sixty to a hundred years if they managed to survive that long. They had one chance at life, one opportunity, and what they did with it showed who they were. The diner's boss spent far too much of his trying to take advantage of her and women like her. Other people lived good lives—donating time to help others, take care of animals, raise children, love their neighbors, etcetera—and her boss was here, trying to put her in a situation where she had no choice but suffer him to live.

Over her dead body. The apples were finished. While boiling a great pot of water for their soup of the day, she imagined her blood. Steaming in her veins. Invisible against the cardinal peel. Obscuring her face in the video.

That voice again. That her/not-her whisper of obsession. It saw the mesmerizing boil of the water, the cycle of its steaming bubbles surging around and around. This time, rather than putting words into her head, the compulsion presented images. Sensations. That water. How hot it was. The LED light above the security camera. Double, double, toil and trouble, fire burn and— Madame Blavatsky, godmother of modern occultism, got out of going to a dance by holding her leg in a pot of boiling water. To the woman's knowledge, Blavatsky had not been immortal; she just didn't want to dance.

She held the gaze of that camera while rolling up her left shirtsleeve—she held it as she raised her hand experimentally above the pot, but from the second her fingers plunged into the boiling water, she could not hold her stare any longer and screamed. The nerves in her hand glowed with an atomic oh-God flash: her forehead broke into a feverish sweat that was no comparison for the downpour of tears springing from her eyes. But she persevered, clenching her teeth, forcing her hand down into the boiling pot for as long as she could stand. The pain didn't matter, didn't matter: it didn't matter. She was certifiably immortal.

The door to her boss's office slammed open. He careened out, his yelling indecipherable over the urgent rush of agony through her nervous system, the out-of-body scream filling her ears. On and on: she used her other arm to keep the first submerged against its natural impulse, and the pain that had begun at a high intensity rose to such an extent that she could only think of cutting off her arm to save herself from experiencing that very burn she'd orchestrated. The experience loosened her mind to new associations. Like she was on a high-intensity trip, the woman's consciousness burst with flowers of spontaneous thought, harried imaginings of favorite books: *Dune*, *Fight Club*, Nietzsche and his superman. The splendor and danger of the human will. The dynamic male will. Texts for men by men. Herbert: fear was the mind-killer. She knew no fear. The storm of pain broke. Nothing hurt.

She awoke on the kitchen floor, boss and coworker stooped over her, both baffled, the pupils of her boss beady with animal fear.

"Hey," said her coworker, brow furrowed with concern. "You okay? Should I call the paramedics?"

Full well knowing what had happened, she asked in a dazed voice, "What happened?"

Her boss looked like he wanted to speak. Now's your chance. Going to tell the world? Do a grand reveal of her strange and frightening powers? Start here. Start right here. If you couldn't tell your line cook, you'd never tell the cops.

Those tiny pupils hovered around her face, then lowered to her arm. "You collapsed," he said as she followed his gaze to her forearm, its sleeve rolled up, its unbroken skin the usual pale hue, pink around the joints of her wrist and knuckles. "I came out of my office and—and…"

She stared steadily into him, stared and stared, unblinking, until all the blood had drained from his face.

He muttered, "And—maybe you should go home for the day. With pay. I'll cover your shift. Come back—tomorrow, when you feel better. Sorry you're… Sorry."

"Hey, brother"—she forced herself to sit up, not having to try to act dizzy—"not your fault. Guess I'll see you tomorrow."

4

HER BOSS HAD REALIZED the same fundamental flaw of filmed "proof"—the same flaw over which the woman ruminated as she lay in her not-kitchen, gaze unfocused beyond the ceiling fan. She had thrilled to see her photographs, evidence of her abilities presented in a sequence of images. But even image was insufficient evidence in that era of human life. There were all kinds of computer programs that permitted, with no effort, the doctoring of photographs. Even amateur editors could create fakes so compelling that one sometimes needed a professional to discern untouched photographs from altered ones. And, as described by the art student, there were deepfake methods.

The woman had recently been sent a convincing but nonetheless synthetic audio clip of late American president John F. Kennedy reading from the Book of Genesis. It was funny until she discovered another, this of his synthesized voice reading a document referred to as "In the Event of a Moon Disaster." Intended for broadcast if Earth's lunar pioneers died during their exploratory mission. They had not. Human beings from the US of A had been on the moon of planet Earth: twelve American human beings, all of whom returned home alive. Moreover, Kennedy had been shot in the head during a motorcade in 1963; the moon landing had not occurred until 1969, under a widely disliked president named Richard Nixon.

But what if that knowledge was lost? What if, centuries in the future, record of the moon landings (which some already claimed to have been faked for public morale, although the faking of such a thing would have been, at the time, infinitely more expensive than the actual achievement) was wiped from humanity's conglomerate of information? What if what remained was not names or dates or statistics but instead this persuasive simulacrum of the assassinated president-messiah, six years dead, solemnly informing the American people that the first men to touch the lunar surface would not be returning home?

Image, audio, video: nothing was suitable evidence.

This was an advantage. In another way, it was deeply frustrating, and the photographs that had pleased her only a few days prior now disgusted her as amateurish edgy attempts to encapsulate the experience that began to feel like reality after the incident with the boiling water. The stranger's outside observation had helped, but in the same way that more than one point of reference was required to triangulate a target's location, her boss's acknowledgment of her alien abilities reinforced her new reality in a way not yet experienced.

How frustrating it was! She wanted to hide, yet to do so without feeling quite so alone. Her boss had video of her boiling her own flesh in soup water to the point of blacking out, so maybe he also had video of the healing process. She felt every day at work like asking to borrow it (he had a new kind of respect or maybe fear for her after that incident and, to her relief, began treating her as if she were a professional instead of a sex object—pathetic that this was what it took), but even that footage wouldn't have done any good. Photographs, video: the only way to experience what happened to her, to prove what happened to her, was to be there while it happened. Present, and fully aware.

The stranger visited with increasing regularity during this time. She supposed that made him more friend than stranger, but you could only ever get so close to somebody who got to know you by killing and robbing you. However, that did not mean she did not like him, or did not take comfort in his company. Better than being alone with the voice that was less a metaphor and more a real voice every time she felt it. When the stranger came by, although he would not assist her in extreme attempts to test her limits (knives yielded polite rejections from him for quite some time), he consented to lay into her with his belt, or an old whip she had from days of more forced kinky experimentation in her early twenties. Her favorite was when he agreed to choke her unconscious during sex: she loved waking after, his material running down her thighs.

It was nice to have a friend. The intimacy of their activities made her feel close to him, and they would sometimes talk about their lives once the acrobatics reached a climax. When she told him about the soup incident, he looked more sensibly concerned than she'd expected.

"You sure that's smart? Letting him get it on camera like that?"

"Does it matter?" She explained her reasoning, but he shook his head.

"Word travels fast. Say he does something with the footage, after all?"

"What's he going to do? Put it on the Internet, slap ads in front of the video… I guess I could always try to claim the copyright, steal his advertising revenue."

"That's seriously a good idea," he said despite her laughter. "No, I mean it—actually." She was surprised into silence by the sharp light rising in his eyes. Cartoon dollar signs. "Do you remember that time around 2015 when all those nude photos of celebrities were leaked on the Internet? Another incident happened later with another celebrity, some singer—somebody hacked into her private accounts and got a bunch of nudes, then threatened to release them if she didn't pay. She turned around and released the pictures herself."

"Controlling the narrative."

"Exactly." After considering the canvas bags protecting her lighting equipment, he asked, "Do you have a video camera?"

"No, film photography only."

"What a hipster." He blocked the slap of a pillow. "I thought people like you grew up about five years ago. I have a camcorder in my closet… It's old, I haven't used it since I broke up with my ex—or since she broke up with me, I guess." After a few more seconds, he advised, "With enough videos on the Internet and enough ad revenue coming from them, a successful video blogger could quit their job."

Her nose wrinkled. "Blogs," a term derived from the portmanteau "weblog," were essentially online journals. Most of them were open to the public, and many of them had been increasingly putting emphasis on video content over written content. A more general sign of the times: overuse of the Internet had markedly impacted the human attention span when it came to prose. People wanted easy content, delivered with bright visuals and bubbly hosts capable of keeping their messages under four minutes. Blogs and vlogs had their own genres, tropes, and narrative arcs: the woman could not see at first how her talent applied. "Nobody wants to hear about my life," she protested.

"Are you crazy? Yeah, they do. Why else would the hit-and-run video have so many views? Millions in a week—everybody wants to know what the deal is. Knowing you're a real person and not an actor or a computer-generated scam would blow everybody's minds. Come on—this is a great idea! You're leaving money on the table, tons and tons of money. Independence. Fame."

The photographs of her hands, now stuck to the darkroom door, reminded her of her newfound artistic voice. "I don't know," she continued, but he was on his phone.

"You don't get what I'm suggesting. I'm not saying you do a video diary or something boring like that—though, as you gain followers, you should definitely do videos like those. Make them feel close to you."

"I haven't even agreed to do anything and you're already talking like my manager."

"Because I would make a great manager. Once you see what I'm talking about, you'll give it a chance. Here."

He slid the phone in front of her, and she frowned at the screen. A girl, early twenties at most, shot nose down at a table so cluttered with exotic food that the tableau proved impossible to parse. Seafood, mostly—tentacles arranged in a huge bowl of broth, tempura-fried vegetables, rice, sides beyond reckoning, sauces for dipping, juicy fruits for dessert. The smiling hostess waved at the camera: there appeared beneath her Japanese subtitles, illegible to the viewing woman despite her cultural heritage. Then, with alarming speed and nauseating abandonment of decent table manners, the vlog's starlet loudly stuffed her face.

The woman's lip curled into a sharp sneer of disgust. "What *is* this?"

"It's called 'mukbang,' or 'eating show.' It's a popular genre in Eastern countries, but all kinds of bloggers all over the world make videos like this. People sit there and stuff their faces for the camera…a spin-off genre of ASMR."

"You're going to have to spell it out for me."

"'Autonomous sensory meridian response.'" The vlogger on-screen gagged: stomach unsettled, the woman shut the phone off and handed it back to the stranger. He reopened it and searched for other videos, explaining, "It's the chills you get when you hear, like, I don't know…a woman's nails clicking on a table, or, whispering, or—well. The sound of someone eating."

"But the sound of people eating is disgusting to me."

"Me, too. But to other people, it's practically pornography… though they won't admit it."

"Practically"! What an understatement. The website hosting the ASMR and mukbang videos was mainstream and pornography free at the behest of its accordingly mainstream advertisers. Yet, to paraphrase the famous judge: the woman might not have been able to define pornography, but she knew it when she saw it. ASMR made her skin crawl, all right. Something was spooky about these videos of young women, many of them underage, whispering into microphones to cause what ASMR "connoisseurs" disturbingly referred to as "tingles." Disgusting. Like they were ignorant children who had never experienced sexual arousal and knew not what to call it. A perverse justification to get off on stuff that wasn't inherently sexual.

The stranger was right. Inspiration lived here. He had shown her a second example of ASMR (some weird video of a girl scratching her own itching skin, the microphone poised close enough to hear the movements of nails on flesh) when it occurred to the woman that there were many other types of vapid nonsense content flooding the Internet archives. She'd heard of "unboxing" videos where the host would unbox a recently purchased product in front of the camera, do a brief review, and call it quits; there were videos of people playing video games for the viewers' pleasure; and, from the inception of the Internet through the present day, the proliferation of content devoted to sharing the foibles, accidents, injuries, and even deaths of other human beings had grown at an exponential pace.

Something clicked on in the woman.

"Oh. Oh, oh!"

"Yeah."

She covered her mouth and studied the video on the screen, the itching nails. "Oh," she said once more. "This is a great idea. Or a terrible one."

"Could be both."

Yes, could be both. Most things were not one or the other but both in proportion. The grinning woman lifted her eyes toward the stranger. "Would you really help me? I don't know where to start."

"Sure, I'll help you. We'll split the ad revenue. You'll be making so much money that you won't even notice the difference."

Not unreasonable. If he'd provide the video camera—presumably edit the footage and post it online for her—it seemed reasonable at that point in her artistic career to yield even a large part of her profits to an agent-producer. However…the line between "agent-producer" and "pimp" was a fine one. "You're not going to scam me on this, are you?"

"You don't trust me?"

"Is that supposed to be a joke?"

"I wondered why you won't even let me piss alone… I thought it was a sex thing."

"You wish. I don't want you going through my medicine cabinet."

"I won't have to go through anybody's medicine cabinet if we do this, and you won't have to work. I'm not going to pretend there isn't plenty in it for me, but—"

"Okay," she said, tired of his talking, brain charged with inspiration. "Let's do it."

They shook, and he went home, and that was how her career began.

5

BY THE NEXT EVENING, the stranger had established her page on the video site. White, unadorned, empty of anything but her account name. Plain as her early set. After careful furniture rearrangement, she'd produced enough space to prop her budget photography screen against the kitchen/not-kitchen partition. There was even space for the lights. More adjustment made room for the camera. The barstool normally at the partition became her seat before the background. They were missing just one thing: after discussion, she took her seat with a hammer in her hand.

"Hello," she began on his mark, but he immediately stopped the camera.

"You need more energy than that."

"Do I?"

"Yeah. Think about those videos I showed you! These people were all super excited. You need to understand that you're crafting a character."

She pondered the head of the hammer. Rust lined the metal edge: the result of a leaky pipe in the last kitchen sink under which it had been stored. Time's victim. "I'm so detached from myself. How could I come up with a character?"

"Oh, please, you're the craziest girl I've ever met. You mean to say you're not a character already?" He waved his hand at her. "Tell me what you feel about your situation. Do you like it more or dislike it more?"

"I guess I like it more. I like it a lot more than I dislike it."

"And what do you like about it?"

"Well…" Her thumb pressed to the jagged texture of rust buildup, almost cuttingly sharp. "I guess it's an opportunity to feel things. Things nobody else can ever feel."

"So, you want to enjoy it—I mean, your condition. Your life." Obviously uncomfortable with the true degree of her sadomasochism, he scratched his cheek before turning back to the camera. "Then I think that's what you should tap into. If you want people to watch you, be excited about something. People love artists who are passionate about their art... Nobody likes a singer who's too blasé, not for long."

"Do people really want to see my passion for self-mutilation?"

"Just roll with it," he said, adjusting the focus of the camera. "In three, two—"

6

THE MOST-DISCUSSED viral phenomenon over the next few days was not the disease sweeping the globe but a surreal video of a lovely young woman in front of a white screen.

"Hi, everybody!" The woman giggled as if at herself and continued, "I'm the Degenetrix!" She introduced herself as a performance artist living in the city. Fairly close to true, or was about to be. It occurred to the woman only in the first few seconds of filming that this was a whole new medium for her. A massive shift: from making art to becoming art. The assumption of a new identity, "the Degenetrix," a title suggested by the stranger and immediately embraced like the answer to some riddle.

This realization of new emergence was not apparent in the video's final cut, where her image was superimposed with the familiar clip of her body smashing against a windshield. "You probably know me from the hit-and-run video that's been making the rounds! A lot of people have wanted to know about me: Was she in shock? Is she on drugs? Is it a publicity stunt? No! I'm a real person. And what you're about to see is real, too."

Once the camera panned to reveal the hammer in her hand, the woman known as the Degenetrix stood up, crossed behind the stool, laid her left hand upon it, and attempted to bring the hammer down with her right.

"Ah!"

The first blow made her cry out but was not hard enough to achieve anything stupendous. The second got a knuckle and a "Fuck!" but yielded no satisfying break. "Help me," she hissed through clenched teeth. "Help me, help me, damn you—"

After the shake of the camera upon its tripod resolved to a still frame, the cameraman appeared in the scene to help her. Face obscured by the low angle so all that could be seen was his arm, the man took the hammer and repeatedly brought it to bear upon her fingers.

"Oh, God!" Her screaming pierced the apartment, and she realized at once that this would never fly—they had to get sound-dampening equipment to line her not-kitchen. This was one of a flurry of out-of-place practical thoughts—strange, spontaneous expansions of imagery the way people thought of chores during sex. In the video, she didn't appear to be thinking about anything: only screaming, profaning, gripping her abused left hand by the wrist to keep it in place while the hammer smashed away.

The man stumbled off frame again. Viewers commented that the sound at time stamp 3:14 was likely the sound of the hammer being dropped. For about thirty seconds, the footage showed only the woman, gasping, weeping, her forehead against the edge of the barstool while she stared through tear-matted eyelashes at the pulp of her hand. Gradually, her crying calmed. The camera shook as it was removed from its tripod and the cameraman's arc swung wide to reveal bits and pieces of an apartment, lighting equipment—no substantial wires or special effects equipment immediately visible. Only the woman, who, still collapsed against the stool, lifted her head at the camera's approach and managed a shaky inhalation.

"This is real," she wetly emphasized, reaching off-screen for a paper towel she used to blot blood from her bruised hand. "This is a magic trick. I'm a performance artist. But this is real."

The camera zoomed in on her cleaned hand. Crumpled fingers snapped back into place as if the woman were a blow-up doll expanding into shape. By the time ninety seconds had passed, the woman's hand was healed. The camera panned over the breadth of her grin, eyes bright and cheeks flushed as if by postcoital ecstasy.

"If you want to see more, be sure to like this video, leave a comment, and subscribe to the channel. See you next time!"

One last shot of her waving her broken hand: an auto-suggestion from the website's algorithm that viewers might also enjoy this clip of a man falling from a ladder and smashing his head on his driveway.

7

TO CALL THE DEBUT of the Degenetrix "a smash hit" would have been more than a cheap pun. The stranger distributed the video across key social media platforms, and because these programs permitted anyone with a public account to contact anyone else, it was easy to reach out to the vloggers whose analyses had helped spread the hit-and-run video during its explosive week of popularity. Although social trends moved too quickly for most to keep pace, certain Internet figures had a way of capturing the human imagination just as traditional celebrities. People loved hearing updates or explanations on strange viral phenomena, and it was better if the explanation made the original content stranger. Suffice it to say, the "Hammer Video," as it came to be known, only served to add controversy to the dialogue. What exactly had the video shown? The Degenetrix had stated that what the viewer had seen was both a magic trick and real. How could anything be both?

The art student, a young person with her finger on the pulse of the Internet's latest obsessions, was the first one to recognize her. "You're insane," was the first thing the woman's girlfriend said the next time they met. A mere forty-eight hours after the Hammer Video was posted: that was the viral speed with which a news story spread. "How did you do that? You should have told me you were doing performance art!"

A flutter of pleasure rushed through the woman's body. How flattering to be recognized. Such enthusiasm, too. "Want to help me with the next piece?"

"Sure—but how did you do the last one?"

"I said in the video. It's real."

"But it can't be *real*." Her girlfriend took up the woman's healed hand, twisted it left and right beneath the fluorescent light of the kitchen side of the partition where they sat having drinks. "Look! Not a scratch on you."

"Yeah. That's the magic trick part of it."

"But how?"

"Lucky, I guess."

"What kind of answer is that?"

The woman nursed her drink as she attempted to explain the onset of her strange but intriguing condition. Her girlfriend was not satisfied. Biting her lip, the art student studied again the woman's hand. The woman felt herself seized by the disembodied spirit of sexual anticipation, that shadow of Eros—oh, the sharp tips of those arrows of his: the sweet and fatal sign of love whose image captivated her more than any result of these sacred shafts' penetrations. What she wanted most of all was to find someone who would not stick one arrow in and think it sufficient to keep her eternally. What she wanted was someone who would pepper her like Saint Sebastian—who would pick a few well-placed missiles and stab them in and out of her again. Not arrows of love, but swords, but pikes. To be impaled upon the pike of love! The act, the repeated and eternally renewable act, of impalement. The moment again. That was what the woman wanted most. Could she find it here? She bent toward her friend and wove her photographer's fingers through clay-speckled ones.

"You want to see it in person? I'll prove it." The girl didn't seem to know what to say and stared anxiously back at the woman, lower lip attractively bitten. "It's okay—I think I like it. Really like it, I mean. Here…" After slithering up from her seat, the woman crossed to her apartment's one window, pushed it open, and permitted the cool night air of late wintertime city to permeate her abode. "Do you still smoke? Yeah? Bad girl! You should quit…cigarettes killed my dad. I haven't touched one in two years, I'll only smoke pot." Her deft fingertips lifted to the top button of her black blouse. "Might as well put yours to use— light a cigarette and bring it here."

By the time the girlfriend stood, the woman was down to the jeans and panties of which she made short work. "Are you sure about this?"

"I took the batteries out of the fire detector years ago."

"No, I mean—"

"I know what you mean." The woman removed her underwear, then reclined upon the unmade bed. As her head rested against the iron bars of her headboard, it struck her that they'd better film what was about to happen. There was only one first time: one organic experience. "Would you record this for me? Your phone's newer, it has a much better camera than mine."

The art student considered the glowing cherry of her cigarette and belatedly remembered to put its filter in her mouth. With her newly freed hands, she removed the phone from her back pocket to open its camera. "I think I'm going to freak out," she muttered. After some coordination, she held the phone in one hand to film the cigarette held upright in the pinched fingers of the other.

"Okay," said the girlfriend, sitting uneasily at the edge of the bed and moving a hand forward. "Okay—uh…are you sure?"

"Don't be scared. I want to see what it's like to be burned. Do you want me to do it?"

Virginal hesitance won out over curiosity: the girlfriend passed the cigarette over. Though slightly disappointed, the woman smiled unflappably on at her girlfriend, at the camera, at the future rising in her immediate time horizon. Mostly, she smiled at the anticipation of it, the desire of it, the singing feel of it. The cigarette, its furious orange O of a mouth burning its kiss into her shoulder.

The woman gasped, head tilting against the iron headboard. Any starburst of pain sharpened the substantial pleasure rising with it: pleasure to feel it, pleasure to see it, pleasure to bask in the endorphin-soaked afterglow that remained the only evidence upon the burn's instant healing. The effect was so acutely sexual that it surprised even the woman.

While watching that first burn shrink to a rapid pinpoint of swift-to-disappear scar tissue, her girlfriend's eyes were wider than she had ever seen them. The woman squirmed in place and pressed the cherry down again, this time closer to her breast, and all the while, her girlfriend extolled, "That's wild! You really are like a superhero."

"Superheroes don't exist… I'm not going to do anything altruistic. Secret identities? Trying to hide was never going to work. Might as well share my talents." Gasping, each burn marking a trail that vanished faster than a track of fairy-tale bread crumbs at the beaks of hungry birds, the woman lowered her eyes from the camera and committed herself to enjoying the sensory experience. When wounds healed like this, there was much to be enjoyed.

Maybe the woman should have been alarmed by this inevitable desire to escalate her experimentation, but after the incident with the boiling water, she had come to view the concept of injuries with excitement. There were so many painful sensations! One could easily argue the world was richer with painful sensations than pleasurable ones: at least, the cumulative internal experience of the human body grew, as time marched on, more painful than pleasurable. Bliss put you to sleep. Pain kept you awake. Consciousness nested in pain.

Nobility, too. Nobility sat in pain's experience, its endurance. Most of all, nobility sat in pain's embrace. Religions understood that: so did the woman. When a being discovered they possessed such incredible regenerative properties, what about pain was not worth embracing? When it could be experienced consequence free, was it not just another sensation? When it was not endured long-term, why shy from experimentation? That cigarette specifically: maybe it was the size of the thing, but the pain was precisely enough to rush her blood without proving so overwhelming that she could only enjoy the aftermath—the fantasy, the memory, the recording—as had been the case with the hammer.

"Oh!" The cherry pressed against her tautly beaded nipple, where she would have held it longer if she'd then been disciplined enough. Self-mutilation was a practice, however, much like medicine or meditation or magic. Her hand, still trained by a lifetime of reflexes devoted to the avoidance of pain, flung the cigarette from her body. Her girlfriend caught it before it could burn a hole in the sheets, but the woman couldn't have cared if it had and moaned in sexual frustration. "I didn't expect it to feel so good! I want to try branding—want somebody to brand me like an animal. Oh, I bet the burn from an iron feels amazing while it heals."

Visibly staggered, the art student looked between the woman's sex-flushed face and the cigarette in her own fingers. No doubt her girlfriend would stub the smoke out and say something about the strangeness of the situation. Leave it at that.

Instead, that prior flicker of resisted curiosity must have renewed itself. Lips set in a firm line, the art student leaned her phone against the nearby metal lamp, the lightweight replacement for the ceramic one shattered weeks before. After kneeling between the naked woman's splayed legs, her girlfriend pressed a long kiss to her mouth and at the same time applied the cigarette to the firm planes of her immortal lily stomach. Softly, the woman gasped.

8

ALTHOUGH THE STRANGER WATCHED the video with an open mind and a hard dick, he said, "I don't know if this is the best content for us right now."

"What do you mean? Did you see the comments on the Hammer Video? Half of them were more disturbing than anything I've filmed… People are clearly getting off to this."

Yes, all kinds of disgusting comments stacked up beneath the video. Misspelled variations of everything from "This is so hot, I wish this girl would step on my balls" to "Hey bitch, if you like pain why don't you share your address" to the most pressing and popular question: "Do you do porn?"

All these were interspersed with people calling the video fake, still more suggesting the Degenetrix had mental health issues, and some claiming the video was linked to something called an "alternate reality game." Whatever. This wide variety of chatter was part of having a successful career in Internet video production: a job hazard that nonetheless revealed the main core of her audience consisted of, as anticipated, fellow perverts. "The creeps watching this video and sharing it with each other would do anything to see a sex tape with me," she proposed.

"More reason to hold back. Save it for premium content."

"Like custom videos?"

"Eventually. But for right now—here."

He showed her another website, this designed to connect freelance entrepreneurs of adult entertainment with fans. "Fans" in this context referred to people with disposable income and a devotion to artists they liked. Such users would join the website, pledge monthly donations to their favorite content creators, and thereafter enjoy a regular stream of exclusive content in exchange for anything from five dollars a month to recurring donations in the triple digits.

"The site where we posted the Hammer Video doesn't allow nudity or pornography, and this one doesn't have that limitation…but I still don't think we should jump to posting premium porn right away. That'll make the hit-and-run look like a publicity stunt to start your career as a niche porn actress. Too transparent. You should be more approachable at first—we need to emphasize contrast by amping up your character's personality. What we want is for people to get the sense that you're stumbling into this, naively trying to leverage your fame and getting sucked into the depraved underworld of pornography as time goes on. A character arc."

What else was there to do but go with it? The inherently sexual capacities of even the most intense pain grew clearer to her by the day. The Hammer Video was pornography already, but it was extremely covert pornography for an extremely covert group of sadists. There was wisdom in dragging things out before switching to overt pornography. She had a niche: one all her own. It would be a shame to wear it out before things even got started.

The Hammer Video had racked up half a million views within the first week of its premiere. A second video was uploaded to the Degenetrix's page the following Friday, a week and a day after the first: from that point in time, Friday was their regular upload day. This second recording required no pretension. The Degenetrix, despite the dark aesthetic of her clothes and hair and kohl eyeliner, despite the ominous nature of everything from the moniker she bore to the subject of her films, smiled before the video even began.

"Hi, everyone! It's Degenetrix again—I can't believe the reaction my last video got! Thank you!" Big pink graphical effects bubbled up to spell the words "THANK YOU" across the bottom of the screen. "I love reading your comments and seeing everybody talking about my work. Praise as a performance artist is so moving to me—I've only just started, but I've been a photographer for a long time. See?" One by one, the Degenetrix lifted a series of photographs for the video camera's assessment: her black-and-white sequence of a woman's hand being slashed open with a knife and healing, all apparently within the same short frame of time. "I've always loved taking photos, but I think I'm going to love making videos for you even more!"

With off-camera shifting, she traded the selection of photographs for the same gleaming knife depicted in them. What a big smile she wore as she lifted her pale arm into frame and dragged the knife across her own flesh! As ribbons of blood unfurled, she hissed, gasped, tightened that hand into a fist, and shut her eyes. When she opened them again, they were rimmed with tears and wild with the lust that left her, along with the pain, almost breathless. "A lot of you still don't seem to think I'm real, but I am… Cutting myself like this is one of the first things I tried when I learned about my magic trick. Ah!" Unable to bear it further, the panting Degenetrix paused to study the red coating of her forearm. A hand from off camera offered a rag to clean the wounds. She did so in order to demonstrate the healing, but only after wiping her own blood across her face with a low gasp of appreciation for the iron flavor on her lips.

Smiling again, though with the fatigue of the post-orgasm afterglow, the Degenetrix wiped the back of her hand across her sweat-beaded forehead, heaved a theatrical sigh, and showed the camera that no wound remained. "This is old news for me," she continued, coyly gazing into the camera and the viewer beyond. "I want to try all kinds of other things…electricity and fire and, well…you'll have to subscribe to see more content from me!"

By the end of the following week, the Degenetrix was an underground icon.

· MAURICE TABARD ·

1

NOT EVERYONE ENJOYED the woman's newfound fame. The Knife Video premiered, and she received an unexpected video call from her appalled mother.

"What on earth is that clip! That *is* you, isn't it?"

"Yeah, it's me…" The woman scratched an itch between her ribs, peered into the cotton of her robe at the dry patch beneath, then fixed the fabric before continuing absently, "It's just performance art, Mom."

"Some performance! What's artistic about that? Let me see your arm." Her mother leaned toward the phone, squinting accusatorily even once the woman lifted her limb to her device's camera lens. "It looked so *real*, I— How on earth did you do that?"

"It's a magic trick."

"Is this the kind of 'magic trick' you want to broadcast across the Internet? My coworkers recognized you from the pictures on my desk. What are you trying to do?"

"Trying to get rich and famous making art, which I thought was obvious."

Again, her mother asked, "What's *artistic* about this, though?"

"You've never understood performance art, Mommy. I didn't either until recently. Paintings and sculpture…even photography, it's all so still. I want to make art in four dimensions. I'd make it in even more if I could figure out how, but four is a good start."

"If you want to make fourth-dimensional art, you could always be a musician. Or a dancer!"

Damn her mother and her sensible alternatives. "Except I'm not a musician, and the dancing ship has sailed. Gotta use the skills you have.

I've got a magic trick no one else can do! A stage name, a character, even a producer. This is such an opportunity— Do you think I should let it pass? I'm making something from less than nothing."

"But art should be creative. Productive, not destructive. Can't you come up with another magic trick? I'll admit this one looks real, but—"

But mothers were all the same. You were a doctor, they wished you were a lawyer. You were a photographer—why couldn't you have been a lawyer? You were a sadomasochistic performance artist, and here was a sudden, mysterious interest in the nuances of developing film and the specific types of lenses she used. Private support would have been welcome, but the community support was so unreal that the woman sometimes felt she dreamt, or forgot she read comments under her own videos. This seemed like someone else's success. Ugly things were interspersed, but more of it elated her. People addressed her as if they craved her attention—as if she did them a favor rather than the other way around.

MORE! This is the greatest content I've ever seen on the Internet.

Please post more, this special effect is unreal. Are you using liquid latex?

When's your next video, do you take requests?

She sat up at night, wrapped in her robe, browsing her videos with a crooked grin. It felt so good to be appreciated. And all this before the first check!

2

THE ROAD TO FISCAL stability—what the stranger referred to as "sustainable monetization"—was a rocky one, but nugget by nugget, gold appeared among that hard-trod stones.

At the end of the second month, the first direct deposit appeared in her account. "This is barely two hundred dollars," she complained.

"We've hit a problem I'd like to talk to you about," he responded, turning his laptop toward her. "I didn't notice until the check was deposited, but it seems like a lot of our videos are getting demonetized."

Yes: incredibly, the mainstream advertisers dealing with the most culturally ubiquitous video hosting website on the Internet did not want to be associated with a woman hammering her bones to pieces, or slitting open her arm, or, in the third video, putting a darning needle through her tongue (a sensation she despised and loved for showing her she yet had the capacity to despise any sensation). She would have thought medical tape advertisers would go for it. Red Cross blood-drive public service announcements. No? No hunting knife manufacturers, urgent care providers, bleach companies? Nobody?

"Nobody who works with this video host," said the stranger. "The more I've thought about it, the more I've come to the conclusion that we'll be lucky if our content is allowed to stay up. Since we claim it's a magic trick and that you're a performance artist, we have a good argument. But…"

Two more forms of online video hosting services were introduced to the woman. One bore a name she had seen before: a website linked to videos of grim terrorist acts, or actual war footage, or disasters, or real deaths like the suicide of Senator Budd Dwyer who blew his brains out on national television. Abraham Zapruder, eat your heart out. The website was hard core, and the stranger suggested they start posting her videos there not just to avoid possible censorship but to further muddy the waters as to the reality of her content—to further tantalize those in it for dark titillation. That her trick was real and she was real were facts so far beyond anyone's wildest dreams that the worst of the most depraved basement sadists subscribing to her videos could not even imagine it. Anyone who saw her footage was flabbergasted, disgusted, aroused, or some combination of the three. But after having time to think, every viewer came up with a million ways of faking this or that or the other thing. It was infuriating, which was why the woman was intrigued by the stranger's next point.

"The problem with this website is the same problem we're having right now…due to the nature of their content, they can't get many advertisers interested in working with them. They've got some, so we're going to get some money from it, but we need to diversify our platforms. Have you thought about doing livestreams?"

"Live performance broadcasts?" The woman tapped her chin while the stranger pulled up a popular streaming service ostensibly used by people who wanted to watch others play video games. Viewers could tip their favorite players real money for quality content, and the most popular players could even partner with the website itself to rake in extra cash. The reality was that people doing streams on that website played video games only in part, and sometimes not at all: most of them were there to do comedy routines between the video games, or react to the videos of other content creators in front of a live audience, or earn pocket change by teasing viewers with low-cut tank tops that gave a good eyeful and promised the occasional "accidental" payoff.

The woman laughed. "Wow! I wouldn't have thought so many video game streamers would be girls, but I guess it makes sense when I think about it."

"Yeah. So—do you like video games?"

3

THE STREAMING SHOWS were shot in the stranger's apartment because his personal computer could play video games her portable laptop computer could not. They used the webcam attached to his PC: all the stream footage was grainy and off-color, and the stranger's living room behind her was poorly lit compared to the atmosphere of her usual videos, but nobody minded, and the woman felt that the lower quality contributed to the grimy snuff-film aesthetic. After getting a few visitors in the channel (ten the first week, fifty the next, quickly anything over a hundred), she would open:

"Hi, guys! It's Degenetrix—thanks for hanging out with me! Tonight, I'm playing—"

And she would talk about the game, blah, blah. Nobody was there for that. They could have seen a hot girl on any stream talk about a video game and why she liked it. Viewers came to the Degenetrix's channel because they sought her peculiar content, and they were not to be disappointed. The first twenty minutes of the stream would be dominated by video game playing. Most of the screen consisted of whatever game she played. Superimposed in a box in the corner was footage of the woman playing the game, her facial reactions, and her color commentary bantered to her watching chat room. Always good fun until something went wrong.

During the first stream, around the time viewers started to ask if she'd do anything, the Degenetrix got up to stretch her legs. She returned with a glass bottle of beer and—

"Oops—"

Cue shattering, fizzing as beer suds splayed across the apartment's wooden floor.

"Oh, no!"

Springing to get a paper towel, running back, stepping straight through the glass to leave a diamond-shaped chunk three inches across impaled in the arch of her foot. She screamed. What a clumsy girl! Clumsier still when, lifting her foot to show the audience the surging blood, she managed to fall back into the spilled booze and broken glass.

The real purpose of the streams. Due to the nature of the streaming site, which was, despite its proliferation of girls in low-cut tops, still dedicated to video games, a facade had to be maintained—there were rules about things like displays of violence and gore, but nothing in the terms of service that said you couldn't have a household accident. Viewers understood as soon as the Degenetrix sat up in the broken glass to investigate her shining arms, then lifted her bloodied foot with its staggeringly large chunk of glass for the observation of the audience at home. Something for the sadistic foot fetishists: let them watch her gasp, scream, hiss, curse while she wiggled the primary offender from her arch and released a flow of fluid that soon trickled to a stop.

And as she played up the character of the clumsy bimbo who couldn't manage to avoid falling over and over into the shards of glass, tips rolled in. By the end of the stream, as she sat sniffling in the desk chair and encouraging viewers to come back next week— when she would make a noble effort to continue the game after this disappointing incident—she had made $600. Overall, this was not much, and when split two ways, it amounted to less than an eighth of what she paid her landlord every month: however, she could not help but feel it was the start of a positive trend.

4

NOT EVERYTHING WAS POSITIVE. The world grew unfamiliar. From the treadmill in her apartment building's workout room, the woman watched a courtesy television with her hands in the pockets of her hooded sweatshirt. The camera panned across a field of dirt while scores of tiny insects (ants?) twitched across the frame. Focus shifted in: the writhing insects resolved to excavators, hundreds, each churning the earth in preparation for an emergency hospital built in the country that originated the virus. There, it was already a grave danger. A similar hospital was being established closer to home by the foresight of some banking chain, a partnership with something or other. Things were like that in America—stadiums, hospitals, even schools had to be sponsored by a corporation to be built or funded. Thank God there were so many wealthy American companies. Sounded like they'd need a lot of hospitals... Maybe one or two more big named corporations would be generous.

The woman was so distracted that, getting her free weights out of the rack, the edge of a dumbbell caught in its metal shelf, and all twenty-five pounds slammed back down into place. No injury, but it gave her an idea for her next stream, wherein she played a virtual reality game designed to get fat schmoes working out. After "accidentally" swinging a weight up and savoring the initial explosion of pain at the breaking of her nose (like eating a fistful of habanero peppers: the image occurred amid the delirious rush of adrenaline, blood, and belated natural opiates), the woman blindly dropped the same weight upon her own foot. Staggered, she lay awhile in the fetal position, clutching her crippled toes to give viewers a nice panty shot up her miniskirt for the duration of the recovery.

People loved this stuff. Maybe because they could circulate clips of these injuries on ostensibly work-safe video hosts, like the mainstream one that now served to funnel viewers to the Degenetrix's preferred platforms. Most videos on the original site were free. As long as advertisers weren't involved, users were entitled to post almost anything that didn't involve nudity. A whole underground community on the mainstream video platform was devoted to stuff like this, this covert pornography—a lot of it filmed in countries where real porn wasn't legal to produce. Strange videos at weirdly pornographic angles of fully clothed women cleaning houses; whole playlists devoted to hot women smoking pot or cigarettes; something called "pedal pumping," where women would, perhaps unsurprisingly, pump the pedals of cars. Preferably ones stuck in the mud. This somehow felt related to the questionable genre of quicksand pornography, which depicted pretty models being clumsily delivered to Fate at the slow-moving bottom of a goofy Old Hollywood–style quicksand pit. Fans who understood that the Degenetrix's work was a comment on modern Internet pornography tended to quite rightly draw parallels between quicksand fetishism and the first livestream with the broken glass. On the other side of the fence, fans who were in it to get off had the grotesque double enjoyment of watching her bleed and bash and abuse herself live on camera in a surreptitious way, on a website for people to watch others play video games. The digital equivalent of jerking someone off beneath the table of a pizza parlor while kids shouted in an adjacent arcade ball pit.

How did the woman feel about this? On the one hand, she did feel a little weird, a little gross, for putting on these surreptitious fetish shows—weirder and grosser than she would have were she openly slitting her wrists on camera for the pleasure of her audience. But you had to do what you had to do. When her ideal performances were sure to get her accounts banned, she had to operate in gray areas.

Besides, these performances were means to an end: not the receipt of money but the production of passionate artwork. To experience what it was to be artwork—to experience self-sacrifice. Or perhaps "self-offering" was a better term. She didn't feel it a sacrifice. It was her pleasure to devote herself, and devote she did. Her work never stopped. Like any true artist, she looked, always, for inspiration. Within the aisles of home improvement stores, people saw pilers, rope, nails, garden shears. The woman saw sex toys, possibilities—many questions.

How far could she go with this? Was there a limit to her body's ability to recover? The more she came to enjoy, say, the feeling of a cold knife biting through her skin, the more she pondered the important question of durability. What would happen if something were amputated? What then? Would it grow back? If she cut off a finger or a hand, would a new one bud like an amoeba—replicating yet remaining whole? Would her severed hand then grow a second body? A whole second woman? That would be fucked up! But kind of hot—sibling incest, pseudo or otherwise (though why it mattered when it was all fictional wasn't clear), was at that time all the rage in pornography. Clone pornography was the next logical step.

There went her imagination again. Daydreaming, always daydreaming. Pondering the limits of her art. On the subway, in galleries, in the diner, in her home. Anything she saw, any narrow miss, was fodder for the vast collage she made of her own existence. When the stranger finished filming and she went home, or on off nights when she was by herself in her quiet apartment, she dabbled in new methods and breathed life to the inspirations that alighted upon her. All day, every day, she waited for the moment she was alone: when, heart racing, she was free to do whatever she wanted to herself. The support of her growing fan base was invaluable, but there were as many commenters whose disgust was beyond measure (why were they taking the time to watch and comment, she always had to wonder), and she could see the stranger recognized only fiscal opportunity in her masochistic sojourns. Then there was her mother—always asking questions. "What if you lose your job over this?" "What if someone tries to copy you and they get hurt and they sue? Worse, what if they die?" "What happens when you make a mistake, honey? What then?"

What then? God, she wanted to know—but the fear outweighed the curiosity to such an extent that she spent many weeks slowly escalating. Adapting. Burning herself with cigarettes developed into laying her hand on the panini press, the stove burner; gradually, the cuts of her knife got deeper, faster. Enough to sever muscle and reveal bone.

It had already been many years since the simple in and out of vaginal penetration, along with a bit of clitoral stimulation, had last proved sufficient to bring the woman to climax: now she couldn't get wet without a few well-timed burns around the genitals. Not to say she didn't enjoy traditional stimulation once she was aroused, but her capacity for sexual enjoyment seemed to have been enclosed within an electric fence. Every day, a new layer popped up. Every day, it became harder for her to find excitement in the torments that others provided. A person got tired of missionary all the time—the woman got tired of the same old cigarette burns and choke-outs applied by her exiting lovers, but they wouldn't edge much further beyond those acts that had once been extreme and now constituted the basic essence of necessary foreplay.

Yet she could not help but feel reluctant to look for new lovers to satisfy her shocking needs. After the incident with the stranger (replayed in her head each time they were together, especially while having sex), anonymous liaisons lost their sheen. Now there were no long-term physical consequences to be spoken of—none she had yet found, at any rate—but the potential emotional cost of more betrayal was too great. Greater, perhaps, for her physical immortality. The idea of opening herself to a new person, of sharing this gift of hers, and failing yet again to make a connection…better to be alone than disappointed.

This brought her, as always, to the important question. It was one she asked herself frequently as she sat alone on the edge of her bed, searing her thigh with a cast-iron skillet while working a dildo, sometimes crying out at the fierceness of the agony, the thunder of the pleasure. This was a question that floated up to her in the middle of the night, woke her out of deep slumber like a man pressing his hard dick to her ass. The question. The real question:

Could she ever die?

5

HER MOTHER CALLED AGAIN. Fourth day in a row.

"Don't you think you should cover your face?"

"Are we converting to Islam?"

"Islam" was the name of a faith notable, aside from angering Christians (that was, members of the predominant faith of America, worshippers of that aforementioned crucified carpenter who was also the son of God), for encouraging women to cover their heads and sometimes faces. A terrorist attack rocked the city at the turn of the century, and because the terrorists were practitioners of an extreme splinter of Islam, Americans associated the covering of one's face with fringe religion and, broadly speaking, government oppression. Her mother was not to be stopped by the implication that she oppressed her daughter. "You know what I mean! Your—'artwork,' it's... I've seen the comments people leave on your videos."

The confession merited a childish drop of the woman's stomach. "I wish you wouldn't."

"I can't help it! I need to keep an eye on what you're up to. These videos—I don't know, honey."

"I'm not making them for you, Mom."

"Obviously not! Maybe if you made nice, funny videos for people like me, you wouldn't be so sad all the time."

The computer's clock seemed slower than analog ones. "I'm doing well lately. I haven't thought of myself as depressed for almost six months."

"That's good, but—don't you want a steady boyfriend? Real friends instead of these bums I see you posting pictures with? Don't you want to live in a real house, have a real job?"

"I'm sorry, is the diner not a real job? Is my artwork not real artwork? I'm making money from it."

"Of course the diner is a real job, I'm not saying that. It's—"

After the conversation, the woman went to the stranger's house to lay in his unmade bed while he, up at the computer desk, tapped on the keyboard until she asked, "Can we freeze comments on the videos? My mother is on my last nerve."

"Why is your *mom* watching these videos?"

"That's what I asked her… Can we do something?"

"We can lock the comment sections of all your videos if you want. But—the community of fans you're developing is vitally important to our success."

She definitely saw his point. People were slowly growing obsessed with the Degenetrix; a few commenters had gotten regular enough that she recognized their usernames. The hard-core fans had quickly come to worship her and had taken to calling themselves "the Degenerates," which was, in truth, delightful. Their comments were vile and disturbing, and the haste with which they strove to be the first commenter on all her videos was pretty alarming when one considered the kind of content she posted. But, brother, all she or the stranger had to do was get on the Degenetrix account and post an ambiguous reply to whatever comment caught their eye: the responses flooded in. Something about Internet celebrity made people perceive creators as friends rather than untouchable icons. And the more like a friend, the more obsessed the audience.

So—the woman understood why the comments were valuable, but all the same, she felt restricted in her self-expression as long as her mother's opinion floated through her head. "There has to be a better way."

Arms crossed in consideration, the stranger stared into the screen and suggested, "I was thinking the other day it was time to make a website. Maybe we could start a forum."

"But Mom could still read it, right?"

"It would be harder for her to find, but…" The stranger rubbed his jaw. "We could make it a private forum—now that's a good idea."

"How would we do that?"

"We'd have to moderate users—make them go through an approval process. We'll probably approve anybody who signs up; but that way, if your mom tries to make an account, we'll know…and the Degenerates will love the exclusivity. Oh, yeah, wow—this is an excellent idea. Okay—I'll lock the comments on your videos and look into creating a website. We'll have to pay webhosting fees, though…oh, and we'd ought to get a new camera."

"Shouldn't that come out of your half, since you own the original camera?"

"It's *our* business," was his protest, and from a tax position, he had a point. She let it go. It didn't matter. The next check was a whole lot higher, and delivered the woman a whole lot of confidence that she was on the right path.

6

THE WOMAN MET her first Degenerate four months after the hit-and-run video. If the fan in question hadn't been female, things might have been uncomfortable instead of surreal. "I thought you lived here," had been how the vindicated Degenerate announced herself while the woman exited a bagel shop, glamorously dusting her hands of cream cheese. "You're the Degenetrix, right? Wow, wow!"

Damn! Maybe her mother was right—maybe she did need to reconsider wearing a mask. "I watch all your videos," the Degenerate continued, shaking hands without a thought to the ongoing pandemic that had begun to grip the city. The fan grinned ear to ear, bright-eyed and wildly excited as the woman herself might have been while meeting, say, Diane Arbus. "You're so freaking cool! I haven't figured out a single one of your tricks. I thought it was CGI, but then I watched your livestream and saw the free-weight thing you did, and—I mean, that wasn't a prop, right? It looked heavy in your hand. You could be a great mime, I guess."

The adapting woman assessed the attractive young Degenerate: sort of what she should have expected when it came to her fan base. Bleached blonde hair shaved on one side, green militia jacket, metal piercings filling about every square inch of her face and tongue except for earlobes dedicated to thick gauges. Nice body, too. Maybe unexpectedly nice. "I'm not a mime," answered the woman agreeably. "Just a magician, a performance artist. I'm glad you like my videos, though."

"Can I get a selfie with you?" Degenerate #1, already holding her phone, referred to modern slang for a self-portrait, sometimes of other people, which then was not a self-portrait but, well…the woman tried not to get annoyed by the nuances of modern culture, because when she did, it made her feel old, and, at not yet thirty, she had no business feeling so old. The Degenerate, whose brightly grinning cheek pressed to hers while they posed together, was maybe even younger than her art student girlfriend—old enough for piercings, though, so she was at least the age of consent.

"I don't live too far from here," said the woman, jerking her thumb in that direction. "Want to come see my studio? I'll show you my props."

Degenerate #1, hereafter referred to as #1, turned out to be much more enthusiastic a sadomasochist than either the girlfriend or the stranger—somehow more interesting, too. This became apparent after sex. #1 had, with wide hazel eyes, watched several kinds of injuries heal throughout the course of their rendezvous, and investigating the perfect site of a former cut, asked, "Is this why you don't have any, like, piercings or anything? Most women have their ears pierced, at least."

"I've never wanted piercings…needles kind of freak me out."

"But what about the needle-in-your-tongue routine? I love that video—I think about it whenever I do tongue piercings."

"You work at a parlor?"

"Uh-huh—we do piercings and tattoos, but I personally only do piercings." Turned out that despite her elfin looks, #1 was older than the art student by several years. Finished with apprenticeship, the piercing artist had come to this brave new city world to have a taste of the lauded life. Just in time for a destructive pandemic to pack the hospitals full. #1 summarized after describing her career path, "It's super hard to live here even when business is good, but it's been getting harder and harder over the past couple of months. I think people keep hearing about that virus, and they're worried about booking appointments."

"Yeah, I'd think the spread of a novel disease would slow down people's interest in paying strangers to stick needles in them."

Though #1 laughed, she observed, "You're much—I don't know, drier in person than you are in your show."

Interesting choice of word. The woman hadn't thought of it

as a "show" before. "My character is more excitable than I am… People like the energy."

With a coy grin, the woman's new favorite Degenerate slid her fingers over rolling hills of sensitive flesh. "I don't know…you seem pretty excitable to me." Down, down, down slipped her hand, and the woman splayed her legs to permit investigation. With a bite of her pierced lip in the direction of her sheet-covered wrist, #1 suggested, "You should let me pierce you sometime… I could do a show with you. Maybe the parlor could sponsor an episode somehow."

"That could be fun—but the hole will close as soon as I take the needle out, baby."

"Guess I'll have to do it to you regularly, then."

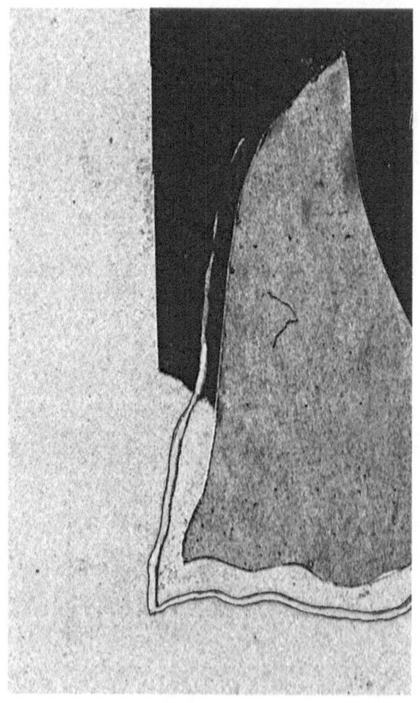

7

AS PREVIOUSLY MENTIONED, not all the Degenetrix's viewers found her content inspiring. There were those who, like her mother, were gravely concerned. It was hard to say if it was one of these concerned Samaritans who called for the police welfare check, or if the culprit was one of her neighbors. For all she knew, it could have been her mother, but more likely, it was somebody nearby. In a building of studio apartments with walls so thin you could hear the neighbor's toilet flush, in a situation where wiser citizens spent more time at home to evade the virus, it was only a matter of time before somebody stuck at home grew tired of the agonized screams peppered with pornographic moans. Still…pretty rude to call the cops on somebody trying to get off. Had to invest in that sound-insulating equipment. Call the stranger tomorrow. Whatever—she threw on a robe and stashed her sex toys before checking the door.

Nothing like seeing unexpected cops on the other side of a peephole to kill the buzz. If nothing else, the younger of the two was good-looking. Big fascist energy, with his pursed mouth and sunken eyes—but what cop didn't permeate the world around with a hint of control issues? If anything, the gestapo aesthetic made him more attractive to the masochistic artist. At least he had not yet adopted the mustache of his fat partner: the lieutenant wheezed an asthmatic inhalation, hooked his thumb in his belt, and turned to face the tenant of the apartment whose door had opened.

"Evening, miss." The older cop introduced himself and his younger partner, a sergeant. "We're just responding to a call—you doing all right? We had a complaint, mentioned unusual sounds."

Unusual to the cops, maybe; the neighbors needed to lean in.

Widening her eyes, the woman rested her forehead against the door and asked, "What kinds of sounds?"

The attractive sergeant interrupted his laser-precision assessment of her face to explain, "Screaming." Hard as his expression was, it somehow lacked the gravity, the concern, expected of a police officer, perhaps by contrast with his more natural partner. "Mostly screaming."

"Noises we'd associate with a domestic situation—with your boyfriend, ma'am?"

"No, I live alone." The woman pushed open the door of her apartment and stepped back, waving an inviting hand in demonstration. "You're welcome to look around if you'd like. I'm sorry, I was watching a horror movie. I'll turn it down."

While the lieutenant stepped into the apartment and nudged aside the vinyl roll of her white backdrop, the sergeant stood in the threshold behind her and continued prying without direct interrogation. "Complaint mentioned this has been going on for a while. A regular problem."

"I watch a lot of horror movies." The woman turned to study him, hands on her hips. What was it about him? The way he watched her— like he was attracted to her, sure, but—

It only occurred to her when the older cop stepped into her bathroom that it was the same sort of look #1 gave her: the same barely contained, wild glint. Predatory recognition.

Her hand landed upon her sternum, where fingers curled around the plush edge of her robe. His pupils expanded. "You boys must not have much to do. I heard the bars are going to close if things don't improve soon."

"Crime has a way of going down when people stay at home. Domestic violence'll skyrocket, but it hasn't yet. Biggest problem right now is people fistfighting over toilet paper."

"Are you trying to recognize me from somewhere?" She theatrically bit her lip, the expression inciting the lust of the uniformed pig unprepared for her sudden veer. "Or do you recognize me already?"

The older officer broke the string of tension between herself and his younger partner while emerging from the washroom.

"These the only rooms in the apartment?"

"Yes, Officer."

"And you haven't had any friends over tonight?"

"No, sir."

The sergeant still hovered so close, she felt the vibration of his atoms. "What was the movie?"

"*American Psycho*. The part where he's chasing the woman with his chain saw—I bet that's what they heard. I'm so sorry, Officers. I'll be sure to keep it down."

"Do your best." Oblivious of his young partner's fixation, the lieutenant squeezed past her and back into the hall. "These places are so small and so close together that it's hard to be sensible about noise control no matter what you do. Maybe try headphones when it gets late the evening, if you don't mind."

"Thank you, Officer, I will. And thank you for checking on me. What you do is so important…it makes me feel good to know that if I'm ever in danger, the police will be there."

"Have a nice night, miss."

The sergeant stared on and on, his interest transparent to the woman despite the camouflage of his uniform until the door had shut. An animal. A Degenerate. In his eyes, his face, his posture. The antagonized desire infusing it all. A shudder rolled through her while she removed the jerry-rigged dildo-screwdriver from under her pillow: the intense predatory vibration of the young cop had given her something fun to think about while she self-abused.

8

WHEN THE WOMAN WAS A KID, the dangers of Internet creeps had been drilled into her skull. But times had changed. Meeting people from the Internet was such a regular thing that nobody remembered how in the 1990s it had seemed a death sentence. Good thing the culture changed. From a networking perspective, great things came of online interactions.

#1 was an example. After they met, #1 continued texting with the woman, and the texting became emailing as she began to more professionally coordinate with the other people at her parlor. While #1 got her boss involved, the woman got her stranger on board, and the team devoted to making Degenetrix films began its steady expansion. The subsequent piercing video filmed in #1's parlor was shared not just with the Degenerates but also the many social media followers of the prestigious tattoo parlor, thereby converting an admirable number of new Degenerates to the woman's proud cult. Many of those who followed businesses like tattoo parlors on social media identified as part of the "extreme body modification" scene and loved videos of acts ranging from extreme corset-binding to self-castration: this made them a natural group to gravitate to the Degenetrix, who could not modify her body permanently and had the pleasure of doing it again and again.

"It's kind of a shame you always heal so fast," said #1 after the second parlor video. The first had been focused on piercings, mostly in the ears and lips and tongue since they couldn't do anything involving nudity and keep their current sponsors. During the second recording session, the woman got her first tattoo, which was half gone by the time the artist finished. The whole thing completely dissolved about twenty minutes after that, which was too bad. It had been a bird, a bluebird of happiness, wings outspread as it reclined in the web-cum-fishing net of an unseen spider. The tattooist's painterly rendering of the bird was pretty as a jewel in turquoise ink, and if she might have had one tattoo, it would have been that one. She commissioned a printing of the design as a wall scroll after the scene was shot.

Truth be told, the instant healing was sometimes dissatisfying in other ways. Take burns. Anything smaller than a nice third-degree sear healed in under a minute. No time to enjoy a prolonged sensation. When she was alone, she had to constantly produce new wounds in order to sustain the pain and avoid being left with mere memory. Not that she complained about her healing. It intensified and changed her artwork. It made her money. It even brought her friends.

Well—hangers-on. Friends of #1 and #1's boss, the tattoo artist who'd collaborated with the woman and the stranger on the second parlor video. #1 had shared the Degenetrix's videos with quite a few of her friends and colleagues; the tattoo artist had done the same. These friends of friends' friends began to drift into orbit around the woman. A pack of them, #1 included, got into the habit of palling around in one of the diner's booths for a few hours near the end of the woman's every shift. Their ruckus grew more absurd by the day, more laden with profanity and inappropriate anecdotes, so it wasn't a surprise when her boss used her friends as his excuse to fire her. A formal warning beforehand might have been nice, however.

"This is a family environment," he reminded her while she stood in his office, dumbstruck to find the contents of her tiny locker (a pair of shoes, a water bottle, her current paperback book, the apple she'd intended to have for lunch) waiting in a cardboard box. "We've had a lot of complaints about your friends and—"

"Then throw *them* out! Not me—or let them stay. They're paying, aren't they?"

"That's not the point."

"Is this about the videos?"

"This is a family environment," he repeated. The woman folded her arms over her apron.

"And we all know how family friendly your fucking behavior is—you prick. What am I supposed to do? I need this job to live."

He didn't have an answer. She left in angry tears. Humiliating! He had fired her not because of her friends or even because of her online content but because she had firmly refused his propositions. She had made herself a sexless entity taking up space that could have been filled by a more compliant, more desperate young lady. Let it happen, then. A few hours later, the woman was in the stranger's apartment, ranting until she realized she repeated herself, at which point she added, "And some timing! We're just starting to take off, but there's no way I can sustain myself yet. This city is so expensive. I'm not going to have to move home with my mother, am I?"

More panicked by the thought of losing his cash cow than his friend, the stranger waved a hand. "Don't do anything rash. It happens I've been thinking about things. Have you looked at the forum lately?"

"On our website? No, I haven't."

The ostensibly private Degenetrix community had exploded. Thread after thread filled the subforums: people asking personal details about Her Royal Highness, as some of the more pathetic posters referred to her; theories about how she managed her tricks; a thread titled "Degenetrix Sightings," exactly as creepy as it sounded and dominated by city dwellers who saw her eating lunch or drinking coffee or going to a bookstore and had to brag; futile searches for comparable performers; a growing collection of "fan fiction" imagining her as the main character in this or that typo-riddled kinky adventure. All trash. All hilarious. The most interesting thread, however, was simply titled, "Requests?"

Does Degenetrix do request videos? asked the original poster. *Probably way out of my budget, but there are some things I'd love to see her try.*

Everybody in the thread was quick to agree, and it had derailed into a list of fantasy requests from Degenerates who wanted to see their mistress stick her tongue in a toaster or take an electric bread knife up the ass. The creativity of the ideas! Battery acid enemas and on-camera lobotomies, oh, she was inspired. Obviously, it was invasive to have all these people fantasizing about her, but when she considered it, this kind of interaction made her artwork an interesting collaborative process. She was the medium as well as the artist, and as a medium, she was open for use by anyone of artistic temperament. The muse was polyamorous. The woman, an exhibitionist.

There was nothing quite like seeing the thoughts people had about you on display in a public forum, and the alarm was real when the Requests thread was juxtaposed with, say, the Degenetrix Sightings collection. There were disturbed people in the city. Not every Degenerate would be as cool as #1—as attractive, as connected. The next time somebody approached her, it might not have been pleasant.

That in mind, the stranger's next advisement had merit in more ways than one. "I think it's time to start taking payments from fans."

He pulled up the payment-based website he had shown her before to reveal he had already parked the Degenetrix's username, "HRH_Degenetrix."

"To do that, we start doing exclusive content for subscribers—on a regular basis, I mean, in addition to our usual streams. We could start with requests from this thread to show we're paying attention to the community, and maybe over time, we'll migrate it to a more crowd-based model. Like, fans throw out suggestions, then vote to decide on the special video of the month. That way, they feel they have a say in the content. They're invested."

And defused. If she was already fulfilling their fantasies on camera, most of the worst weirdos would probably be satisfied. It was a self-defense measure. Wasn't any effort to get money a self-defense measure? Money was not something inherently valuable. It was valuable because the government, along with a bunch of dead people, decided it was valuable. The capitalist system was brutally rigged to ensure anybody without money or credit was punished. There were people in the city working themselves to death to maintain their dwelling, and many, having failed, now lived on the street. The woman hoped it would never be so bad for her—in addition to her friends, she now had legions of fans to keep her afloat—but it was still sobering to wake, that first morning after being fired from the diner, without certainty of income.

Her next video was a good way to work out her emotions.

Method acting! Better than therapy. Before her white background, the tearful woman explained her heartbreaking circumstances. "It's Degenetrix," was how she opened, leaving out the chipper, "Hi, everyone," that usually proceeded such an intro. "I'm here to talk to you about a situation… I've lost my job, and I'm in dire straits." She hammered it up, sprinkling truth into the damsel-in-distress fantasy: abusive, would-be exploitative boss; distant mother; the hard life of a girl struggling to make it as an artist. All of it was true, but the opinions in the video were those of the Degenetrix. A more sensitive person than her real counterpart. In real life, the woman felt not disheartened but insulted. The Degenetrix was the Degenetrix, the woman was the woman.

At the end of the video, the Degenetrix explained the establishment of her new subscription system, assuring viewers that the streams would always be free and the video page always populated with complimentary content. However, this new system was better! Users could contribute whatever they wanted and would receive benefits depending on the tier: first-tier fans who gave a token amount like five dollars a month would receive access to a private fan-only forum on the Degenetrix's website. There, the Degenetrix herself would occasionally post (or the stranger using her account, but nobody needed to know that). A chance to talk to your favorite performance artist! Kind of. Maybe. Pay more if you wanted guarantees.

At $25, second-tier fans could access monthly videos, and $50-a-month fans sitting pretty in the third tier had the privilege of voting on what those monthly videos would be. The ideas that went into the voting pool every month were, naturally, generated by those who contributed $100 a month or more to the welfare of Her Royal Highness: and, finally—at that time, the dream of a fantasy of a delusion—those rare and repugnant birds willing to pay $500 a month or more in support of a young woman's full-time devotion to artful self-mutilation were tantalized with the opportunity to receive their own custom videos up to once a month. A private gift from the Degenetrix to her most generous contributors. Most people, the stranger advised, would stick to the first tiers, and anybody who dropped $500 once probably wouldn't let such a fund ride monthly—that was more likely a tier belonging to those who wanted one or two custom videos to sate a niche interest for which content was scarce. Even $100 fans couldn't be counted on long-term, he advised, but the woman didn't care about long-term: she needed to think about paying rent next month.

And all of this, from the moment she first cut herself until the time she began collecting fans, these months speeding by like days, was how the woman met her beloved.

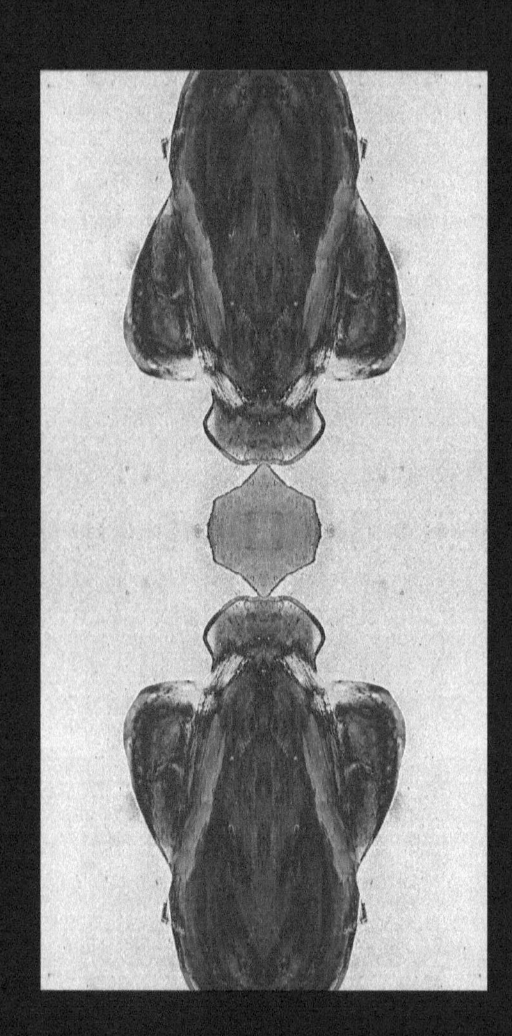

· S A L V A D O R   D A L I ·

1

SHE ALMOST DIDN'T NOTICE HIM. There were a lot of Degenerates out there, and a shocking number had been sufficiently moved by their mistress's plea to shower her with financial support in exchange for increasingly extreme content. Within the first forty-eight hours of posting the announcement, the stranger showed her she had already elicited the kindness of twenty-six noble souls. By the end of the month, the number had bumped to seventy-nine: most of them, as the stranger had predicted, contributed five dollars, but to her surprise, five had contributed as much as a hundred dollars a month. In other words, the forum already had five power users responsible for prompting new videos. By the time the first check from this new service came in, the amount garnered from supporters of the arts—combined with money she made through tips on her stream along with payouts from those few advertisers unethical enough to accept space in front of her videos—meant that even after her split with the stranger, she was still raking in $1,800 a month. Pretty nice for a freelancer in her first year of working from home. "You'll have to worry about taxes," advised the stranger while they crouched together before his laptop to bask in the glow of her fans' usernames. "But, as far as worries go—"

"One of the better ones I've had in a while. So, these are the real perverts, huh?" Kindred spirits. She paused in scrolling through the list to study the handles of the five who had agreed to contribute $100 a month to their favorite, most unique camgirl. These were the people who saw what she did: *really* saw it. She hoped they saw the artistic merit in her work, anyway—but it was all right if they saw her getting off on the extreme tortures and got off on that in turn. That was part of the experience of the artwork: it was a challenge of the nature of titillation, the nature of sadomasochism, the nature of Internet pornography. The woman liked to think of herself as somebody trying to make porn less solipsistic, more mindful.

Maybe she hadn't shown her body yet, but people didn't pledge pretty women $100 a month for no reason. She wondered now if she'd ever need to show her body. These freaks were satisfied to watch her punish herself with clothes on. Why go the truly seedy route? Clothes on or off, it was the same. Still porn. Her genre of work had to be called something, and though she was reluctant to label it "erotica" and stubbornly referred to it as "performance art," looking at her list of fans cooled her ego's hot need for the defense of cognitive dissonance. Of the top contributors in the spreadsheet, she recognized four usernames from the forum and recalled all their suggestions for the first monthly video: a list that had included fun requests involving things like railroad spikes and gasoline but had ultimately yielded to the tame prompt that she slit her arms up to her elbows and die while on camera. She had died for about twenty minutes on a stream once, and it had been a pretty hot experience. The Degenetrix had put on a big show of "accidentally" getting tangled in a lamp cord hanging from the stranger's ceiling and had intended to black out but had hanged herself, and she knew that was true because when she came to, it was with the same degree of stark disorientation and limp body that had come after the incident with the stranger. That feeling of having been stolen somehow—snatched from out of the ocean of time and thrust back in at another point entirely, although spatially it seemed the same, being as it was all ocean.

She didn't enjoy the death experience itself because she was not there to enjoy it, having been dead at the time—but she liked to think about it after, once the stiffness in her neck from breaking a vertebra with her accidental suicide loosened to its usual mobility. Viewers had loved to see her die, and she could already guess snuff videos would be the most widely selected content from her voters. Fine by her. She could love anything. She was a professional.

Professionalism was why she tried to contain her curiosity while assessing the subscriber list, but she could not help asking, "How come this fifth guy hasn't made an account on the forum?"

"You noticed that too, huh? I thought he didn't get the email inviting him to set up the account, or maybe he didn't know how, but I sent the invitation a second time. No response."

"Worried about his wife or something? Too bad! I like reading everybody's posts, getting to know them…they're all so bizarre."

Not the healthiest habit, but better than smoking. With her new glut of free time, the woman had taken to regularly perusing her own forums. Like some well-meaning mother spying on the conversations of her children, she watched cliques develop and hierarchies devise themselves among the regular posters as all socially scrambled to prove themselves first-class Degenerates. Any thread the woman graced with her presence was at once inundated with responses: eventually, she learned to post only in the subscriber forum to avoid derailing threads into endless off-topic lists of well-wishes and praise from an abundance of adoring weirdos.

All this was why it might have been easy to miss her beloved. Having no personality by which to remember him, the woman began to remember him as the guy she didn't remember. She wanted to remember him, though. She wanted to remember all her fans and, most importantly, keep all of them paying her—and she wanted to view herself as a professional. Professionals were as gracious as they were ingratiating. While the stranger wasn't looking (she didn't want to hear his opinion and give him a chance to micromanage her email writing, but how glad she was later that she had hidden this from him!), the woman jotted the email address affiliated with this fifth high-rolling account and, at home, drafted a digital letter.

Dear "Mot",

Sorry to address this to your username—you didn't give a first name anywhere that I could see! I notice you've agreed to give me $100 a month in support of my performances, and I wanted to tell you how much I appreciate your commitment. It seems you've opted not to make an account on the forum—but it's your privilege to suggest videos and vote with the other subscribers! I don't want you missing out. If it's your privacy that's a concern, would you like to send me suggestions directly? I can add them to the idea pool on your behalf.

Please let me know what I can do to express my appreciation! Supporters like you make it possible for me to work full-time on the art that's proven the most important part of my life.

Thank you again for your commitment!

Love,

The Degenetrix

She sent it from her official Degenetrix email account, didn't think more about it, and went to bed. When she woke up, it was not to an emailed reply from her donor but rather a call from the stranger. "All right, prepare to freak out: we just had somebody bump their contribution to five hundred dollars." She knew somehow what his next set of words would be. "Remember that guy who won't post on the forum? Well—I hope you're down for a custom video. Maybe whatever he wants is too personal for him to post on the forum."

If her mother was right about one thing, it was evidently thank-you notes. "Guess I'll send him an email. What's his info?"

After the call, the woman opened her work email account, found nothing of note in the inbox, and sent another message. Her heart thudded in her chest. When had she last felt this excited? It wasn't the money that thrilled her. It was the gesture behind it. The intent. What kind of person pledged $500 a month for her to hurt herself? Oh, she died to know.

Wow!

You must love really me. Thank you, thank you! Can I make a special video just for you?

Xoxo

Your Degenetrix

2

NOT EVERYBODY LOVED the subscription system. Many forum posters called her a sellout. One in particular wrote a manifesto-length condemnation declaring he had been "with her since the beginning and watched her get stupider, trashier, greedier every week" before summarizing, "Now she's a literal whore."

Cool—sweet opinion. Not worried about the haters. You know who was surprisingly cool with it?

"I'm so relieved you're not working at that diner," her mother said. "I'm sure they'll shut their doors soon. Our governor shut the state down—we've all got stay-at-home orders, and any day you will, too. Making people pay for your movies is a smart idea. That's a much better strategy than putting them up for free. I always said you'd make a good businesswoman."

"It was my manager's idea actually, but—you know, somehow I thought you would be more upset about this, instead of less."

"Oh, no! Gosh, are you kidding? We're living in a state of emergency. These are unprecedented times—my office is closing. We're all indefinitely furloughed, who knows when we'll be back."

"No wonder you sound so relieved to hear I'm making money."

Flustered by the woman's laughter, her mother said, "No, that's not—"

"I'm teasing."

"Anyway, you're going to have extra money if you're sensible about it. Think of how cost-effective it'll be when you're not partying every night!" Then, after hesitation: "You're not still partying every night, are you?"

She did still party, though with different people. Her art student girlfriend only came around about once a week, appearing more distracted each visit—instead, #1 began to frequent the apartment to smoke pot and bum around throughout the day. Her parlor's owner had closed up shop temporarily as a result of the virus, and the piercer had no place else to go: #1's was not the only parlor doomed to close, lose business for a few months, and possibly shut forever if they couldn't catch back up with their stacking bills once evictions were permitted again. Forgiveness, like federal financial assistance, was a temporary measure in America. Everybody struggled. Closures of tattoo and piercing parlors as a consequence of a pandemic did not alarm the woman as they should have, maybe because of tacit association between this novel pandemic and the AIDS epidemic of the 1980s. Nor was she fazed by the occasional face mask among pedestrians, professionals, even police.

The woman only realized something was historically wrong when she walked past the shut-down diner to find her mother's prediction had come true. Yes: closed. Not just for the quarantine but for good. The chairs were gone from the tables, and a "For Rent" sign brooded in the window.

American industry throttled by plague, so sad: yet the same sight filled her with sadistic glee. That son of a bitch got what he deserved. Wanting one last hurrah before the bars were forced to close at the end of the week, the woman called her friends to celebrate in one of those rare occasions where her girlfriend was invited to a work function. Through it all, the art student sat feigning smiles at jokes and otherwise mirthlessly consulting her drink. When the woman could stand it no longer, she pulled the art student aside to ask what was wrong. Huge mistake. The girl shrugged and admitted, "I feel like you've changed."

The woman rolled her eyes. "Yes, I've changed. Change is good, it's healthy."

"Not all change." Adjusting her big Buddy Holly glasses, the frowning girlfriend consulted the woman's face. "You haven't asked me how I'm doing in weeks. Do you even know they've canceled my classes 'til further notice, maybe the end of the school year? We have to meet online. I have to schedule my time at the kiln so I don't bump into anybody, and I'm freaked out all the time. You didn't even know that."

Guilty as charged, the defendant began, "Well—" But the prosecution continued.

"I walk through the door, and all you want is to talk about how well you're doing, or sex, or—my grandpa has it, that virus. Because my cousin's an irresponsible idiot." The student's face screwed up against the urge to tears. "I think I should go."

"Oh," said the woman, trying to touch the girl, frowning as she jerked away. "Oh, I didn't know, come on, let's talk—"

"No! There's been tons of time to talk. You're an awful friend to me. I sit in your apartment and I feel like I'm wallpaper while you tell me about your girlfriend"—she jerked a hand at oblivious #1 chatting in their booth—"and—"

"Woah! Wait! *You're* my girlfriend."

The poor art student's face was pink as that month's artificial hair color. "I didn't even know that!"

Oh, man. The woman, hand resting first upon her own cheek and then covering her mouth, tried not to feel. There would be other people out there. They were both better off. They'd been stunting each other. All undeniable facts, but, well…she liked her girlfriend.

Ex-girlfriend, she supposed. The art student shook her head, tone solemn as it was decisive. "No, no—if I didn't know it, I was never your girlfriend in the first place."

Seemed another matter of opinion, but whatever.

3

HER RELATIONSHIP WAS ANOTHER VICTIM of the virus. Sector by sector, prudent businesses—yes, schools included—shuttered indefinitely to prevent the spread of the virulent disease. Those remaining were essential services like grocers, banks, pharmacies. Police presence, already prevalent in the city, increased beyond anything the woman had seen.

And somehow she felt nothing. The first day after her ex-girlfriend broke up with her, the woman awoke thinking to send that same art student a text message. An activity so regular the phone was in her hand by the time she remembered. Numb, the woman sat up, rubbed her face, pushed #1 aside a few inches. Her phone's screen glowed with icons indicating messages that had come in overnight: at the envelope heralding an unread email, her heart skipped with hope. Her girlfriend, contrite after time to think in solitude?

No. Somebody else.

Dear Degenetrix,

No need to thank me. No need to do anything. Your shows are enough. I watch them every week. To request any special material from you would be far beyond what I deserve. Just to receive these notes fills me with an awe bordering on fear. I dare not extend this response except to say I have watched your clips many times over, and am certain you are real. Your talents are real. I would test them if I could—but you see, the longer I permit this note to grow, the more my passion reveals itself. How embarrassing.

I won't frighten you or say the profane things I think, as there are enough idiots commenting on your material to provide that service. Even the questions I have for you reveal too clearly the machinations of my fantasies, so I will stop but to beg you: the next time you hurt yourself, please think of me.

With burning lust,

Your Admirer

Wowee! Who wrote notes like that? Face flushed, the woman made her way to the end, read it a second time, then, on hearing #1 shift in bed, crept to the bathroom to read it yet again. The woman's pulse raced. This was not like the vile commenters who talked about wanting to see her hit by a train and thereafter dragging her severed torso, entrails dangling, across the tracks in pursuit of her lower half. Nor was this like #1, whose appreciation of sadomasochistic body modification combined with artistic sensibilities to leave her little more than an anointed fangirl. No…this missive, this—face it—love note, was from a different sort of person altogether.

In the shower, the woman touched herself while thinking of the note and grew all the more excited to find herself aroused without self-injury. Boy, when was the last time she'd managed that? Middle school, maybe. No, high school—the skater boy who had only one testicle as the result of a childhood accident. "Far out," she said at the time. "Do you know about Hitler?"

After her shower, and explaining to groggy #1 that Her Royal Highness needed time to herself, the woman rifled through her disorganized drawers of clothes, found a flattering blouse that left her neck and shoulders bare, then set up her studio background, stool, and phone. Its camera wasn't good, but was better than nothing, and the intimacy of the letter made her want to exclude the stranger from this production. Maybe it was time to get a video camera of her own once rent was covered. She adjusted the frame, pulled her top down to reveal more of her décolletage; then, after pulling back her hair, she hit the red record button.

"Hi there." Her grin widened. How silly she felt! Almost shy. Focus on the camera, go on. "I don't even know what to say—five hundred dollars a month, and that letter! Oh, thank you." Her hands folded, and she bent forward in the grateful posture of prayer that permitted a thorough flash down her bust. "I wish I had a name to call you. A proper name. I want to say it out loud… Oh—"

The erotic thought of the money, this devotional, shuddered through her. Lips parted, the woman slipped her hand into her jeans off-screen. "You must be a special kind of sadist to give a girl five hundred dollars a month and not request a custom video in return. Or a masochist, maybe…is that it? Financial domination? Are you one of those men who likes tithing e-sluts until you're bankrupt? No…I don't think so. You want something…you just won't say. Oh—you're shy, like me… I don't seem that way on camera, but I am. I'm shy." The woman's eyes shut. "This is the hottest I've gotten without hurting myself in months. Who are you?"

Softly gasping against the touch of her own hand, the woman opened her glassy eyes to the camera again and squirmed with roiling desire. "I want to know what you want. What you want to see me do. Whatever it is, I'll do it…you deserve a reward for being so sweet. Please, oh—I wish I had a name to call you!"

She gritted her teeth. The woman's free hand reached off-screen and returned with the loyal kitchen knife. "Is this what you like? Tell me. Tell me what you like, and I'll do it." Her hand moved of its own volition, the cool metal pressing her cheek, biting in. Oh, the sting of its blade! The hot rush of blood streaking her jaw to drip down her neck, her collarbone, her bust. She cried out, applying the blade to her other cheek, her shoulder, the visible swell of her cleavage, begging, "Don't be shy, please, don't be shy. You can tell me anything you want. My producer doesn't know—I'm making this video all alone on my phone, sending it to you all alone, I'll bet you wish you had me all alone. What would you do to me? Tell me, tell me—it'll be our secret, between you and me. Oh, oh! Oh—oh, God, oh, Mot, oh—"

Her climax, violent as her proclivities, tore through her body: for a microsecond, she felt herself bob to the surface of time, catch her breath in the nothingness, the not-black sky beyond all things. In the unconscious seconds of her orgasm, the woman forced her body to sink the blade into its own throat and jerk the jugular open. She stayed unconscious—stayed upon time's choppy surface, looking at something so beyond her comprehension she could not see it and exist.

Ten minutes later, the woman awoke slumped back against the garnet-stained background, her front covered in a bib of drying blood. Delirious from her extended death orgasm, she sat up, moaned, laughed at the smartphone to find it still recording.

"Thank you for your patronage," she summarized, smiling coyly. "Please tell me what you'd like in the next video…and remember, these are between you and me."

A couple of hours later, she had lightly edited the video to cut off the awkward opening and closing of her reaching for the camera; despite her temptation to do otherwise, she kept in every second of her still corpse, thinking her patron might like to watch her throat heal as a reward for his belief in her. (The first fan who genuinely believed in her before meeting her in person—no wonder it was love at first contact, whether she then recognized it or not.) Then it was a matter of finding a file-sharing service she could use to privately link someone to a video of such a length. Voilà. Only somewhat nervous, she sent the link and kept her note short.

Hope you don't find this too forward. Your love letter got me excited. Tell me more about you.

Love,

Degenetrix

4

A FEW DAYS LATER, she got a note back and read the simple words with almost sexual pleasure:

Would you like a new camcorder?

5

POST OFFICE BOXES were blindingly expensive, but it was time for the Degenetrix to have one. Viewers had begun to ask her about it in the stream's chat room, and she had brushed it off, but there were evidently props people wanted to send her to use on camera, or gifts they wished her to have or wear as tokens of their admiration. Then there was this guy, this reserved but tantalizing mystery man who kept his desires to himself while everybody else chattered on—simpletons falling all over themselves for her attention. This man, he sparked a golden curiosity until then unfelt.

Besides…even cheap video cameras weren't all that cheap.

Lucky thing she got a post office box at all—most locations offering even private mailboxes had waiting periods and required hounding to obtain one—but more than a few forward-thinking people had seen the outbreak's inevitability and fled the city, in some cases canceling their boxes. Or a few less-than-forward thinking people had expired and lost theirs by default. Either way.

After sending the box's information to her new mystery friend, not expecting him to follow through on the offer, the woman talked to the stranger about getting her mailing address onto the website. "Great idea," he responded. "I'll empty it for you once or twice a week, and we can—"

Bzzt—that was a big old no. "It's my PO box. I don't think I want you in it. Maybe we can do a second stream? More people are home all the time, so maybe once a week we could do a show of me opening the latest PO box haul."

Still processing the first part, he said absently, "That's a good idea," before rejoining, "but what do you mean, 'you don't want me in it'?"

"Just what I said."

"You mean you still don't trust me?"

The woman couldn't help the sharp titter at his wounded expression. "You're kidding me, right?"

"We've been together for six months and—"

Oh, no! "Together"? Maybe her ex-girlfriend was right: the woman needed to figure out how to communicate with the people she screwed. "Okay, wait—when you say 'together,' why don't you specify what you mean."

"*Working* together," he corrected, sour. "Working together. Don't look so relieved!"

"Just wanted to make sure… My girlfriend dumped me because she didn't realize she was my girlfriend. The last thing I need is a lesson in empathy—a boyfriend I didn't know about."

After all, there were enough weirdo fans who thought they had a chance to be her boyfriend and were furious to remember they weren't. Pleased to present for your consideration the frequent forum poster "Wildtown90," who insisted the Degenetrix's growing collection of paying fans was tantamount to prostitution. Apparently loose change in the form of tips had been fine, but seeing other people give her money on the regular had blistered this weirdo's ass. She'd known men like that, like her boss—eager to throw her scraps and furious when scraps weren't enough. This guy's posts on the Degenetrix's forum grew, by the day, more profane. She would see his avatar and leave the thread she'd been browsing, unwilling to read yet another post about how she needed to be raped into reformation. Sure, yeah, this guy wasn't the only one spouting off depraved fantasies, but the posts of the Wildtown90 account bothered her immensely. Everybody else shared slavering fantasies they would never dream of acting out, even given her physical presence and full consent. It was all an elaborate sexual role play inspired by her phenomenal powers. But Wildtown90, this guy meant it.

The day after she announced her PO box's address was the day he finally stepped over the line. It was the first time they were forced to ban a Degenerate from the community. The post that got him banned was a response to the "Degenetrix Sightings" thread.

I'm sick of this. What a trashy whore she is—first expecting people to pay her to make her smut, then demanding they send her tributes. Why are women like this? I've known this cunt's address for months but haven't said anything because I hoped she'd straighten up, but I guess it's time to dox her. Maybe somebody'll do something and I won't have to.

With bone-chilling clarity, there it all was: her real name and street address.

Her mind raced through questions so abundant they could not be sorted. How did he get this information? Who was this person? Was he somebody she knew? How long had he known this address? Had he somehow hacked the website, or perhaps the stranger's email? Had she ever even written her address in an email to the stranger? No—why would she? Not even in the dating app. They'd met up at a bar the first time, and she'd brought him home from there. Who was this? Who was Wildtown90? How did he, maybe even she, have this information?

The screaming panic didn't stop until long, long after the woman had gone across town, roused the stranger from a dead sleep, and made him ban the guy. Not understanding, the stranger was at first reluctant, saying, "It might set a bad precedent—censorship, the Internet hates it," but when she showed him, his face whitened with horror. "Shit—oh, shit!"

"Yeah, I know."

"How does this person know you?"

She wanted to scream: if she knew that, she'd instead be over at their house and in the process of removing the teeth from their mouth. Instead, she calmly insisted, "I think we need to delete this post and move on with our lives," even if, inside, she trembled.

The woman spent that night at the stranger's apartment; the next, at #1's. When Wildtown90 appeared, stupidly bearing the same username, in the weekly stream's chat, the woman had the pleasure of personally banning him, saying only, "That's the guy who tried to dox me," which was well-known Internet slang for the nonconsensual release of identifying documentation. Her chat filled with the sympathy of outraged Degenerate drones who could not believe such an offense had been enacted upon their queen bee. The woman resumed her show.

6

IT TURNED OUT the woman found #1 to be kind of annoying, but she didn't realize this until after the art student became her ex-girlfriend. Maybe the attraction had only developed because, in addition to flattering the woman's ego, #1 had been appealing in comparison to the meeker student whose body modification interests were limited to changeable things like hair. Without the more down to earth and sensitive student to make her seem fun, #1 came off as a try hard. Always doing her makeup with a thick and juvenile hand (which may have been why she came off a couple of years younger than she actually was), only watching the edgiest slasher movies she could find, constantly partying. #1 reminded the woman of the worst parts of herself—made her want to excise those parts of herself. The art student had wanted to hang around the apartment and make out when binge-watched episodes of televised baking competitions became tedious. The better parts of herself. She missed the art student.

What a bummer. The woman had to stop thinking about her ex-girlfriend, but you didn't realize how much you appreciated something until it was gone. Her mother was optimistic she would find somebody else. "You're such a sweetheart, you'll do great once all this blows over. Are you staying indoors?"

"Mostly. Are you?"

"Of course—what do you mean, 'mostly'!"

"I'm still visiting friends, Mom…and I've got to check my PO box."

"You can't be visiting your friends, that's the whole point. Do you understand we're in quarantine? The whole country, the whole world! This is a pandemic. Do you know how many applicants submitted for unemployment subsidies in one week?"

"Yeah, it's crazy."

"Don't sound so blasé. I thank God every night that you can pay your rent and that Daddy paid off this house before he died. Oh! And did you see the CDC advisory?"

She had, the same article written in two different ways. On a liberal news website: "American Center for Disease Control urges use of cloth masks to prevent viral transmission." On a conservative one: "President says CDC wants Americans to cover faces with cloth amid virus."

Incredible. Was there anything that couldn't be politicized? Most people in the city were not stupid and, face by face, people shielded themselves while out in public, but there were those on social media already making noises against the prudent practice. The woman laughed at her mother's question, saying, "The one about masks? Yeah, I saw that. Weren't you ahead of the game!"

"You say it so lightly—just because you're young doesn't mean you're invulnerable. The city isn't safe. Thousands of people are infected every day. You need to be careful."

Did she? Not to be hubristic, but the woman didn't think she was capable of getting sick. She didn't need to eat, either. It had occurred to her she might starve herself to permanent death, but when she got out of the habit of eating, she realized that what she had felt until then was appetite rather than hunger: not a need for food but an instinctive urge after years of eating at least a few small meals a day.

What started as an experiment became a new way of life. She didn't eat for three days, four, five—a week passed, and she maintained her exact weight: 144.4 pounds. Great number. American television's gentle Christian grandfather, Mr. Rogers, had interpreted his own constant weight, 143 pounds, as God telling him "I LOVE YOU," the numerals resolving to the number of letters in each word. For the woman, the number 144.4 was the faceless divine screaming at her, "I KILL YOUR BODY," "I FUCK YOUR MIND," "I RAPE YOUR SOUL." Always made her smile. She flirted sometimes with the divine, and things like numbers were how the divine flirted back.

Would it ever change, that weight? Would anything change for her? She knew one thing that had frozen: in another experiment, she was two months off birth control and still hadn't had a menstrual cycle. The natural explanation, given her body's healing abilities, was that her uterus could no longer shed its lining. The question was whether she was permanently infertile or more fertile than ever. Would her miraculous immune system perceive an implanted egg as an attacker to be expelled? It somehow wouldn't have surprised her if her body aborted life's every mutinous effort to claim control of this, her stupendous ship.

Probably for the best. If she had a kid, would it end up with her power? How would she raise somebody like this, like her? Worse—what if the kid didn't have her power? What if this young person who would someday be a big person had to adjust to the fact that their mother was, well…sort of a porn star? Obviously, she'd be in a good position to raise them sensibly and instill open-minded values. But it would have been nice to be considered an artist, an avant-garde professional, rather than a digital sex doll.

Her disconnection from her original intentions for her artwork had become depressing to her. With the art student gone, no more clay-covered fingers to depict while holding cigarettes or pressed ponderously to the part of relaxed lips, the woman felt a shift—a loss of grounding. It had been several weeks since she'd picked up her film camera to do her own photography. Maybe this was because photography had been reduced to a hobby. Perhaps her body was no longer subject to change, but something within her was now in a constant state of flux: always shifting, three-dimensional life and the world around her reduced to a flickering magic lantern projected in the back of her skull while her thoughts, her fantasies, her wild inspirations (all of which were the most real things she knew), proved more important and captured more attention than these stultifying four walls, these beings with which the woman increasingly failed to connect. these dream characters from a different dimension.

Yes, she lived a dream. The checks rolled in. She was a celebrity. People were obsessed.

Speaking of obsession: One day, the woman went to her post office box and discovered a padded envelope. How exciting! The trickle of mail had begun a few weeks prior and was already interesting, containing such fun tokens as love letters, books (at her request), and at least one vibrator. Well—you could never have too many. Why look a gift dildo in the sculpted rubber urethra?

This manila envelope was not big enough for something like that, and its contents were much better. Since, based on its size, it harbored nothing especially obscene, she opened it there in the lobby of the post office to discover a key attached to a short note.

Hello—

This is one of two keys to a safe-deposit box. Its information is listed on the back of this note. The other key is mine. Keep whatever you find. I'll check it once every other week and do likewise.

Love always,

Your Admirer

As, shuddering, the woman turned the letter over to see the address of the corresponding bank, a symphony of fragrance blossomed up her sinuses. Oh, how wonderful—she pressed the dense paper to her face and sought for the essence of that aroma, scenting like a hound, overcome by instant imaginings of hard male hands and dark wood cologne. Hm…cedar? Hard to say what else. Whatever it was, the woman could have stood all day huffing that letter. She swayed beneath the dreamy enchantment of her emerging desire; somebody came into the lobby of the post office, and, jolting, she stuffed the letter away, then hurried to the street while looking up the bank on her phone. Everything in the city was a subway ride and short walk away. This one specifically was located in an area called Wall Street, where money was made, American's future was divined, and the whole thing was overseen by a beautiful statue of a bronze bull too crowded by tourists to touch. Someday, someday, she'd pet its flaring snout! A silly desire for a citizen of the city, but the motion of the ostensibly still bull inspired great ideas in her heart.

At her destination, a banker wearing an N95 mask, having guided her from the six-foot distance prescribed to prevent transmission of the virus, left her alone with a great silver box. The woman, primed by renting her **PO** box, couldn't help but think it must have been staggeringly expensive to secure a safe-deposit space of this size on a monthly basis. Almost trembling with excitement, feeling involved in strange subterfuge, she slid her key into the lock. *Click* said the tumbler. The lid opened: inside, already packed in a soft black carrying case, a brand-new digital camcorder of a size indicating cost as well as professionalism. Another note lay on top.

> *I wish I could give you a name. I wish I could tell you anything. I wish I could do more to repay you for your gift. Such a lovely video. Thank you for sharing yourself. What a woman you are!*

7

"I DON'T SEE WHY you had to waste money on a new camera," chided the stranger when he saw her playing with it on his next visit. "The one I upgraded to is perfectly good."

"This one is even better, though. Look at all these settings—"

"Extra features don't make a good video recorder. Anyway"—he loved to change the subject whenever she was about to prove him right in an argument and hurried on to admit—"it's good quality, but I don't think we need to worry about that level of equipment. Especially because—here." He showed her his phone, an email already open. "This is why I came by today. I thought you might be interested."

Word by word, she began to understand what she read. "I know about this magazine! My friend"—Degenerate #1, she meant—"reads it all the time. Her boss knows somebody who works for it, I guess."

Yes: everyone at the parlor, or what had been the parlor before it closed for the virus, was a big fan of a certain body-modification-themed magazine covering everything from extreme tattoo transformations to literal limb amputations. The more extreme the modification, the more intense the fantasy. These people had a way of getting absurd and had even once released an infamous shock video, the sort of thing kids showed their friends to freak each other out—a video of self-castration that was probably fake. This e-magazine was a known commodity within certain sadomasochistic art circles online, enough for the woman to get excited to realize the email proposed a collaboration.

"They're not as big as they used to be," the stranger was fast to caution, "but it'll help our audience grow, and help us get our foot in the door with other bigger publications. There's sort of a problem, though."

She saw what he meant. The suggestion was to do corset piercing, which was a kind of superficial piercing that the body naturally rejected in short order compared to the usual more permanent decorations. A number of rings were implanted along the back, mounted in the upper layers of skin, and ribbons were woven through to resemble the heavily fetishized Victorian undergarment synonymous with sadomasochism as with sexist subjugation. In a normal person, a corset piercing was temporary. By the time all the piercings were made on Her Royal Highness, the first ones would be extruding from her body.

"You think I should turn down their offer?"

"I just think we're going to have to find a solution. Deeper wounds? I don't know. I'll think about it."

So would she. Incessantly. Like any good artist transfixed by a problem in their work in progress. It didn't help that this issue was one that had rested uneasily for some time. Most people would have enjoyed the security of immediate healing, and she did—but every once in a while, she wanted a cut to last. Sort of like an orgasm. She was "over" orgasms as a general rule. Not that she minded having them; but the sexual climax felt like an interruption of pleasure rather than a satisfactory conclusion. Couldn't pleasure be infinite? She saw in the orgasm the time limit of pleasure: the temporary nature of all things. It was more acute now that her consciousness seemed incapable of similar conclusion. No, she was tired of hollow sex for the sake of the orgasm. The woman had enough reminders of finality everywhere she looked.

Everywhere except when she looked at the camera that her patron had given her, or when she pressed her face to the still lightly scented note stuck like a child's drawing to her otherwise blank refrigerator door. Ah! Then came upon her an exquisite frisson, not remorse for inevitability but anticipation of it. The passage of time was a pleasure when she considered this faceless man who was evidently interested in showering her with gifts. The ticks of clocks pushing all human beings toward their graves now pushed her nearer to the inevitable moment she would read his name, or learn how he looked, or maybe even meet him face-to-face. Oh, this man! Who was he?

Touching the camera felt like touching him. She smiled into its recording iris once the stranger left her apartment. "I can't believe you would send me something like this." The woman shook her head. "This is the nicest camera I've ever seen. Are you a director? Or a photographer… I'm a photographer, you know. Maybe that's funny to say. It's already been so long since I've taken pictures! This is a kind of photography, though, isn't it? Cinematography."

Lip still hidden behind her top row of teeth, she laughed again with more self-consciousness and drummed her fingers upon her chin. "I better be careful or your videos are going to turn into blog entries. You don't want to be my diary, do you? I don't want you to be… I feel silly talking about nothing. I feel silly just talking."

Still gazing into the camera, the woman folded her leg up, foot poised upon the stool's edge so she could hold her ankle in reflexive habit. "I bet you're beautiful. A really beautiful man. I don't know why I get that idea. Maybe it's the silk lining inside of the camera bag. The way your letters smelled. I don't know. Who sends letters? You must be old, too. Older than me."

Her cheek rested on her knee. "Will you still like me when I'm popular? There's this electronic magazine—you might have heard of it if this is what you're into. Anyway…they want to do some project with me." The woman hesitated. In the distance, far beyond the camera and the open window, lay the vast nighttime, that temporary visibility of outer space so faint amid the light pollution. At least the city was quiet with its citizens formally told to stay home. "I don't know why, but it feels like this shoot is something important. Something that might have a good influence on me—a change for the better. I want to be taken more seriously. I think I like you because you take me seriously… You wouldn't have bought me this camera otherwise.

"You still haven't told me what you like. I think I'll tease you until you share something good with me. Send you videos like these. Minutes and minutes and minutes of me just talking, on and on. Talking about nothing. That's the worst! Nobody likes to listen to somebody ramble. Boy…I can't believe you sent me that camera." One last time, she laughed in disbelief and wondered if she had laughed so much while thinking of anybody since her breakup with the art student. "Thank you. I wish I knew your name."

When it was all edited, the woman burned the footage onto
a digital versatile disc used for storing data and left it in the safe-
deposit box. Nine days later, she opened it to find another note, and
a silver-handled shaving razor.

*I could listen to you read the phone book for sixteen hours and never tire
of hearing you speak. I'm not a director, but I enjoy classic film. What
do you think of* Un Chien Andalou*?*

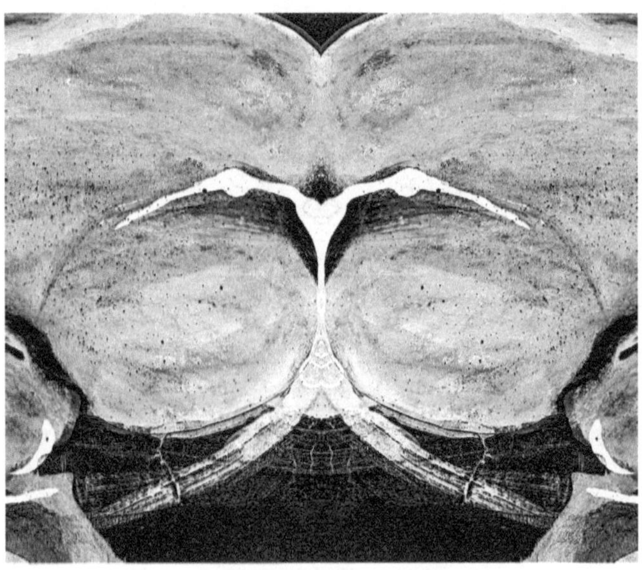

8

FOLLOWING A GREAT DEAL of discussion, the usual delicate loops of the corset piercing were thrown out in favor of fishhooks designed to catch largemouth bass. Given their pronged tips, her body would need to work harder to reject them; the hooks might even require tearing out. This pleased her to think of and was the suggestion that inspired a new inclusion. Why stop at the ribbon weaving of a corset? For all her dabbling in sadomasochistic pastimes, she'd never experimented with bondage. Capturing her first time on film served more than a few purposes.

The tattoo parlor had been out of business for a month, but so had been everybody in the city, the country, the world. Yes, the world shut down to slow the proliferation of the virus that had torn from one side of the globe to the other in the span of months.

For the woman, nothing changed. Without a need to eat, she was content to laze about her apartment day and night, watching weird art-house movies for inspiration and flipping through news broadcasts when she wasn't thinking about her works in progress. If she didn't need shut-down time for her brain, she wouldn't have had to sleep—but what would she have done with that extra time? Watch even more news? Let's see: the head of an overseas nation had the virus; that new hospital serving the tri-state area around the city was full to the brim as swaths succumbed to the brutal disease; the federal government hoarded medical supplies, including masks and ventilators, of which states were in desperate need; a foreign finance minister had literally killed himself under the pressure; and, oh, here was a fun video of a dairy cow sleeping with a litter of kittens. Gosh, wasn't life splendid? Were the kits fed on beef pâté?

No: being awake and home alone bored her. She wanted to fill the time with creative pursuits but dared not experiment with her talent too much. Practicing a concept before performance took the fun and freshness out of the performance itself. This meant that for her own titillation the woman was left with methods of stimulation already tried—she was mostly stuck with knives and burning implements, but there was always room for ingenuity. A curling iron had potential. Wasn't all bad. Do-it-yourself projects were fun if you let them be, and necessity was the mother of invention.

Likewise, boredom was the mother of pornography. A user-driven porn hosting website—the hard-core equivalent of the mainstream site on which the woman's work had started out—reported a staggering uptick in views worldwide as a direct result of the pandemic's isolation. People, single or committed, craved distraction when locked in their houses. Porn was an easy route to empty-mindedness. The Degenetrix's forum gained new users at an increasing rate, and (perhaps against expectation, as so many were out of work and should have been saving money) she had over a hundred paying fans who had pledged to support her videos in exchange for exclusive content. Her admirer had not reduced his $500 payment after the first month as the stranger speculated he might. Quite the opposite. When she checked the safety deposit box a few weeks after delivering her own take on *An Andalusian Dog*, the woman found a bouquet of thorny crimson roses and a cashier's check for $2,000 dollars. The attached note: *The check would have been bigger if I didn't worry about coming on too strongly.*

On the next video, after thanking her patron, asking more sure-to-be-unanswered questions ("What's your deal? Why are you so shy? If I bothered giving you my phone number, would you call me?") and molesting the rose petals with her fingers and lips, she deep-throated the stems to discover with delight that the high-quality lens and attached light of the camera could get a good look down beyond her bleeding uvula. But the important thing was the bouquet! Such wonderful roses. She loved to look at them and hung them over her bed like a crucifix, where they remained once dried.

When she went to the bank to deposit this third video, the woman examined the lobby on her way back out. Her first time there, only the banker who'd led her to the box had worn a mask; now everyone there wore one, either a professional fabric mask or a rare-as-gold N95 mask or sometimes something crafted at home out of old pajamas or used bras. Even the woman wore a mask, if only for the sake of blending in. Day by day, the city self-anonymized. The men waiting for the teller, each six feet apart from the other, faces all obscured: Was any one of them this patron, this benefactor of hers? No, probably not. Whoever he was, she had the feeling he was the type of guy who called up his personal banker to issue checks or deal with the financial minutiae for which the common man now had to risk his life.

The woman went straight from the bank to the closed tattoo parlor, where the store's lights were on and the curtained windows emitted a great bustle of noise even before she entered. There was the standard group: the stranger, #1, #1's boss, these (ir)regulars accompanied by new people who stood nursing beers of a brand that happened to share its name with the type of virus killing city dwellers in droves. Such misfortune left the beverage cheaper than water and provided prominent availability for those more alcoholic than superstitious. After accepting a bottle, the woman was introduced to a few people associated with the magazine: a writer, a photographer, and, most fatefully of all, the *kinbakushi*.

"*Kinbakushi*," also called "*bakushi*," was a term derived from "*kinbaku*"—a Japanese word meaning "the beauty of tight binding." If *shibari*, an elaborate form of almost sculptural bondage commonly depicted in sadomasochistic pornography, was a term to be thought of as referring to the final product of being bound, kinbaku struck the woman as a term that contained both the final product and the process of that product's achievement: a noun that contained a verb, the perfect superposition of progress and completion. A lifelong connoisseur of vintage pornography as much as was any photographer, the woman had been from youth acquainted with shibari and found the concept lacking in eroticism. This was why she had not much dabbled in bondage over the years. The bakushi, a short intergender individual with a sharply defined undercut hairstyle and about twice the Asian stock of the woman, listened to her opinion in open-minded interest.

"Have you watched many videos," was the response of this person, "or only seen photos? Photos don't do the process justice. Especially photos from this country. And to fully appreciate it, of course, you have to see a live performance. Imagine looking at still photos from a Broadway show and thinking that, because you don't like the look of the stills, you don't like the play—that you don't like theater! Kinbaku and theater are related, you know."

"I didn't."

"They are—it began with *hojōjutsu*, a rope-based fighting style used by samurai to subdue and transport prisoners. Sometimes even torture them. Edo-era Kabuki actors, when showing torture on stage, would use variations of hojōjutsu as part of the show, but had to adapt knots to be less painful and more exaggerated so audience members could see them. The artist Seiu Ito, in first developing kinbaku, drew his influence from Kabuki and hojōjutsu. He did produce a lot of two-dimensional art, but...let's face it." The bakushi took one last swig of beer before setting the empty bottle aside. "His illustrations were an excuse for the process of tight binding. Great as his drawings are, they don't demonstrate the beauty of the experience—the connection between the artist and the model, the way the model is transformed. Change is an action, not an image."

Yes, yes. She could fully relate to that concept and was, with that thought resting in her mind, far more open to kinbaku than she'd been before arriving at the parlor. Once it was time to strip down to her underwear and lay out for #1 to open with her piercing magic, the woman was excited. She let it show in the interview shot while another camera steadily recorded the process of the Degenetrix's back piercings, which #1 applied with fishhooks in sixteen places. Was the woman nervous? A little—new things were always a nerve-racking, especially in her line of performance. But once the piercings were in and the bakushi stepped up to do the work of weaving the first rope through the hooks, the woman's hesitation changed to a natural state of artistic flow—something between artistic and sexual.

Trance was a fundamental aspect of the sadomasochistic

experience, just as it was for the artistic experience and the sacred experience. No matter how painful things were when they began, any such situation's rhythm had a way of tuning participants' psyches until their minds fell into harmony with the experience itself. Meditative clarity came to the average dominatrix cracking her whip perhaps easier than it ever had to Prince Gautama, who spent over a month meditating beneath his Bodhi tree: and on top of her efficiency, the dominatrix, like the Degenetrix, had the sense to monetize her samadhi. Better still, the trance of the dominant party in a sexual encounter was shared by the submissive party: participants connected through the pain, the pleasure, the delirium of the experience without the prerequisite of traditional sexual contact. The solitary confinement of the human prison cell lapsed, dissolving into an endorphin-rich flow of consciousness where focus was nowhere and everywhere at once.

To her surprise, the woman found that the slide into this more free-form state occurred faster while being tied up and enduring pain than while enduring pain alone. Perhaps it was the stillness required, the tranquility of it, the hypnotic quality of the rope's cruel tugs of her flesh as it passed around her again and again like the hypnotist's pendulum. The sensuality, too. Her sadomasochistic activities tended to be blunt, cut-and-dried, even ostensibly accidental in the case of her livestreams. Now she floated upon the air, suspended by her own flesh, the body harness woven by her new friend so well crafted and so supportive of her weight that she barely even noticed the piercings from which she was partially hung.

Most of all, the bukashi was right: kinbaku, like all erotic experience, was an unfolding process. The failure of still photography to stoke her imagination with the possibilities of Japanese bondage seemed correlated with her own feelings on the passé nature of the orgasm. Wrapped in the ropes, face flush with sensual peace, the woman thought of the flowers her patron had sent her, and the silken kiss of the petals against her lip, and the aesthetic throb of their inverted suspension above her headboard, and stared, unseeing, into the fluorescent lights of the parlor.

· JEAN ARP ·

1

AFTER HER PLEASANT EXPERIENCE, the woman traded phone numbers with the bakushi and was invited to call anytime. Even in what should have been isolation, her social circle grew— though, not without consequence.

That damn forum. Why had they put it up again? Oh, right—her mother. If her mother knew the trouble this closed-off community caused, she might never have complained about the occasional obscene comment beneath her daughter's videos. Not all the Degenerates were problems—before the ubiquity of masks settled across the city, the woman had been identified by other people audacious enough to reveal their proclivities in a public approach for a handshake. These viewers were nice, polite, and gracious…but what was the saying? A few bad apples.

What a true cliché. She had been on the fence about collecting all her pervert fans in one place to share their thoughts and daydreams with each other, but when a clip from the ex-girlfriend's cigarette video emerged, the woman couldn't help but feel sharp regret. The ninety-second segment was shared to the "Miscellaneous Media" subforum, where posters discussed movies or artists in the vein of the Degenetrix but not necessarily pornography or performance art in the traditional senses. An account that was all of six hours old at the time of sharing had posted it in a new thread titled "RARE: Degenetrix Sex Tape (Real!)" with the comment: *Check out what I found! This should be behind a paywall. I knew she did this for more than just the money. Check out time stamp 1:12 to see how wet she gets.*

Worse grammar than that—but her brain, even swamped by the stress hormones, couldn't help but translate the post into actual

English. By the time she had clicked on the link to download the video, the statistics on the file-sharing server indicated she was the forty-fourth person to have downloaded it.

Fuck life. Good Lord! People had already asked in the thread if the video was an official Degenetrix release. While waiting for the download to complete, she called the stranger twice, got his voice mail both times, and ultimately hung up without leaving a message.

Where had this come from? She hit "Play." Sure enough: ex-girlfriend, burning the squirming, moaning woman with her cigarette. It wasn't the whole video, but that was almost more disturbing. A tease that would make its viewers desperate to find the whole video. Collectors were completionists, and porn collectors most especially. The worst thing in the world to them was a hot clip from an unknown source: the existence of such a snippet implied an unseen source video unusual enough to ignite desire; pornography was about the immediate satisfaction of desire; therefore, rare pornographic films and unseen sex tapes were antithetical to what pornography was. In being desired, these records of eroticism had ascended the label of "mere pornography" and needed to be chastened by the act of observation back into the realm of the perceptible, the definable—the detestable. This was the motive driving disgusting people who liked to hack into the personal computers of famous women and steal footage of their most intimate moments.

Hackers. Goofy, but that was where the woman's mind went while she got ahold of the ex-girlfriend via video call. The art student's hair was now auburn—its first natural color since they'd met. Had she been coloring her hair to seem fun for the woman?

This call was the first time they'd talked since their argument-cum-breakup at the bar. The woman was glad they could talk like friends. Maybe when the isolation-quarantine-pandemic nightmare was over, she and the art student—who would by then be an art school graduate, whatever that meant—could hang out to smoke pot or watch movies together. But as they ran out of mundane topics, and the woman steered the conversation as far as she could from the changes in her lifestyle (like her recent eschewing of food and even water), she gave in to her pressing internal need to address the reason for her call. "Hey, so—you don't have an account on my forum, do you?"

"No. Your videos are, uh—sort of extreme for me. Sorry. I tried to watch one, but—"

"No, no, I understand." That was one of the most frustrating things about her artwork: nobody who knew her personally wanted to watch her videos, to see what she worked so hard to produce. The output of her creative libido was too alarming. Real people didn't want to look her in the face and reconcile the relatively pleasant woman she could be with the shocking acts that demonstrated her soul. She had been selective about sharing her photography with visitors and friends because many people weren't interested—but absolutely nobody she knew was interested in her work. No one except #1, a Degenerate who arrived in the woman's life as a direct result of the videos. Therefore, the notion that her ex-girlfriend didn't watch her movies failed to faze her. Really. Didn't affect her. Why would it? Clearing her throat, the woman went on, "I guess I should lay it out for you, since it's your privacy, too. Somebody posted that, uh—that video of us to the forum." The girlfriend's eyes widened while the woman explained, "It's just a clip, but—"

"Did you take it down?"

"I'm trying to get my webmaster"—aka the stranger—"to answer his phone."

"Why can't you do it yourself?"

"I guess my account doesn't have privileges to do that. I need to talk to him about it."

"No kidding…not that deleting the post will do much good. Man—you could see my face."

"Not much of it, though. And your hair's different. I like it, by the way."

"Gee, thanks." A sigh. "Sorry, I shouldn't be sarcastic. I really appreciate it. It's just—"

"I understand."

"—this is super violating."

"Tell me about it. I'll go over in person and get my guy to take it down. He might even be able to help me do some kind of cease and desist, copyright claim thing on the file-sharing site, but—"

"Once something's on the Internet, it's there forever."

That was the conventional wisdom. And that was why the stranger's solution left the woman uneasy. "Shit," he said while watching the clip. "Yeah, that's the video you showed me, all right."

"How do you think this person got it? You haven't shared it with anybody, have you?"

"Hell no! I would never share proprietary content with anybody—that's good money we're wasting."

"My ex- said that she didn't share it, either." Faltering, the woman asked, "You don't think—do people in real life really hack into computers? I thought it only happened in movies from the 1990s."

"Yes, they really do…I told you about that stuff with the celebrity nudes. You should probably change your passwords just in case. I'll change mine, too."

"Good idea. Hey"—speaking of passwords—"could you fix my account on the forum, or give me the password to yours, so I can delete posts without having to call you? I tried to get you on the phone three times before I came over."

Irritation tensed his features. "Don't you think that's too many cooks in the kitchen? If I'm doing work on the website and you log in under the same account, I might get booted and lose all my work."

What was she, a kid? Having to beg: "Then give me privileges to delete posts. I swear I won't be indiscriminate; I'll only use the option in emergencies like this. Please? If you'd pick up your phone—"

"All right." He faced his computer with a melodramatic sigh. "All right, I'll change your account permissions."

"Be sure to change it so I can ban users, too." Again, he made a noise of displeasure, and she insisted, "It's important! What if we have another case where my address gets posted, and this time you're not there to answer your phone?"

"Christ, okay—but I don't think it's a good idea to ban anybody from the community unless it's for a real infraction like that one."

"I promise. I barely even read the thing—you can oversee me if you want."

Shaking his head, the stranger scrolled to the top of the screen to delete the thread, passing on his way about five new posts that had popped up since the woman looked at the conversation. "I will say… people are loving this video. Hey—well, I don't know."

Hook, line, and sinker. Embarrassing in hindsight. "What?"

"You originally talked about filming more erotic stuff. Maybe now's the time? If this video is out there, and somebody could release it, the right move might be to take the initiative and just treat this clip like the trailer we don't have to make."

Not a bad idea, especially considering the outrageous comments left by Degenerates horny enough to think she cared for their opinion. Still, the woman couldn't help but feel reluctant. When keeping her clothes on already made rent money, why take them off for more? Besides: "Won't one person pay for the whole video, then share it?"

"If they do, you can ban them…but at a hundred dollars a video, why would somebody release one of these films for other simps to enjoy pro bono?"

"A hundred dollars a video! Do you expect anyone to pay that?"

"Are you kidding me? If anything, that might be cheap. Your content is so sought after—I mean, there's nobody in the world who can do what you do. If there is, they're definitely not forthcoming about it, and they're definitely not making movies like yours. It's legal snuff. You've died on camera more than once, but you live. No crime to speak of. Nothing for anybody to complain about."

2

NOTHING FOR ANYBODY to complain about. Anybody except the particularly pathetic segment of the Degenetrix's fans. The subject of what to do with the sex video was difficult because so many of her followers bought the specific image of the Degenetrix as the "girl next door" —an archetype embodied by the stock image of the shy but accessibly flirtatious neighbor girl curious about all forms of experimentation. In the Degenetrix, extreme sadomasochists had their answer to this fantasy.

What even some of her paying fans failed to understand, however, was that a large part of the present attraction to the girl next door was dependent on that girl's future corruption: her untapped sexual potential, that pure crystal wellspring waiting to be struck by the well-aimed drill. The commodity was naivete, but the paradox was that this naivete's value lay in its temporary nature—was dependent on that naivete's destruction, as the value of oil was in its eventual refinement and burn off as fuel. A broad number of mechanical uses that would graduate a girl next door into being the cougar down the street, the Mrs. Robinson of American sexual myth. Yes. The more the woman pondered, the more innocence had in common with oil.

Incidentally, oil futures had recently cratered. Americans just weren't driving their cars. There was so much oil, nobody had anywhere to put it: for the meantime, it had little to no value. Everything inside her also appeared outside her. Such a thing was defined by a much-admired psychiatrist as "projection," but it was more than that. The mystery of time perpetually expressed itself within and without the woman. She contemplated it daily. Time's most visceral effect was not in entropy but the reactions of people to entropy. Like the values of oil and innocence, time and entropy were not to be inherently weighed this way or that. Like pain. There was nothing that she could find inherently good or bad, but the human beings around her demonstrated a more black-and-white opinion set.

Most posters on the forum were desperate, absolutely gagging, to finally have actual sex tapes of the Degenetrix. Everything led to this—the inevitable development of her career from coy gray-area soft core to actual nudity, actual sexual acts, actual penetration. Yes, yes, yes! This was what the majority had clamored for. "Please be real" was the general response to the video clip, whose thread exploded to a hundred-plus replies by the end of twenty-four hours in what proved to be the most popular conversation, and most burning flame war, yet seen on the Degenetrix's forum.

The large faction praising this development was met with a splinter protesting almost violently Her Royal Highness's new turn. These voices intensified when the full video was released at high cost. People who had been iffy about her selling any content crowed that they had seen this coming from a mile away and weren't surprised by what they perceived as her trashy devolution. Proponents responded quickly that it was only natural for an artist who called herself "the Degenetrix" to devolve. On and on, each side continued, until a poster called "LouFord2020" got himself banned by revealing that this was not his first account on the Degenetrix's website.

I've posted this before and nothing came of it except a ban. She's a whore and she's always been a whore. If you go to her apartment and listen through the door, you'll probably hear something interesting going on. We can all only hope if somebody does drop by, they'll do more than listen. No need to bring a camera, she's obviously got one.

There again, in bone-chilling black-and-white, her address. She had been obsessively watching the sex tape thread and received an email notice every time a reply was posted, so as soon as she saw the troll, she decided it was time to exercise her new moderation powers. In a few seconds, "LouFord52" received his second ban. A few seconds more, and the post was deleted; about ten minutes after that, the Degenetrix made her own post, sprinkling in a pinch of disinformation to keep anyone from following through on "Lou's" advice, locked the thread, and stuck the whole thing to the top of the board.

I've had to ban a poster for attempting to release private information. The address is old, but it's definitely real and I'm sure somebody lives there, so I've deleted the post in question because I don't want a random person getting harassed. Let me make this clear: if you disagree with my artistic decisions, you're welcome to join the community of another immortal performance artist. Oh! Wait, that's right.

Guess I'll see you all back here, huh?

Maybe not the most popular of responses: in this annoying parental habit he'd adopted, the stranger chided her for her tone. The woman would not be persuaded to delete her post. "I'm tired of this stupid girlish image you insisted on—a cartoon character. The Degenetrix has been naïve long enough. Let's let her grow up…"

3

"...BECAUSE WHAT DO YOU DO with rude children?" The Degenetrix lifted her eyebrows defiantly at the camera, the viewer, as she wrapped the video, which worked as a second response to the situation. "Every parent loses their patience after enough ingratitude, and I think more than a few of you have been ungrateful. It's a privilege to look at me—to see me do what I do. None of you deserve to look at my body, but artwork is the great equalizer. No matter how gross and pathetic you are, I'll let you look if you'll support me. Paintings don't have their choice of who looks at them once somebody's paid to walk through a gallery. But—if you don't like my artistic direction, like I said: Go somewhere else. Don't act like this isn't why you came here in the first place."

Camera off, the stranger sucked a tooth. "People aren't going to like this."

She didn't care. The woman wasn't interested in being the sort of person who tried to be likable if it meant she couldn't speak her mind. If her harsh opinions lost her fans, fine. Her real fans would reveal themselves. The important ones, the good ones, would express approval of her response. #1, for example, applauded her moves and overall shift of attitude. Most importantly, the mystery admirer's already avid support continued to intensify. She communicated with him once a week, sometimes twice. It depended not on him but on how often she could get to the bank, part of a list of errands that included checking her post office box and dropping off groceries for housebound friends like the bakushi and, from time to time, the art student, who had started messaging her again. The woman was over her ex-girlfriend. Quick as that. She only cared about one set of messages now.

You must be the most hypnotizing woman in the world, read the note she received with an exquisite Egyptian blue bangle, an antique decorated with chariots and plated with gold. *Such beauty inspires in me only the most reprehensible urges— O goddess! I long to speak with you in the instant. To consort with you as the priest with God. I cannot; I cannot approach you, cannot take the veil from my face in your immaculate presence. My skin burns to imagine holding you, my ears ring when I imagine your voice addressing me. Have I ever told you? The first time I watch the videos you make for me, I have to watch them with the sound muted. The experience is too intense. You always ask for a name, something you can call me, but there is no name of mine I could stand to hear pronounced by that sacred tongue. Look how I go on! Look how long this note is. Look how insane I am. This is pathetic. I've never even met you. You could have anyone in the world. Oh, you agonize me. I have been pierced by a Holy Spear, and the wound will never heal until the selfsame weapon that tore me open has touched the oozing gore.*

"*Parsifal,*" she said in her video reply, cheek resting against the window frame through which she gazed. "I've never been to the Metropolitan Opera House. I don't know why not—I love opera music and I've lived here for years. What a waste! Will it open again soon? Next year, at least? Will you take me?" She smiled crookedly at the camera. "Wear a mask if you're worried about being seen with me…everybody's wearing them these days."

Nothing would please me more than to be seen with you—nothing. At this moment in time, however, open admittance of appreciation for your work is tantamount to publicly confessing what form of adult entertainment one prefers. My career and related image are such that I cannot take that risk. Soon your work will be accepted by the mainstream. How selfish I sound! But there are more reasons than privacy for wanting to wait to meet you. Above all, I am terrified that when I meet you, I will no longer be capable of being apart from you, nor you from me. The distance I maintain is not for my career so much as for my sanity, and my own peace of mind. I would not have you meet me and kick me away like the mongrel I am.

"You write like you're in love with me…like, really in love with me." Grinning despite herself, she turned away from the camera, which for that response video lay in bed with her. "I feel like you understand me. That's so rare."

The knuckles of her left hand bounced against her teeth. "You still haven't told me anything about yourself. Even what you like about my videos. I wish I had a name for you." She covered her eyes with one hand. "I wish we could talk more. I make these videos for you, and it's like you're here with me. Then I turn off the camera and my apartment feels empty. Maybe I feel like you're in love with me because—well." Her smile widened; her hand lifted to permit her to look at the camera. "What's your favorite painting? How old are you? Do you like dogs or cats? Where were you born? Do you have any kids? Do you want them? If you're not married, have you ever been? What time of day do you watch my videos? I wish I knew you. I want to know you. I like that you're scared of me, or scared of the way you think of me, but…I wish you could approach me. Oh—I wish I hadn't let that idiot release the sex tape, I wish I hadn't ever shared it with anybody. Maybe I could be mainstream sooner. You don't think it's lame I'm doing porn, do you?"

Oh, no, no, I love your body, I love to watch it. I love all the things you do with it. To it. I loved last night's video—this was mid-June, and the Degenetrix had released her first full penetration video in a ten-minute clip involving the stranger and a cattle prod—*too much; your body deserves to be loved by men, by women, by everyone. Loved and tenderly abused. Oh, you demon, you shape-shifting succubus!*

I have thought about the questions in your last message. What do I like about your videos? So difficult to quantify. I don't know if I can answer other than to suggest the aesthetic of your face holds the same meaning and purpose to me as a bouquet of flowers. Each soothes my aching soul with a short look and, with a long look, steadily reveals to me the omnipresent signature of the divine. Only a great artist could produce something as incomparably sublime as you, and the juxtaposition of that sublimity with the brutalities of violence and sex and the death they both imply—that conjunction is what I like about your work, of which your videos are mere record.

Oh, God! Literally swooning, the woman sat on the edge of her bed to read the note that had come with a box of gold-dusted bonbons and a silver letter opener whose sharp blade glinted in the light. Its cold metal bit into her unconscious lip as she read on.

As to the rest of these questions (so many questions!) and your desire to speak with me—I have already said that I think my life might end to hear your voice address me without warning, and that I am quite private…but you're a shrewd woman.

What followed was an invitation that made her heart race:

he suggested the use of an encrypted chat program that would permanently delete read messages after a certain length of time. He explained that he had set up an account to talk to her, should she choose to humor him. A strange giddiness overwhelmed the woman, but that giddiness was in and of itself a warning to go slow, to avoid looking overhasty. She spent a sleepless night tossing and turning and made it a full twenty-four hours until she was warm and fuzzy from the healing afterglow of a flaying scene shot in the stranger's apartment before inviting the user known as "m0t" to a chat in the program suggested. Maybe she shouldn't have worried about looking too desperate: he accepted her invitation within ten minutes. Her arms went numb from her elbows to the tips of her fingers.

"I'm going home for the night," the woman announced while looking for her pullover. The stranger frowned at the clock.

"It's so late."

"That's why the subway's there." Head already over her phone to check an incoming message, the Degenetrix waved a hand that she then used to get the door. "Anyway, if you're really worried, then rest assured I've been seeing cop cars in my neighborhood all the time—they've got nothing to do but hang out at night since things got quiet. It's safe. Catch you later."

In the elevator to the building's lobby, the woman laughed like a schoolgirl while opening the waiting message. The excitement was so intense that she had to grin up at her reflection in the doors, then at the blank panels of the ceiling before her vision could withstand the instant message.

m0t

I never thought you'd actually bother to do this.

Grinning all the wider, the woman typed her response and hit "Send" as the elevator doors released her to the lobby.

HRH_Degenetrix

Why are you surprised?

m0t

You must have better things to do.

HRH_Degenetrix

And you don't?

m0t

What could be better than flirting with a goddess?

I can't believe this. I feel like I'm ten years old on Christmas. Is it really you?

Before descending into the subway, the woman snapped a selfie beneath the saffron beam of a streetlamp. She sent it without a comment, and his reply, though still text, seemed breathless due to its speed.

Oh, God! You are glorious.

I wish I could save this image—look at me, already regretting this chat will delete itself.

HRH_Degenetrix

That's okay. That means we need to keep chatting. I have to go in the subway; don't worry, I haven't gone to bed yet.

4

THE ALMOST-thirty-year-old woman would not go to bed until three in the morning. From the time she emerged at her subway stop at 11:42 p.m. until 2:57 a.m., the woman was hunched over the phone, brain pinging with dopamine every time the device buzzed with a response from her friend. Sometimes chains of responses, her favorite. Words never meant so much to her. Each sentence he produced was crafted then and there for her. Each one sent from elsewhere in the city as, with equal absurdity, a grown man several decades older than the woman was also up until 2:57 a.m., also waiting with bated breath for each message to come in, each question to be answered—best, each picture to be sent.

She didn't receive pictures from him, didn't need to. How exhilarating to message back and forth! It was one thing to read a note painstakingly written, perhaps revised, then copied down with immaculate handwriting and sealed for at least twenty-four hours. It was something else when the messages were instantly delivered, vast as the difference between leaving a voice mail and connecting a call.

HRH_Degenetrix
Do you actually mute my videos?

m0t
Always the first time through. Sometimes for several more viewings.

The thought of you addressing me is so intense, so exciting, that my poor heart can hardly stand it. More than once, I've had to stop the playback completely and rest on the couch before I dare continue.

HRH_Degenetrix

Yeah, "rest."

m0t

That kind of resting happens around viewing four or five, once I'm able to turn the sound up.

HRH_Degenetrix

You're so funny. You could do more than rest at the thought of me if you'd meet me in person.

m0t

I would expire.

HRH_Degenetrix

No, come on…I want to meet you. Don't you want to meet me? Don't you want to touch me?

m0t

It is all I think about. All day. Every day. I wish I exaggerated. From the time I wake to the time I sleep with your imaginary double on the empty pillow beside me, I think of nothing but how it would be to make love to you. What it would do to me. Every thought that's not of you feels like a sin. An intrusion at best—at worst, an infidelity.

HRH_Degenetrix

Then let's do something! If you don't want to be seen in public with me, I understand, but that's why hotel rooms exist. The backs of cars. Grimy alleys. Anything!

m0t

I cannot, no, I cannot. It is so beneath your dignity—you deserve more than cringing and hiding in even the finest suites. Let me worship you as you deserve, from a safe distance—as I deserve, without benefit of your touch.

HRH_Degenetrix
No wonder you like the new videos. You love it when I'm mean, huh?
m0t
Oh, yes.

HRH_Degenetrix
What a gross, perverted thing to like…it makes me smile when I think about what a weirdo you must be. You want to watch me hurt myself and want me to push you around?

m0t
Yes.

HRH_Degenetrix
And you probably want to hurt me, too, huh? That's why you won't tell me what your favorite things are.

m0t
The performances I crave from you are not solo works, no. But, oh…to be involved stands not within the prospect of belief.

HRH_Degenetrix
Worthy thane! If you were my slave, I'd let you do whatever you wanted to me…once you'd begged enough.

m0t
Oh, God.

HRH_Degenetrix
I'd be such a nice mistress to you! Wouldn't you be a lucky boy?

m0t
Luckier than I deserve.

HRH_Degenetrix

Oh, you don't deserve it? Okay. I'll be cruel instead of nice.

You're being cruel to me, anyway.

m0t

Am I?

HRH_Degenetrix

Uh-huh…you give me all this money, all this wonderful stuff, that camera (which is so nice, by the way), but you won't give me the one thing I want from you.

I want to meet you so badly.

m0t

Yes, yes. I want nothing more. Oh—yes. But there is a vast gap between fantasy and realization.

You will meet me and find me old.

HRH_Degenetrix

I like dirty old men.

m0t

What if you decide you only like me for my money, the reason we met in the first place?

HRH_Degenetrix

You could stop paying me and I'd still send you videos. Talking to you makes me so hot I can't stand it. I don't care about your money—well, I do care, I'm grateful for it. But there's always more money somewhere, from something.

I'm not the jewelry type, but I like the jewelry you've been giving me because when I wear it, I think of you. It's like wearing a love note. I'm wearing your bracelet right now, and whenever I notice it, I feel happier than I have in almost three years.

Probably longer.

m0t
Maybe you're just saying that.

HRH_Degenetrix
Maybe if you met me in person you would know that I'm not. I don't "just say" anything.

m0t
Would that I could…I didn't offend you, did I?

HRH_Degenetrix
You're cute. Of course you didn't offend me.

I mean, yes, how dare you, you pig. If you were here, I'd flog you bloody and make you kiss my shoes.

m0t
Oh, dear—I'm dizzy. If I stop replying, it means I've fainted.

HRH_Degenetrix
Maybe you should send your address in case I have to call the paramedics.

m0t
Yours first.

HRH_Degenetrix
Okay!

Giggling, the Degenetrix typed her address and swore she could hear his gasp from all the way across the city.

m0t

My God! I didn't mean that—oh my God.

HRH_Degenetrix

Better write it down before the message deletes.

m0t

I shouldn't have this. You shouldn't let me have this.

HRH_Degenetrix

Strong temptation to come and visit, huh? You should give in. I'm waiting for you.

Hesitating, her lower lip pinned between her teeth, the woman typed again.

I want you.

m0t

I want you. Oh—look at that shameful sentence. It isn't enough. It's never enough. God help me, Degenetrix, I can't get enough of you.

HRH_Degenetrix

Do you want to know my real name, since you're so good at keeping secrets? I want to think of you whispering it while you go to sleep.

m0t

What a gift! I would love to know your real name.

His enthusiasm pulled from her another laugh of girlish delight, and after pressing the phone to her lips in contemplation, appreciation, disbelief, the woman lowered it to type again.

5

FROM THAT NIGHT FORWARD, the woman was always on her phone. When she awoke, when she went to bed—when she'd finished filming, finished sex, finished checking email, finished monitoring the forum, finished a call with her mother, finished her shower, finished a thought, she was right back on that damn phone in anticipation of another message. It soon became apparent to her that her patron was an early riser, and that he, too, was always waiting for her pings. What he did for a living, she couldn't guess, but he was sporadically in demand because there were days when they would chat with minimal interruption from dawn until dusk, and others where for long and itching hours, her hopes were dashed every time she picked up the unconscious device. Telepathy would have been so much better!

As a young person in high school watching couples perform such nonsense overcommunication, she had no idea what two people could talk about for so long. With most people, even lovers, she wished they'd shut up and let her think. With this unmet lover separated from her by socioeconomic barriers and social taboo, the woman wished they could talk forever. Forever and ever. Talk about nothing, talk about everything: about movies, food, theater and opera and art. He wanted to hear more about her photography, and she was so embarrassed that she hadn't taken any photos in months that she went out straightaway and took her first deliberate batch since the hand images that had begun her career. Simple black-and-white snaps of the bakushi whom she now visited at least once a week were received by the admirer like Annie Leibovitz portraits. The glow of his praise was so addictive that she began a sort of photo diary, supplementing the videos still faithfully delivered to the safe-deposit box with a few photo prints taken over the course of the week. A mangled pigeon in the gutter, chest still struggling for breath despite its broken neck; the disgraced and empty facades of famous theaters, which, anticipating a second wave of infections in the pandemic, were unable to reopen in any meaningful way that season; a self-portrait taken in bed with #1 in the background staring off into space, the dragon smoke of a cigarette pouring through her metal-filled nose.

The woman had been hesitant to talk to her patron about her interpersonal circle, but when conversation inevitably made natural turns there, she was thrilled to find him extremely accepting of her other physical friendships. *It would be a crime to pretend you spending time with other people is anything but erotic to me. Even if you were mine, I would want to watch your desires fulfilled by others—to see you in constant ecstasy no matter the source.*

Damn! Why weren't all men like that? Why weren't all fans? Take #1. No, she meant it, please take #1. The piercer grew clingy and took notice of the woman's new addiction to her phone, especially because Her Royal Highness was so fast to put the device to sleep whenever #1 leaned in to see what she was up to.

"You're always on that stupid phone," #1 actually had the audacity to complain one day, producing a sharp scoff from the woman.

"Yeah? I have a business to run, a forum to check. Sorry, it's not part-time."

"Hey, no, I get it. If I'm taking up your time, I can go."

So passive-aggressive! The woman put her phone away and said, "No, it's not that," because #1 was a valuable player in her network of colleagues and Degenerates alike. That said…the gloss had worn off around the art student breakup. It wasn't that #1 was a bad person. She was a nice enough girl. She was pretty likable. And she hinted a lot. "This apartment sure is small," she would announce, hands on her hips and eyes big as if the time she had spent in the bathroom had erased her memory of the studio's cramped geometry. "You could live someplace nicer with the new videos!"

It was true. A nipple here, a penis there, and the woman was more successful than ever. Like discovering fire. For the first time in her adult life, she was not concerned about this month's rent, or next month's.

When one took into consideration all the money and time she saved on food preparation, she had begun to develop a cozy savings account of the sort her mother always nagged her to create. What older generations didn't seem to understand was that in order to save money, you had to make more money than you spent on bills, and even before the virus, few employers paid wages permitting financial stability. Especially not to somebody like the woman, a college dropout whose primary skills were photography and the production of antisocial pornography.

Better to make your own way in the world than be somebody's slave, but not all self-made trades escaped the virus without monetary impact. #1 was among these and, as the tattoo parlor struggled to get back to business and serve its customers in a way that made the employees feel safe, that position of unemployment looked to be more or less permanent until the completion of a vaccine. Work-at-home was the wave of the future and that was rough on certain creative types. Oh, #1 could work at another parlor, but even if that didn't put her in competition with her old boss/current friend, a new job was no guarantee of long-term work. Businesses were reopening early due to political and financial pressure, but viruses knew no politics. Everyone in the city was unsettled by the plague and braced for the second surge, a second isolation period. Even if she did find another job, #1 might be unemployed again in months or weeks. And as for working someplace "essential," as previously mentioned, most "essential workplaces" where workers were forced to continue exposing themselves to the public were places like grocery stores, banks, and subways, and most of these were at a full boat of staff—even if the size of a "full boat" had been reduced to prevent viral transmission.

Everywhere she went, it was the same set of upper faces. At her own bank, the masked banker who tended to lead her to her safe-deposit box, and who had begun to smile at her from behind his fabric shield (in a pandemic world, one learned to discern this by the crinkle of crow's-feet at the eyes, like the puckered evidence of an amputated limb), was joined by a regular cast of other masked staff members and city-goers. Security guards, tellers, and customers alike bore increasingly ubiquitous masks in infinite variations. Fashion companies had stepped in to offer designer masks, and these were particularly popular around the city; the woman had several, herself. Fashion designers, seamstresses—say, there were some jobs that were never going away. If only because the seamstresses tended to be tiny, subjugated women cloistered in overseas sweatshops. Still, a movement had developed toward national independence from other countries in the global economy: maybe a few of these sweatshop jobs would start subjugating cloistered American women and the immigrants, legal or otherwise, living around them.

"You could learn to sew," was the woman's unhelpful suggestion to #1 as the latter lamented her limited skill set. "Both deal with needles."

"You could pay me to do videos with you," was the counteroffer a long time coming. The woman had been so braced for it that she had already prepared an argument.

"My producer is against involving performers we have to pay separately, and I kind of agree. There's all kinds of legal health and consent things, and—"

"Oh, come on! I'd be great. People want to see you with a woman again. I read comments like that all the time."

"So do I, but I ignore them." Her phone buzzed and, driven by Pavlov, she flipped the device faceup to smile at a response from her admirer. When #1 leaned in, the woman flipped it facedown again. "Anyway, I'm at a point in my career where I'm trying to save money instead of living above my means until I'm poor again."

"I've wondered why you're still living in this dump."

"I love my apartment!" Genuine insult infested her tone, and she tried to tamp it down but could only snidely respond, "Sorry it's not a mansion."

"You don't have to move into a mansion—but a living room would be nice sometimes, wouldn't it?"

"This *is* my living room. At least, it's the room where I'm living."

"But you could live in a bigger space. You'd be happier."

"Would I really be happier? You get a bigger space, and people think you want them to fill it. I get a living room, next thing I know, people want to live in it with me."

"What's bad about that?"

"I don't like people," she said as the phone buzzed a second time, still facedown on her thigh. "They're always doing the opposite of what I want from them. When they want me, it's when I don't want them. And when I finally want them again, they're nowhere to be seen."

"So, you do like people."

"Not their decision-making, I guess."

"They can be good to have around, though. Somebody to check in with you and notice if you don't come home. I know this girl who's a sex worker? She said she was raped by this— Are you listening?"

m0t

Every time I pass your street, even from the other side of the city, I feel you trying to lure me in.

Do you think about me as much as I think about you?

When #1 left and the woman, having narrowly avoided an argument, was alone with the bad taste in her mouth and the coveted cell phone, she sent her response.

HRH_Degenetrix

It's like everybody in the whole world exists to distract me from you. Filming for you now. Xo

6

IT WASN'T THAT THE WOMAN didn't feel bad for the suffering in the world. Not everybody had the good fortune of waking up immortal but not invulnerable, and for those who did, sharing their talent with the Internet might have never crossed their minds. For all its depravity, all its pornography, all its bizarre and disturbingly specific sexual fetishes, the Internet was still a relatively level playing field in terms of the content available. Its lighter side was full of foolish, innocent souls who wanted to look at funny captions on pictures of cats or watch pretty but ultimately less hard-core women play video games. This inability of the entire Internet to appreciate the Degenetrix and her talents was what got her weekly stream downed for good, or so it seemed: it was sort of hard to nail down an exact reason, or at least one that could be delineated within the terms of service policy of the streaming website.

The stranger was a lot angrier than she was and read the email to her with one hand open in midair as if to support the weight of his baffled disgust. "It says we've violated the community guidelines agreeing to not 'create, upload, transmit, distribute, or store any content that is inaccurate, unlawful, obscene, pornographic, abusive, or otherwise objectionable.'"

"We sort of did. In fact, we sort of have from the start."

"We have not. The whole point of the streams is that they're *not* obscene or pornographic. They've basically banned you for being accident prone."

The woman laughed despite herself and sent the message she'd been slowly composing between the stranger's annoying interruptions (*That sounds fun, but what would you do with the barbed wire?*), then set the phone aside with a shrug. "I mean, they're not stupid."

"They are stupid, though. This is in response to user complaints—people have reported us, and instead of thinking about it, they've decided the easiest solution is to ban us outright."

"Forget them. We don't need their money."

"This show is an important part of our income stream! I mean, for me, it's bad timing—I showed you the new apartment! Even at a discount, it isn't cheap. Plus, these streams are advertising for the rest of your videos."

"Yeah, it's not nothing…but we'll work through it." Buzz: *What else but construct a crown of thorns for you, my industrial divinity—oh, to crucify you, to spear your side and drink the fountain of your blood…I wish I had you here with me.*

Man, oh, man. What was she discussing with the stranger, again? Whatever it was, he droned on in the background. She lowered her phone once more as he continued, "—try to appeal it, but I don't think it'll do much good."

"Then it's time to find another way to advertise. Or another place to stream."

This might have been difficult, however. Because pornography could so easily go to a bad place for the performers involved, most websites for it were carefully regulated. Adult hubs of the mainstream variety had to vet performers, professional or amateur, not just for age but for consent. This was especially true thanks to the trend of "revenge porn," where—in private iterations of Her Royal Highness's public problem—bitter exes posted intimate photos to any number of sick websites for all the world to see. A pixelated molestation of the soul: digitized rape with even longer-lasting room for consequence. As in the rapist's memory, when a woman's image joined a sea of other women's images on the Internet, those images were there forever, accessible by the initial abuser and anyone who felt like it. The dignity of another human being meant nothing to one with a raging libido and a pornography addiction.

This was where oversight was needed but also where oversight was flawed. A mainstream porn site would want evidence that the Degenetrix was all right. There would be hoops to jump through, contracts to sign, maybe even doctors to see. She didn't want to deal with it. She didn't want to deal with any streaming problems again.

Good God! Leave her alone.

The woman was turned on after exchanging messages with her patron; the stranger, oblivious to the private conversation being had across time and space, was incensed into a passionate rage by the removal of the stream. After assessment of these two moods found them compatible, the pair decided to film a couple of different routines. From a sexual standpoint, it was fun. Nothing compared to the psychodrama that unfurled as soon as she read the words "Good morning" in the instant message application—but the films she and the stranger made, especially now that they were more explicit, were still pretty fun, still seemed sexy to her, still felt good. Felt better and better every time, actually. A time when she had ever perceived pleasure and pain differently was by then a fantasy to the woman. It hadn't even been a year since she'd discovered her talent. In retrospect, it was incredible how quickly she met the mother in the wake of that discovery—but death was the woman's meditation, and she made fast progress in its methods of consciousness expansion.

On the other hand, things had regressed for the stranger. Though during that first video, he had been reluctant to hammer the bones of her hand, day by day, he grew in his willingness to cause her grievous bodily harm. Once the first check cleared, the range of acts that were acceptable to him had changed, and although she suspected he used some combination of Viagra and speed to facilitate their sessions of gory intercourse, she was just glad he made the effort. Her most recent suggestion had been to reenact the method by which serial killer Jeffrey Dahmer hoped to turn nubile young men into zombie sex slaves. Following an on-camera power drill trepanation that caused an obscene burst of primary and unknowable colors and scents (oh, cedar, oh, oh, lover, lover), the woman gave a blow job while hydrochloric acid obtained from the stranger's chemist friend was funneled into this newest hole. Industrial divinity, sacred whore, would her unknown lover treat her half so well?

Beneath the stranger's hand, the Degenetrix worked automatically; her mind stuttered in its efforts to construct and process reality as birds fluttered past the ridge of her brow. No more vision in one eye, then both, sight flooded away in a swirl of ink. The pain was so immense, it was beyond pain: her thoughts fell down into her jaw, down, down, down, down beyond the bed and into the center of the Earth and beyond, until it was obvious that going down was going up and the only place to go was in. Recede back and away from the senses: that was where that divinity sat, the immortal spider-goddess weaving the veil upon the other side like a great black widow winding a sack of webbing about her sacred egg, speaking to it from without of all the insects it would kill. *Back again, my child,* spider-mother trilled in the woman's oozing mind. *Back and forth, back and forth, like the way I weave. Come here. Mother will protect you.*

The woman felt spider-mother trying to assume control of her consciousness, which had happened before, she realized, in states of death; she did not remember it because spider-mother wiped the memory of the transition state away, wiped memory of death away, wiped everything away, when allowed to control the woman's mind and guide it through the death process into the rebirth one. It was so very tempting to lean into the arms of the mother, the generous mother who would protect her, because the woman seemed so tired and so desiring of sleep—but if she slept, she would awaken once death was over, once she was alive again, like a person who had an orgasm but didn't attempt to enjoy the conscious experience of what an orgasm actually was to the perceiving mind.

No. The woman was so firm-set in the still eye of the hurricane that she dared not give in to these gentle offerings, this autopiloting of her mind and self through the unconsciousness of death. The woman resisted the possession attempt, trying to keep awareness of the hard prick in her mouth, the theatrical grunting of the attached man, her throbbing skull beneath his pushy hand. *You'd rather feel this than nothing?* Spider-mother laughed. *If that's what you'd prefer.*

The woman came to with a stifled scream of pain, an itch in the top of her head as her brain healed and her skull knit back together. Her scream? No—the stranger's scream. She'd had a seizure during the regenerative process and her teeth had clamped down on his prick. Mouth full of blood, she laughed.

7

SO FAST. Sex, memory again. Apologies, explanations of job hazards. She did not mean the apology. In fact, she did not care. She was lost in thought. She did not have to ask herself what spider-mother was, because spider-mother was inherent. Self-explanatory. What the mother was, it was beyond human expression. She could only be felt, experienced, interpreted, over and over again. If only the woman could find a way to communicate verbally what the mother was! Such communication would have been in and of itself spider-mother's incarnation. Such was her unknowability—her dangerous and all-containing nothingness.

"I can see you're not listening." The stranger, waving his hands in annoyance (had he even been speaking? She was slow to recover from the brain injury), rose and said, "I'm going to take a shower, let yourself out please."

"Sorry again," she said. The stranger sighed on the threshold of the bathroom.

"You didn't mean to do it…valuable lesson."

But as the bathroom door rattled behind him, the woman wondered. Had she meant to do it? She herself, the time-child aping free will in three dimensions, had not meant to. Yet who was to say what accidents, what pains, were part of the mother's perfectly constructed web? That web draped across the woman's face, that web that was the woman's face and all things beyond it. Her veil.

Oh, yes. The prick in her mouth, the stranger and his pain, the taste of blood still tinny on her tongue, her feeling hands, her clothes as she dressed, the dust of her coworker's imminent move and the sneeze it tickled from sinuses still shaking off chemical burns. The notions of sight, of taste, of touch, of scent, even sound, pure ethereal sound—all these things were constructed by the mother, threads making up her web. This body, this mind, all of this. The woman felt like a performer who had woken up in the middle of an act and become overwhelmed by self-consciousness, thinking of themselves not as their character but as an actor playing their character.

Rather than feel anxious at this notion, however, the woman was empowered. It was a cherished opportunity, rare and exquisite, to wake in this way, or begin to, without the use of drugs. The woman felt it was the responsibility, at least in part, of her absent lover. Evoking her divinity had made the woman conscious of that divinity: granted her the strength not just to resist the mother's call but to pull the dark mother down into time's ocean with her.

Spider-mother was awake within her, or she was awake to the consciousness that had always been within her. Quietly watching. That veil. What were these hands? What was this world? What net was cast eternally down into time's terrible waves? What was the pearl for which she quested down, down amid this frightful net, this web, this veil, all three images interpolated like the fearful blended face of a screaming Francis Bacon ghoul before a misty black ocean?

Old pipes groaned through the bathroom wall as the stranger showered their depravity from his body. The sound returned her attention to time's unfolding play: its lead actress discovered she stood near the apartment door, fully dressed, hand on her purse. The body was capable of so much while the mind was occupied…and for a woman whose mind was always occupied, she now had more to ponder than ever before. She tried to think of other things. The stranger's rooms overflowed, boxes on boxes of possessions packed away in anticipation for a move to the furnished apartment of some tenant dead by the virus's hand. Why was it so easy for everyone else to move house? She found the notion such a paralyzing one. It was a more permanent kind of death, maybe. A living death that mattered more because the deceased consciously contemplated it. A cicada, studying its own husk.

Once, when the woman's father was alive, when she was a girl, when she was seven years old, she found one of those cicada husks clinging to a cedar in her family's backyard. That yard! Truly home to her. A verdant patch of lawn in an area of the Pacific Northwest where any lawn was a status symbol, or maybe a warning sign of decadent values. Her nose had wrinkled in disgust to see the brown shell. "It's a dead bug," she said, and he had come over to study it.

"It's not dead," he said, "it's molted. That's its casing, its old shell. Almost like a hermit crab."

The girl had contemplated the shell for a few seconds and, more repulsed than ever, stepped away while concluding, "So it *is* dead."

Every time she moved, she thought of the cicada's dead old shell. What was truly left behind when a human being changed their apartments, sold their houses, moved from place to place? Could a house, a cicada's shell, hold memories? What if ghosts were not the spirits of people but the memories of houses—the fond recollections of allegedly inanimate objects for their absent owners? Now, knowing the secret presence of the mother, the woman could not help but feel sure there was some consciousness within it all. The same electrons that adapted their behavior based on observation, perhaps.

That was why she could not move from her apartment. She could not yet molt. Not without a reason. It was a movement to another part of time's ocean too soon. Her apartment's memories of her would be sad ones. She wanted its walls to see her happy: wanted it to see how she learned, grew, fell in love. Yes, fell in love.

What a funny world. No wonder she couldn't stop descending into these dark trenches even when the alternative, the mother, was so comfortable. The real pain of being alive in it, this, whatever this life was, was to be alone in it—to bear the weight of the seeing and the feeling, that visceral witnessing of life, as if in a void. That was how she felt until the mother was within her. Awake in her, void-weaver, that great transdimensional diving bell fisher of crustacean and insects and men.

How she wanted to explain the mother to her lover! Full comprehension of the mother, the woman saw while ruminating on the empty subway home, was the same thing as awakening the mother within the self. Her lover, her admirer, he was a sensitive and intelligent man. If anyone could understand, could be stirred into the mother's awakening, it was this man who spent his days and nights chatting away with Her Royal Highness. What might happen? What splendid acts of love might they share, what alien intimacies, with the mother awake in both at once? That was where her dreams of telepathy perhaps lay. And there may even have been others in the world capable of enduring the mother's presence in them. But how? How was it possible to communicate the mother by any means at all?

While tripping on a step on her way out of the subway and imagining her fall back to a death evaded with reflexive grip of the handrail, the woman felt the answer rise within her. Artwork. Somehow, she could derive a creation, an act—a performance, perhaps, or another form of art—that was a true expression of the mother.

She just had to keep creating, and one day, there it would be.

8

THE STRANGER WANTED HER to care about the stream more than she did, and she tried. But with so much going on in the world from which she daily disconnected, it was hard to worry about the loss of one small source of income. Her fans were devastated. She posted a few conciliatory videos, but within the walls of her apartment and the privacy of the instant messaging application, she felt no remorse. With no further need to pretend their acts of violence were mostly accidental, the production team could get as extreme as they wanted—and not only that, but they were liberated from the constraints of the format, permitted the potential of new realms. There was room for her to master the art of constructing real performances: to shift emphasis from titillation and into her pursuit of embodying the mother.

A week after the brain injury scene, the closeness of the mother remained. The positive glow of a psychedelic trip would have faded in that time for most people her age, and the woman felt comforted that spider-mother might remain awake in her forever. She had told no one of the experience, not even her benefactor. It was all too new and intimate—she did, however, share her desire to hone her artistic expression with one person. The bakushi, who occasionally had her over to drink beer—evidently feeling the woman's regenerative abilities also prevented her from being even an asymptomatic carrier of the virus—appeared to give real thought to her vague desire for growth. "I think you're approaching your art the wrong way if you're trying to enrich, say, the physical acts themselves. Your extremity is evident—that dimension is captured properly, in other words. At this point, the importance isn't in the types of injuries or even your willingness to experience them. It's what they signify, what you're doing with them."

"I haven't been doing anything specific with them."

"Right, because in your unpaid content you've been posturing. That posturing has been the act. There's no room for narrative flow when the narrative is already one of a girl having an accident."

The woman lowered her bottle upon the iron of the fire escape outside her friend's apartment. "The narrative of sadomasochistic stunts?"

"Every piece of art has a narrative. Painting, sculpture, flower arrangement. Even kinbaku has a narrative, tells a story. Show a person the stillest, simplest painting, and whether they know it or not, they start constructing a story about it to themselves—even if it's only to respond, 'My kid could paint that.' That statement alludes to an instantaneous internal narrative, an imagining of their kid reproducing a painting. Even more true of they're not a parent and say instead, 'A kid,' because then they might have derived a whole imaginary child just from looking at the painting. You can't help it. It's human nature to explain the world in stories. Art is the unfolding of deliberate narrative within the confines of a creative medium—an attempt to transmit a specific story and connect two people, creator and viewer, by that experience of empathy."

"If you had been in my 'What is Art' freshman seminar, I might not have dropped out of college."

"Only a liberal arts college could waste an entire semester on that."

"It was fun at the time, but you're right, it could have been a two-week unit in a better art history course." After another swig, the woman again set her bottle aside to tend to her buzzing phone.

m0t
If you're by a window, the sunset is positively outrageous tonight.

She smiled and typed a rapid reply while the bakushi looked politely in another direction.

HRH_Degenetrix
On friend's fire escape, heading home soon. It really is something! I wish you were here.

"Sorry." The woman lowered her phone a few inches. In the corner of her eye, the text of another reply appeared on-screen. She forced herself to look at her friend. Amazing: she hadn't told anyone about this man messaging her around the clock. She hadn't even told her mother, knowing full well what that opinion would be. But why hadn't she told the stranger, or #1? The anticipation of jealousy perhaps, and the added factor that the stranger, as her purported manager, would contrive a way to control the situation.

The bakushi, however, was emotionally detached yet friendly enough to take an interest in a fun, un-possessive way. "It's this guy," the woman explained to the perk of her friend's ears. "He started out as one of my highest contributing fans, and—I don't know. We got to talking."

"Damn, is that who you're always chatting with? Got a picture?"

"No, actually."

"No picture? Do you know what year it is? Fine—what's he look like?"

"I don't know."

"What! What do you mean, you don't know?"

"I mean, I don't know."

"You're messaging this guy all the time, and you don't even know what he looks like? Are you crazy? He could be five hundred pounds! He could be that serial killer dumping girls in the park!"

"I don't think he's five hundred pounds." At last, the woman succumbed to her craving and looked over at the phone.

m0t

And I wish I were there with you. So sorry to bother you with your friend. Tell me when you're ready?

HRH_Degenetrix

I will! So excited xoxo

"You two message like an old married couple," observed the bakushi, putting two and two together with a gasp at the bangle around her wrist. "Is he where you're getting all this couture stuff?"

The woman explained the safe-deposit box.

"And you haven't met?"

"No, we haven't."

"Girl, you've lost your damn mind. You have other people writing to you, don't you?"

"Oh, all the time. My email is so full of unsolicited dick pictures that the spam box smells like smegma."

"Well—obviously don't talk to the guys sending you dick pics, but, I mean, you could probably find your share of randos to send you jewelry and kiss your ass if that's all you want."

"I don't think you understand." As best as she could, the woman listed a few tokens collected from the safe-deposit box; she tried to articulate the amount of money he had given her over the past several months; most of all, she tried to explain the other things. The obvious care he had for her. The songs he had started to send her when they made him think of her. The interest he had in whatever she said and the interest she felt in return; the endless stream of questions bandying between the two of them like elementary schoolers on the playground getting to know each other in the limited time frame of daily recess.

There were things she couldn't tell, however. She couldn't tell the bakushi about the exquisite alignment of their proclivities: how she wanted to feel herself turned inside out by this man, this patron, this mysterious benefactor of hers. How she wanted to present her internal organs for assessment, receive his caresses quite literally along her spine. How his devotion had, without his meaning to, awoken spider-mother within her—had renewed her desire to make art that was more than mere art.

These most important things were beyond explanation, and what she expressed didn't sound like more than puppy love. The bakushi's nose wrinkled accordingly.

"I'm not convinced this guy isn't five hundred pounds. Or maybe he's, like, a cripple. Or an amputee. You said he seems like he's into amputations, right?"

"Yeah...but he seems like he's into everything that's violent if it's a natural development of whatever we're talking about. The acts in question don't matter to either of us; it's the acts in the context of the fantasies we share." Something in her mind snapped into place. "Okay—maybe I do sort of see what you mean about narrative in my art."

"Ah! Yes, that's exactly what I mean. The sexual act also follows a narrative structure, and within that narrative, the action is driven by the accumulation of many small movements, gestures, rituals. Stories climax like people do. Of course"—with a steely glint, the bakushi slid a suggestive arm around the woman's waist—"women have multiple climaxes…most stories have only one."

There was a minute or two to make out, but in a rare divergence, the woman had somewhere to be by the end of the hour. When home, she assessed her clothes, picked out an old coral dress that had gotten three prior wears (she was not a formal woman and the dress was intended for cocktail parties, the extinct sort hosted by 1950s housewives alongside square-jawed spouses), and slipped into it after finishing her hair and makeup. Then, feeling only a bit silly, she took a picture of herself and sent it to her patron.

HRH_Degenetrix
Ready for the opera! How do I look?

m0t
My own Violetta! How exquisite you are. Did you have fun with your friend?

HRH_Degenetrix
Yeah, but I've been looking forward to coming home and hanging out with you. Give me a couple more seconds.

After rifling through the clutter of her nightstand, the woman located a card she'd removed from the safe-deposit box. Many entertainment companies and streaming services had seen booms in subscriptions as a result of people isolating against the virus. This had increased the number and quality of programs available on demand. The Metropolitan Opera House, one of the city's finest centers of culture, had taken great steps to improve their own service; after the woman's lamentation that she had not gotten a chance to go to one of its prestigious shows before it was forced to close for one, maybe as many as two or more years in a row, her benefactor surprised her with a subscription to the opera house's streaming service. *Come to the opera with me*, said the attached card.

Human courtship was not to be deterred by a pandemic.

· MAN RAY ·

1

THE WOMAN COULDN'T BLAME spider-mother for her increasing disconnection from reality. Her benefactor was also responsible. Plunging into love with someone you'd never seen had a way of devaluing the tangible realm. Her emphasis was, of late, on the mind. Especially, well—the stranger was always complaining since the stream had gone down, and #1 harangued her for attention all the time, and nobody cared what she felt or wanted. The stranger criticized her for no longer posting on the forum and slowing down her use of social media platforms, but every word she typed was now like gold, and she wanted to give her gold to this man who intrigued her. Her words, her attention, her mind—day by day, every day she lived was lived increasingly for the sake of communicating with her benefactor. Filming activities not related to producing footage for his private enjoyment were wastes of her time, which was why she was ultimately relieved when she found the lovely dead rat in her post office box. Finally! A perfect excuse to stop doing the weekly PO box haul videos.

To be fair to the post office, the dead rat was in a package addressed to the Degenetrix's box. They couldn't have known. Still—after the experience of getting home, tearing back the brown paper and opening the package beneath to be bowled over by the horrific smell, the woman was so repulsed by the mere idea of returning to the post office to cancel the box that she actually employed #1 to do it. When the stranger came by a day later to film the weekly unboxing video, she directed his attention to the freezer.

"Why is there a dead rat in here?" His lip curled as he resealed the flap of the cardboard carton, then the freezer door.

"I can't say since there was no return address."

"What—you mean somebody mailed you that?"

"You think I make it a habit of keeping dead rats in my freezer? I canceled the box—"

"What!"

"—and I think I'm done with receiving and replying to fan mail in general. If somebody wants to send me an email, and it's nice, maybe I'll respond, but I think I'm officially through kissing people's asses because they've sent me a butt plug they expect me to use."

He had no choice but to accept her judgment on the matter, although it visibly displeased him to do so. The box was already canceled and, given the nature of the latest "gift," it seemed more a safety issue than anything else. Too bad. She did like getting viewer mail. Packages had come from as far as Norway (members of the black metal scene were in love with her work), and some gifts had been nice. Nothing touched the treasures from her friend, however. Nothing fazed her. As the holiday season approached and a new wave of viral infections was formally defined along with it, the woman watched a steady drop in paying fans, felt the impact on her videos. Didn't matter, didn't matter. Her benefactor gave her anywhere from $4,000 to $8,000 a month when you put all the checks together, and, what with her address being known to him, he had volunteered to pay her rent, as well. Money was not nothing—it was the means, the substrate in which she nourished her ideas—but it meant less to her now that she did not need it to live.

Such a change made her see how clearly money impacted the people around her. The stranger, for instance. All he thought about was cost-effectiveness: how much he made every minute. He rolled his eyes when she offered him her first script during a business meeting in his new apartment.

"What's this?"

"It's a loose idea. I'm willing to change things."

"No, I mean—what is this for?"

"I feel like we could add structure to our videos and make them more engaging."

"Oh, no…you want us to start incorporating plots?"

"Only in an abstract way! Imply them with setting and gesture. I don't want to end up like porn studios making bad stories about pizza delivery drivers getting blown in exchange for food, I want to… I don't know how to describe it. Establish an aesthetic, I guess."

His eyes scanned the contents of the page, expression tight. "Wh— A tarantula?"

"Tarantulas, plural."

"Where are we going to get— Do you know how much live animals cost? And in the middle of a pandemic?"

"I probably know a guy who knows people who could hook it up. Seems like he knows everybody."

"Seems like this is a huge waste of time and money for no payoff," the stranger insisted, handing the script back to her. "So you're an artist now, huh?"

The hairs down the back of her neck stood up. While, in her hand, her phone buzzed with a reply from her lover, the woman said, "I've always been an artist," and saw the stranger realize his own mistake as she raged on, "I can't help if people want to project their perversions all over me. All I wanted from the start was to make art, and now— If you don't like the tarantulas or whatever, that's fine, I get it. I have other ideas. But do you ask? No. You don't care about my ideas, about me as a person— I told you some psycho sent me a dead rat, and your response was to be pissed that I canceled *my* PO box, that I was renting under *my* name with *my* money."

"I just wished you would have talked to me first."

"Why should I talk to you about something that's mine? Just like this. You want to act like you have a greater share in this than I do because, what—you contributed our first camera? It's my body, dude. It's my magic trick. Not yours, not the fans', not anybody's but mine. And if I have to cut you out—"

"I get it," he said, body tensed beneath the burden of her fury. "I get it, sorry, calm down."

"'Calm down'! An asshole sent me a dead rat last week, and you want me to calm down— You're right. I think I'm going home. I'll manage to 'calm down' when I've had some time to think."

"Hey, wait—"

Outside his apartment, she could breathe again. Beneath the light of the building's stoop, the woman checked the new message and couldn't help her grin to read her lover's saucy addendum to the erotic conversation paused while she dealt with the stranger. Maybe that was why she had snapped so hard up there: if he had the least idea the conversation she'd interrupted to have a useless fight with him, he wouldn't have cared, but he might have understood why she was so quick to anger.

Woof! Her benefactor made her face flush with lust. How she wished he was around—that she knew where he lived! What a fantasy: to drop in on him, make love to him, stay the night with him instead of going back to her lonely apartment. Ah, well. She was never alone—not with the phone.

HRH_Degenetrix

That's so hot—you sure were raised Catholic, huh? Did you go to a private school? I'd dress up like a nun for you.

m0t

Only if you promise to be strict. I'm glad you wrote me; I was thinking about you just now.

HRH_Degenetrix

Something mean, I hope… I'm on my way home, but I'll message you when I'm there.

2

THE COP CAR WAS REAL. He was a real cop. Everything about him—hat, uniform, badge, handcuffs, gun (especially the gun)—was real. The cop was real. The woman would never have been stupid enough to get in the car if the cop had not been real.

It wasn't all the uniform, the car. In part, it was the circumstance. She was flustered after the fight. Not to mention, it was nighttime in the city. The bastard knew how to play into a woman's natural fears because he was every woman's naturals fear.

But the real reason she fell for it was the worst reason of all: she recognized him. A block from her apartment and the promise of privacy, bed, and chitchat with her intriguing older man, she passed the prowler in its parallel space, and it rumbled alive. The passenger side's window rolled down; a cop with sunken eyes looked out across its empty seat before she was far enough away to ignore him, calling, "Excuse me, ma'am," in the clipped tone favored by former military men. After introducing himself as a sergeant, he asked, "Do you live in that building up there?" Not only did he gesture to it, but he named its landlord with such confidence that the woman didn't think twice of answering in the affirmative. The cop went on. "We've had reports of unusual activity. I know it's late, but could I ask you a few questions?"

Christ. This had better not pertain to her. Her apartment was so close. Too bad the cop car was closer. The woman stooped to see the driver and smiled in recognition. "Oh." She connected the sergeant's name to the sunken eyes above his black cloth mask. "Oh! I recognize you! You came to my apartment with your supervisor one time. Hi, how are you?"

"Fine. Go ahead and sit in the back of the car while I ask you the questions I'm about to ask you. They may be extensive."

The locks of the cop car clicked open. She studied the officer without removing her mask. "I'm not being detained, am I?"

"Not unless you're the loiterer we've been getting complaints about."

"Sorry for violating your six feet of social distance," she joked while opening the car's rear door and getting into the back. She would have left it open, but he said, "Shut it," in a way that made her realize alarm bells had already been ringing for a few seconds. Only now was she hearing them.

"It's only going to be a few minutes, right?"

"I don't want to draw attention to us in case somebody's lurking around."

Right. She looked hard at him through the screen separating the back of the car from the front—at his state-issued laptop in the front seat, at the hat sitting on the dash. Like an absolute fool, the woman buckled to these trappings of fascist authority. With one reluctant glance at the sidewalk, she drew her legs into the car and shut the door.

Everything was fine for a few seconds. He began, "Do you come home around this time fairly often?"

She nodded. "Yeah—I work late three or four days a week and come home about now."

"Ever seen anything unusual around your block?"

"Just you."

"Nobody lurking around your building in the dark?"

"Like I said: just you. Officer."

"Talk to your neighbors often?"

"Not really."

"Think you could identify them?"

"Some, but a lot of people live in that building."

"How long have you lived here?"

"About six years. Sort of sad." She laughed weakly; he didn't, and his lack of laughter drew attention to the eyes that pierced her reflection in the rearview. "Six years," she repeated.

The radio on his chest emitted a burst of static, the indistinct voice of an operator emerging from its speaker. He shut it off. Had he shut off his body camera before picking her up? Probably. Too bad; she understood they recorded for several minutes after being turned off in hopes of catching dirty cops. This one had foresight. Experience.

"Ever become aware of any pervasive problems during that time? Any issues?"

"No. It's an uneventful building. I don't think we even had any cases of the virus—no, wait, some outbreaks on the second floor, but I never had any contact with them. And there was a shooting a couple of years ago."

"Well…as I said earlier, we got calls pertaining to a loiterer hanging around the building." The message from her patron flashed through her consciousness—*I was thinking about you just now*—and was gone as the sergeant continued, "I thought I'd check in on you. Don't want anything happening to Her Royal Highness."

All thoughts of her unseen friend were gone as quickly as they'd come. Glad for her mask and the way it hid her pallid face, the woman asked, "Excuse me?"

"You shouldn't be using your body this way, Degenetrix. These new videos—you know the ones I mean. You're a whore now."

"Lou Ford." The woman's hand eased toward the door handle. "He lived in a small town. Not a big city."

"Why do you have to do this to yourself? It's so humiliating—degrading. You were perfect before."

"Is that why you sent me the rat?"

"I hoped you'd finally stop, but instead you got rid of your PO box. Guess we're giving you enough money for your porn that you don't need our gifts, huh, you whore."

Her fingers were against the door handle; the locks snapped shut at the touch of his button. She gritted her teeth and still tried to release herself, slapping her free hand against the door while jerking the handle as the cop went on. "I used to watch your streams every week before you changed. They were fine, everything was fine. You didn't need to prostitute yourself like this."

"Don't be jealous, Sergeant." The woman slid forward in her seat, jerked down her mask. His pinpoint sociopath pupils bloomed with animal lust at the sight of her uncovered face. When he looked away, she gripped the grill between them. Already a prisoner. "Those videos don't mean anything more than any of my performances do."

"That's the problem."

"No, but see—see, my apartment's right there. Look at me—" He didn't, and started the car while an overeager note sharpened her pitch. "Hey, maybe you could take a break from your hard shift! You could come upstairs with me."

"Shut up."

"I mean it—you could do whatever you wanted to me, I promise. Hey, look at me—"

"Shut up, goddamn you—"

She recoiled in her seat like a slapped child. Quieter in the aftermath of his visceral scream, the sergeant said, "You're a lying whore. Trying to manipulate me. You'll say anything to get out of my car. Like you'll say anything, do anything, for money. I can't believe you're making these awful videos."

Was he actually crying? That sentence deserved an interrobang rather than a question mark. Yes, his eyes were filled with tears. He even wiped them while pulling the car from its space. This guy was straight out of Crazytown: the woman lowered her hands and, grimacing, slipped her phone from her pocket. Was it possible to use it without his notice? That screen was so bright. Up front, the cop continued, "What I liked about you was that you seemed like such a nice girl. I thought, here's a girl who could understand me—somebody who could help me, even."

"I'll still help you, Sergeant…look"—they passed her apartment building, and she tried to will her blood pressure down, down, stay calm, don't panic, stay calm—"it's not too late! Why don't you turn here? Go back around the block and—"

"But I saw it growing in you more and more by the week—money. You used to greet all your fans. Everybody who piled into the room, you'd say their usernames and smile and wave. It was like having a friend. Then you only acknowledged the people who tipped you; and now you barely do that. So many people have supported you, and you don't even care about our opinions. You're shutting us out."

Sure at last that seductive indulgence was not going to save her, the woman let her annoyance show and tried the door handle a few more times. "You know what? I don't care about your opinion, no. When a performer pisses you off by taking a new direction, it's not a personal betrayal, dude. Let me out of your car."

"I'll let you out when— What are you doing?"

She didn't care: the phone's fluorescence lit her face as she hastily sent typo-riddled messages in the one application always left open.

HRH_Degenetrix

Help help don't know what u can do

Crszy guy has me he's a cop don't call the police

"What are you doing," the cop demanded, eyes darting between her reflection and the road.

m0t

Where are you? What's happening?

"You bitch—texting? Who are you texting?"

HRH_Degenetrix

I think he is trying to kidnap me and it could be bad bc I odnt know if I can even die

The car skidded along another curb as she constructed the final hurried words of the message. Her face pressed against the window, eyes squinting, thumbs flying to type the cross streets. Okay. Okay. Okay, he was getting out, be ready— She snapped the button on the side of the phone to put it to sleep and became not a human being but a series of muscles reacting to stimuli. This was the veil. This was karma. This was spider-mother as much as everything else was spider-mother, and spider-mother willed the woman's survival.

Eyes took in the drawing of a gun. *Click* went the door, and the observing body flew against it, slamming into it, squeezing out of it, crying aloud, gripping the phone, a hand flying wildly, a jab in the eye, cops scream like humans do, amazing, amazing. Scrambling, the woman careened upon the blacktop, scraping her knees, pushing herself up to scream. The explosive noise of the gun's triple discharge manifested as fiery pain in her hand—but her body ran, two fingers and a dead cell phone left behind, no big loss, come on, go, go, sprint, keep running, keep running, he drove you only three blocks, keep running, run, run straight to the apartment, don't stop, don't look, don't think about lost fingers, just run, run like he pursued even though he didn't, even though he knew he was as lucky as she was, just run, run, run and

    run and

    run and

    run and then

    be home, be inside the only exterior door of the apartment.

    Be there. Be there.

    Cry a little: it's okay.

    It's okay to cry when you're thankful.

3

HER FINGERS were still gone. Okay. Okay, that was scary. Would they ever come back? It was her first amputation and the first time in months she felt consistent pain: not just pain but long-term pain, burning, screaming, hellfire pain, that signature of the wound's attempt to gestate infection.

But she was alive. Oh, she was alive. Unkidnapped, unraped. Undead. Thanks to her patron: she saved herself, but without him, she might never have had the opportunity. The act of reaching out to him had given her the opening. Eyes full of tears, the woman wrapped her three-digited hand in medical tape, fashioned from a belt a makeshift tourniquet, then used her one good set of fingers to log into her laptop and install, in the eerie quiet of her isolated apartment, the desktop version of the chat application that connected her to her absent savior. The instant she managed to log in, a spate of messages crowded the screen.

m0t
Wherever he takes you, try to keep the messages going.

I may be able to have someone trace your location, I've got your phone number somewhere here.

Did you see his badge number/name? Give it to me, ASAP.

Oh, darling, I'm so worried. Are you getting these messages? Tell me you're all right.

Are you still there?

When this event was memory to her, she would smile to think of his concern. Touched in the adrenaline-numb depths of her psyche, the woman typed her response with one hand and a pinky finger.

HRH_Degenetrix

Hey, I made it out. Home safe. Thank you so much, sorry to worry you.

No sooner had her message popped into the box than the words "m0t is typing" appeared at the bottom of the screen. Her eyes filled with new tears to think of somebody she'd never met sitting in front of the computer, overwhelmed with worry. This man, this man.

m0t

Thank God! Are you all right? What happened?

What exactly *had* happened? She had been stupid. That was what happened. One hundred percent, the woman blamed herself: for bowing to authority, for not trusting her instincts, for coming home late, for fighting with the stranger. She might even have blamed herself for making videos in the first place if the videos hadn't also brought her the patron whose existence was her salvation.

HRH_Degenetrix

Want to do a one-way video chat? Hard for me to type.

Amazing that this was their first time. While constantly texting, each evidently felt the other so present that the idea of private live shows hadn't occurred. The haste with which he replied, *Of course*, gave her the endorphin relief of a genuine smile; after typing, *Hold on*, she got up, popped a few aspirin pills, changed her blood-soaked bandage, then of all things checked herself in the mirror to run a brush through her hair and wipe the tear tracks from her cheeks. Turning the camera toward the headboard so he couldn't see the cluttered not-kitchen but could instead enjoy the inverted roses mounted above, the woman activated the video-chat feature. He accepted a one-way call, and their chat box remained, now devoted only to his messages, at the bottom of the screen's presentation of her face.

"Ta-da." She wasted no time in waving her bandaged hand before the screen.

m0t
My heart! What happened?

"I feel so stupid about it that I don't even want to tell you."

Don't say that—you're not stupid.

"I don't know if you'll agree once I've shared my story… This guy was a real psycho. I've seen him before. He came with his partner one time to respond to a noise complaint—he's the one who's been posting my address, and he sent me that rat I told you about. Probably the one who finally got my stream banned, too, now that I think about the timing…seems like he's snapped. Honestly I'm just glad all this turns out to have been one guy, if it was more than one—ugh." She leaned forward to read his response, grinning despite herself.

It shouldn't be a surprise that your work attracts predators.

"You would know—"

Are you sure he was a real police officer? When he responded to the noise complaint with his partner, what was it like?

"Oh, I don't know. Maybe weird, but all cops are spooky to me since they choked that guy to death for selling loose cigarettes— Oh, yeah." He had shot out another fast line, the question: *Did you post your video announcing the takedown of the PO box?* "Yeah, I posted that, um, yesterday."

Perhaps he watched that and felt his campaign of harassment insufficient.
"I guess…what a loony. He *cried* over my *porn*."

Pathetic.

She laughed in reassurance while he typed on.

Did you get his badge number?

"Just his name…it doesn't matter, though. I mean, I'm sure he was smart enough to shut his bodycam off before I came by." Another spark of nausea crawled through her limbs, its genesis point in her torso. "He was waiting for me. Has he been stalking me since that night he and his partner came to my house?"

It doesn't matter—tell me his name, please.

Yes, he has probably cased your apartment.

"Is that what *you're* doing?"
No immediate response: she smiled in a teasing way. "It's okay…I like the thought of you stalking me."

I prefer to think of it as walking past the closed Met and feeling the artworks inside.

"The artworks would probably like it better if you would come visit them…but unlike the artworks at the presently closed Met, I have a say in it. I gave you my address for a reason."

Will you tell me his name?

"You're so persistent." She told him, asking, "Happy?"

Measurably more so, yes.

"That's good." With a light laugh, she said, "Even in a fucked-up time like this, I like to make you happy," and reflexively lifted her right hand to hook her fingertip against her lip. But—ah! Wait. That fingertip was gone. Yes, yes. Her nose wrinkled as she assessed the bandage soaking through at a slower pace than the first. "I can't believe this—I feel sick. My fingers are property now."

You think he kept them?

"Come on, wouldn't you?"

Fair enough.

May I see?

What a creep! She bit back another inappropriate grin while contemplating the bandage one more time, then said, "Okay."

With the slow, lurid concentration of a burlesque starlet undressing on the stage, the woman stripped the bandage from her hand. A wad of stained gauze fell away; a bloody shift lifted; when she showed him the oozing scabs crowning the stumps of her index and middle finger, he was quick to type a message.

How wrong it is for me to be consumed by lust at this moment, but your mere existence is so erotic to me.

"You're such a pervert." Real delight filled her giggling voice and relieved her body. Her worries likewise began to lift. The ugly world still had room for happiness, but—

"What if they don't grow back?"

You don't think they will?

"I don't know what to think. I've never lost fingers or limbs or anything before, and these aren't healing yet. I don't know what to expect."

Maybe that's your problem.

Does it hurt?

"Uh, *yeah*." Though it came in good humor, her withering tone indicated the question's stupidity. "Yes, it hurts terribly, like my whole hand is on fire. All my fingers, even though I don't have two and the others are still in one piece."

Poor doll. Would I were there to kiss the pain away.

Oh! Now she understood. It wasn't a stupid question—it was a lewd question. She coyly bit her lower lip. "I think you're just sad it wasn't you."

Would you hate me if that were the case?

"No, never! I'm sad, too. He stole my amputation virginity; I would much rather have given it to you." With a reflexive look at the clock, the woman studied her mutilated hand. "You'd really think I was sexy if I had eight digits forever?"

Oh, yes.

"Two limbs?"

Yes, yes.

"None?"

God, yes.

"You're a sick fuck, huh."

You have a way of bringing it out in me.

"Blame the victim…it's sure fun to talk to you live like this and wonder what you're doing on the other side of the screen."

I think you know what I'm doing.

"You make me want to do the same thing. Wish I could! Oh—I wish you were here."

I would give anything to be there with you.

"Come *over*, then!"

I can't.

"Why not?"

Because I will give up everything to stay with you. My entire life will end as soon as I enfold you in my arms. There will be nothing for me but you.

Already, there isn't.

"I feel that way about you more and more and more." Drumming her two good fingers against her lower lip, the woman leaned off-screen, opened a drawer, and took out one of her homemade toys. At the touch of a button, the screwdriver-tipped dildo wiggled into repugnant motion, head thrashing back and forth like a captured snake, an agonized worm, a metal-headed maggot. She demonstrated it for her benefactor's admiration and laughed as, according to the application, he stopped typing whatever he'd been in the middle of typing. Sudden silence.

"Will you stay up with me a while longer? I feel so scared and lonely… I don't want to go to sleep."

4

HER ADMIRER'S MOST REFRESHING QUALITY was not the elaborate and frequently religious erotic daydreams he shared with her, although the woman enjoyed all he had to say about matters of sex, desire, divinity, etcetera. It was the simplicity of what he wanted from her outside of their violence. When their mutual pleasure was satisfied (as much as was possible in virtual circumstances), the woman expressed reluctance to end the stream and, oh, how eagerly he volunteered to sit up—to watch her sleep as though they were in bed together. She found lovers watching her sleep to be invasive, but that night, the suggestion relieved her, and at any rate, his invasive qualities sparked her desire. She figured he would hang up once she slept, but this distant intimate of hers was still online as a viewer of their private stream when she awoke late the next morning. "Did you even go to work," she teased, lifting her head while the screen lit with the message: Good morning.

I can afford to take a day off.

"I get that sense. Oh…" The night before rushed back like hangover vomit. Limply, the woman lay her head back down upon the pillow and regarded her hand, its two fingers still missing, the wound fetid from a night of exposure and the scab crusted with unnerving ochre pus. Certain infection. "This has never happened."

You're still experiencing the trauma. Still in it.

"No kidding."

I mean that you didn't expect this. It was nonconsensual. The injury is current, active, still happening. In your mind, maybe in your body. Do you see?

"Kind of." She still trembled: as affected as if the sergeant might leap out of the bathroom. That image so frightened her that she squeezed her eyes shut. "Uh— H-ey, listen, will— This is stupid, oh, I'm crying—"

When she had rolled off-screen and back for a tissue, another message waited.

Wait! I love to see you cry. Come back, cry for me.

Even as she cried, she laughed at him, and called him a creep, then wept more, pressing the tissue to her forehead with the heel of her mangled palm and tingling arm framing free-falling tears. "I'm so freaked out—oh, I was so stupid. What's wrong with me?"

Stop saying that. He is a police officer. They tend to have an advantage over the average sex offender.

You heard about that fellow in Canada at the start of quarantine, didn't you? The one that got their assault weapons banned—he wasn't even a real police officer. Just some costumed troglodyte.

As much understanding as those victims should be shown, I'd grant to you, or more.

"Still! I should have realized something was off. I go back through it in my head, and it's like—I don't know! I saw his cop car and all his cop shit, and it made me lose about twenty IQ points." She squinted through her tears at the new message and snorted at its contents.

I'll give you money to stop saying that.

"You don't have to give me money…I want my fingers back, man."

Don't worry.

"It's—" Words soaked with tears, the woman gave in and used her left hand to hastily sweep saline from her cheeks. "It's easy for you to say that sort of thing when you're not feeling this—feeling like this, alone here."

You're not alone. I'm with you. Always, always with you, a message away.

Looking at the ceiling through her watering eyes, the woman battled a streak of self-pity and wanted to point out he wasn't there— but wasn't he? Hadn't he been? Had she thought of calling the stranger for even half a second? #1? The art student, the bakushi, her own mother, 911? No. She hadn't thought to tell anybody. Nobody except the man she'd never met.

Instead of arguing, she nodded at her tear-stained, whole hand, turned her head, stared again into the screen of her laptop. "Who are you?"

Someone who loves you.

It was sex and obsession at first, but since we have been talking, I am so in love with you.

You make me weep, make me mad.

Her eyes filled with new tears. She shielded them with her ruined hand, unable to bear his words. "Oh, man—I wish I didn't love you back, but I do. I do, I do."

Why would you wish a thing like that?

"Because it hurts me. Because the way I love you is so painful."

I should think that the sweetest part.

I love you.

The isolated phrase on the screen, oh! Her hand throbbed with the pain of love, and she wept, then quieted herself with a late thought for her neighbors. She gasped against the suffering provoked by the words, by what it meant to love another person the way she meant it. The way he meant it. "I love you, too. I need to be alone for a while. Is that okay?"

More than okay. Anything you want is okay. I understand.

"Thank you. Thank you—thank you, thank you."

I love you.

"I'll talk to you soon…I have to get a new smartphone. And that's not a hint, so don't—"

Oh, I ordered one for you while you slept.

Damn him! She wept again. "Why are you so wonderful to me? Why do you spoil me like this? You don't need to do this."

The things I want to do to you are so incomparably horrific that I feel driven to shower you with splendor. I must compensate for these urges. You say I don't need to spoil you, but I do. Will you tell me when you're up to talking?

And that was what she found so refreshing in her patron. Her beloved, still unseen, Eros's shadow bending over Psyche in the dark to press ghostly kisses upon her yielding mouth. What the woman found so refreshing about him was the notion that, in spite of his lurid interest in her potential, despite his divine fascination with her powers, he first cared about her as a living human being.

Could she say that of anyone else but her mother?

5

WHEN THE TIME CAME to talk to people again, her beloved would be the first to know. After ending the nine-hour video chat, the woman sent an email to the stranger and copied #1. She dashed it off without a second thought about tone, being as she was in a constant fury at the typos produced by her gangrenous hand.

Hey ya'll,

Good morning. I was almost kidnapped by a cop last night and it's a long and stupid story so please excuse me if I don't feel like sharing. Think I'm going to take advantage of the stream and PO box videos being dark to have a week or two off. Or three. There's plenty of previously filmed content to pad things out until I'm up to leaving my apartment.

Try not to gossip, although it's inevitable, I guess.

Peace out,

And she signed her name, and sent it, and shut her laptop, and lay awash in the sound of traffic there in her nest of pain. Somewhere in the city, a man tried to catch up on sleep after spending a long and strange night helping some woman on the other side of a webcam. What was he like? She'd never even heard his voice. The idea was incredible. The only sense she had to go by was her sense of smell, and that had been deadened by her use of the masks that also ended her brief spate of public recognition. Everybody with an iota of intelligence was now anonymous. It was great, and it was awful, because police in the city had already once touted the right to stop and frisk pedestrians for dubious reasons related to skin color. Although that legislation was no longer valid, with everybody in a mask and expected to engage in social distancing, the high-strung city cops had justification to be suspicious of anyone. Previously the woman had not cared. She always had her ID and legally speaking was never up to no good.

How quickly that feeling had changed! Now the mere thought of the word "police officer" made her nauseous. "Cop," "sergeant," by extension "lieutenant," "pig," even "doughnut" summoned up the kind of bloodcurdling, reptile-brain disgust that signaled danger to the human nervous system. The woman retreated to the floor of her shower and regretted immediately letting the wound get wet because the scab and pus had a chance to moisten, to comingle and create a tawdry brass scab over the twitching stubs of her mutilated digits. To think something as quick as a gunshot had done this! Jacqueline Onassis probably felt the same way. "Guns don't kill people, people kill people." Ad campaigns from the National Rifle Association, years of propaganda shoved down public throats, had turned out to be funded by and large by foreign interests. Untold amounts of antagonistic money had been devoted to training Americans to think that if the government so much as tried to control the private ownership of assault rifles, violence and oppression were sure to follow. After all! How could domestic terrorists and uneducated quarantine protestors oppress other people when they themselves were oppressed?

Such low expectations of the basic bad intentions of government spoke volumes of the same mindset that had engendered such a fascist democracy. Large pockets of the country, frantic at the request to keep their faces covered, loudly protested the need for masks and economic shutdowns. Violence seemed close at hand. The woman felt more every day that she watched the collapse of an old epoch and the nascent moments of a new one. Straddling the transition point. What a time to be alive.

Alive, living. What was living now? It was not just America. The world had changed overnight beneath the burden of the pandemic.

Many things would be back someday—the opera house would reopen, masks would fade out, the value of oil would once again rise beyond reason—but much more would never be the same. This virus was the first true consequence of a global culture and the hyperconnected man. Increased nationalism was the guaranteed, assuredly heavy backlash. Humanity was forced to come together or be driven completely apart, and, in the city at least, the woman feared the latter the more likely result.

Look at the woman. She had always been isolated but now felt alien: truly stranded. Seeing strangeness in the stranger, for instance, because she projected. And thinking of the stranger, she had to wonder: would she even have had the experience of losing those fingers had she not gone to his apartment that night—if she had backed down from the fight and stayed longer?

Didn't matter. Especially didn't matter if she didn't leave her apartment. No phone to obsessively check, either. Thank God! She needed a break from the thing. Needed three dimensions. Not that she was happy to have lost it. Setting up the new device and salvaging data from her various accounts was, to her beleaguered mind, such a monumental task that the mere idea was sufficient to make her weep again. Who could be a person in a world like this? Who could be anything?

Her mother tried to contact her, and with the phone out of commission, the call program on her computer rang loud through the studio. She ignored this weekly contact for the first time in history. When the ringing stopped, she looked at her hand, her remaining fingers contorted by the loss—or by the painful heat of infection. She did not even think of going to the doctor, in part because she had no health insurance, but really because she didn't know what to expect. Her patron had a point in an emotional, metaphorical sense as well as a physical one. The wound was still happening because it was infected. Once the infection was gone, what would happen? If doctors witnessed a miraculous occurrence while she was in their care, what then?

The hit-and-run video came back to her for the first time in a long time. Cops, asking people to be on the lookout. How long had the sergeant followed her videos? Had he made another account on the forum already? Christ! She wanted to delete the whole thing. It made her sick. It made her palms sweat—but maybe that was the fever.

And what a fever! Made her realize she hadn't been sick since well before the apple incident. When she awoke from the second nap of the day to a clock that read four p.m., she became aware of the thin sheen of sweat covering her body, then promptly slipped back into the heavy slumber that kept her plastered to the mattress. When she awoke again much closer to midnight, having soaked through her bedclothes and stained even the box spring with putrid fever sweat, she nonetheless suspected she had not even begun to reach the peak of the brain-boiling fire in her body. Had to get that fever down if she didn't want to wrestle off spider-mother's control again.

She sat again beneath the crystal hail of her showerhead's cold jet and this time kept her festering hand's bandage dry with a plastic bag. When she got out, she stood staring at the absence of fingers and, not knowing what else to do, splashed hydrogen peroxide on the stumps while thrashing against her sink in very real, very not-fun agony. Although there was something to be said about the gentle sizzle once the cleansing pain had reached its high point—when compared to that jagged peak, everything after was a tingle of pleasure.

That was what she liked about her talent, she supposed. What so dissatisfied her about even the current state of her work. The pleasure was not in a first experience of pain. Novel pain was never fun, seldom expected—and even when it was, the body could not physically prepare for a pain it had never felt. But on second, third, fourth, repetition, when one was equipped with the knowledge of instantaneous healing, something happened with certain types of pain. Some pains were novelties not to be sought more than a few times, but with those ethereal breeds she'd come to seek, the pain transformed within the hermetic vessel of the mind. Elevated from a sensation of warning to a sensation of pleasure; a simple experience like any one of infinite other experiences available to the human mind. Once the dizzying first try was over, there was no way to again achieve that shocking hit of new-felt pain: only lesser echoes, reenactments, where pleasure was the one thing left as surprise dried up.

What were her videos? Not even reenactments. Records, yes. But it was not as if they contained the events, or that the events were experienced over again. No atoms engaged in the ritual of pain for which the Degenetrix had laid out requirements. She had once read, however, that the human brain responded to fantasies about a thing as if it were truly experiencing that thing—that books, for instance, impacted the human mind as if the reader lived the protagonist's life. This was the result of empathy, that product of mirror neurons, and the woman wasn't sure if she felt too much empathy or none at all. Difficult to say what was and wasn't normal when one spent a lifetime as oneself.

But…in imagination, the woman could be anyone. She could live any event, and her mind would respond as if it had truly happened. She could continue thinking of her trauma from the night before as she remembered it, keep reliving it second by second and feeling sorry for herself as a victim who lost her fingers, a victim who was so feverish that she had lain under the icicles of her cold shower for twenty-five minutes and still felt her body struggling to burn off the violence of the infection, a victim who could not even dream of leaving her apartment or setting up a cell phone or answering the calls from her mother. Calls that rang endlessly upon her ignored laptop until she stumbled from the bathroom to turn the whole thing off.

Yes, she could keep revisiting her trauma. Or she could think of it another way. What about the sergeant? What was it like to be so petty but so wild about somebody that you'd rather see them dead than experience pleasure elsewhere? Kind of hot. She hadn't been bluffing: if he had come to her apartment instead of trying to kidnap her, she would have gladly fucked him. Maybe they could have been friends. Better it didn't work out, of course. He was insane. Who knew what happened to make him that way? She didn't want to guess.

Still…they clearly had interests in common. Similar things might have happened in their lives. Sympathy was easier than empathy, but it was hard to give either when somebody was so bad at emotional management that their response to strong feelings was total hostility. Yes, that was what lay in the sergeant's eyes. Hostility. Ire. Humiliation that she had made him feel something, some normal human feeling like desire. If a person didn't comprehend feelings, it must have been frustrating when one occurred to them—even if it was a basic one like the coveting of an object, sexual or otherwise. People already prone to frustration tended to go into careers like the police force, something permitting the exercise of authority over others. Control over situations. Theoretically avoiding frustration.

And, oh, he must have been frustrated tonight. Yes! Furious to think she escaped. Why, he even knew where she lived and couldn't do anything about it—it made her laugh, and laughter against the fever felt like laughing underwater. So difficult and hollow a noise that she soon gave up and let her eyes fall closed beneath that water's pressure. Wasn't she always laughing underwater, in a way?

The sergeant had been handsome. Hard-jawed and imposing at her door during that wellness check. The piercing cobalt of his eyes seemed less frightening before the proliferation of medical masks. Divested of a face, glinting into the rearview mirror, they had become eyes belonging to a demon. With the lights out, the curtains shut, the door locked and bolted, she still felt those evil eyes on her.

How well had she locked that door? Say it wasn't really bolted. Say he got in. It was three in the morning: What if the door burst from its hinges, and there he was, wild-eyed, still in his uniform, fresh off the beat? Already with his gun out, the fascist. The slam of the lock behind him, the rattle of the bolt thrown in place, his voice twice as derisive amid this feverish miasma as it had been in the prison of the car: "What a stupid whore you are to have stayed here. I guess you really wanted me, after all."

The woman was too weak to respond. Her eyes couldn't so much as follow the blade of the ceiling fan. His scoff was punctuated by the leather grunt of a re-holstered gun.

"What a mess you are. Look at that hand! Didn't go to the doctor? See, you're asking for it. I could do you a favor and shoot you in the head if you begged for it. Hey—are you listening? You cunt...here, maybe you'll pay attention to this—"

6

A 2009 UNIVERSITY OF NORTH TEXAS study titled "The nature of women's rape fantasies: an analysis of prevalence, frequency, and contents" found that 62 percent of women sexually fantasize about rape; of these, the median number of occurrences for such fantasies is four per year. And 14 percent of respondents reportedly experienced such daydreams once a week. In an effort more nuanced than previous rape fantasy catalog attempts, fantasies were ranked across an erotic-aversive scale: 9 percent were considered entirely aversive, 45 percent completely erotic, and, best of all, 46 percent were judged a combination of the two. However, as the research was limited to a pool of 355 female undergraduates, one cannot help but take the study as a look into the fantasies of the young, unmarried American woman (some college education) between the ages of eighteen and twenty-two, as well as finding in it no small measure of wishful thinking on the part of UNT researchers.

7

HER FEVER had broken the next morning, but her hand was still not repaired. She could not bear to look near the front door and might not have moved from bed at all if she didn't need to correspond with her mother to say she was down with a cold (no, not that virus) and didn't feel like talking.

All day, nothing happened. All night. Somebody a day later knocked on her door and inspired a bolt of fear, but after she recognized the stranger's voice, she told him to back off until further notice. Nothing continued to happen for the following day. Nothing happened again the day after that. Nothing the next day, the next day, the day subsequent. Nothing continued to happen until quite a few mornings after the incident when she forced herself to edge down to her overstuffed mailbox on the building's first floor. A package. No dead rats, please!

No. A brand-new cell phone four years better than her old one. Very nice of him to send it directly to her instead of her safe-deposit box, but it would have been even nicer if he'd hand-delivered it. Maybe even helped her. Gee, it was sure a blast setting it up one-handed; but when it was done, she was back in business…with twelve voice mails waiting to be reviewed, all of them from the stranger, #1, and her mother.

Whatever. She deleted each one without listening. Everything was a distraction from her patron, whom she contacted as soon as she installed their conversation app.

HRH_Degenetrix
Hey, I got my new phone. Thank you so much. You make me feel taken care of.

m0t
You deserve to be taken care of. I've missed you.

HRH_Degenetrix
I'd like to say I missed you, but I've been too sick. Mind if I stream again? My fingers still aren't right.

m0t
I hope that once your fingers heal, you'll still let me watch you privately. Just to see you go about your day, I mean. I felt so close to you watching you sleep.

When the camera turned on, she smiled already but laughed to see herself on-screen. She rubbed her eye with her good hand. "You've never seen me without makeup before."

You are magnificent. How is your injury?

"I think it was infected, but it seems better."

I would imagine such things run their courses faster in you.

"If this wanted to wrap up, that would be great."

Maybe it's a state-of-mind issue. Have you seen the news? Probably not. You would have said something.

Hold on, let me flip around so I don't waste your time. I'll find it. It's sure to be on.

After a delay of about forty seconds, he returned with the news station number. She punched it into her remote and sat against the bed as the screen's image resolved to the round head and mustached face of an officer mid-interview with a reporter holding a boom mic from a six-foot distance.

"—and, uh, basically, uh—"

"Wait, I know that guy!"

"—we want to know if there are any living women who have—have experienced an, a, uh, assault at the hands of Officer—"

"He's that sergeant's partner, what's going on?"

"—and if so, we're encouraging them to come forward with information so we can perform a thorough investigation and keep him from hurting anyone else."

"Police say," resumed the blonde in-studio reportrix to whom the camera cut, "that if not for an anonymous tip in the first place, the alleged serial killer may have been allowed to claim dozens more victims. We'll report on this developing story as updates become available. Next—"

"What the fuck," the woman softly intoned, looking down at her crippled hand, then over at the screen. During the report, messages had appeared, and a fourth continued to be typed.

I love you more than you could ever believe.

My first instinct was to have him killed, but then I thought, "No, that's what this sort wants in the end." Do unto others. Better to put him in prison for life, solitary confinement if possible—not even other men, let alone women, to project fantasies upon. I hope you don't mind. I'm sure I could find someone to kill him in jail if you wanted me to, but please do think about it, first.

Good thing these messages delete themselves, eh? Anyway, you ought to stop by your safe-deposit box soon.

As soon as possible. I don't know how long they'll last in there.

One by one, she read the messages, smiling in astonishment from behind her right hand. "You're crazier than he is."

I suppose—but it seems basic common sense that anybody who would abuse you without your consent doesn't even deserve the kindness of being put down like a dog.

"Oh my God," she said, belatedly realizing which hand she'd used to cover her mouth.
I haven't upset you, have I?

"My hand! Look at my hand."
While she wasn't looking, the fingers had reappeared. At last! Mint condition again.

8

IN SOME STRANGE WAY, it made sense that fingers blown off in an instant returned instantaneously. At this point, she was beyond questioning it. What did it matter trying to determine the physics of an instantly appearing pair of new fingers? What did it matter trying to explain any of the hows or the whys behind her own experience? Spider-mother willed it, and the woman was but a fly in her web. A fly—or something more.

She did theorize with her patron about the whole finger debacle. She petitioned for the material explanation that infection had caused the delay in healing, and timing was incidental. He, firmly crediting her divinity without even having heard of spider-mother, stood by his original theory: the trauma of the event had kept her so focused on the pain, on the experience and emotion and fear, that the wound had no choice but stay open because her perception was devoted to creating the experience of that fiery agony, that terror of lost fingers. Like living a dream where your teeth fall out and still having the privilege of waking to find them all where they belonged. When the trauma bubble of this proverbial dream was collapsed by new knowledge—in this case, the capture and imminent prosecution of the sergeant—her attention freed up, the pain was forgotten, and her body healed.

After they had talked for an hour or two, their speculation devolving into obscene banter, the woman excused herself with a blown kiss and hurried off to the bank. The sky outside was turquoise, and the gold eye of the sun blazed hatefully within it, blinding even as winter crowded in, high rises and skyscrapers catching its light on their edges to direct the glare into her pupils. She wore sunglasses over her mask and hurried into the subway: under her coat, the subterranean heat the platform was infinitely worse than had been the sweat-inducing internal forge of her fever. Happy neither above nor belowground. God, spider-mother, get her back to her room! It only occurred to her as she stepped into the subway train that this was the first time she had left her apartment building since the incident with the sergeant.

Worth it, though. She hit the bank at a slow hour. Not seeing the usual private banker guy waiting in the open for somebody to help, the woman interrupted a pair of masked tellers in the middle of a not-very-quiet (nor particularly work-safe) conversation about the incessant presence of the bank's CEO at their location—it clammed into a pair of awkward smiles when she appeared on the other side of their glass.

The woman was brought back to her box by the younger and more high-strung of the two. Once alone, she made short work of removing a small brown parcel from the locked box. She did not look inside—merely slid it into her coat and immediately returned home. The package sat unopened until that night when she hopped back onto the private stream and let him watch her open the package. As suspected: her own two fingers, sitting pretty in an aromatic cloud of the cedar-laden, almost-incense-like cologne she'd come to associate with her beloved. Notes of sandalwood and Earl Grey tea.

"And to think I was worried about having eight digits…now I have twelve."

The possibilities are truly endless.

"You're telling me. I mean, what am I supposed to do with these?"

I'm sure we could think of something if we put our heads together.

I was tempted to keep them, but I wasn't sure if you'd need them to repair the wound.

"You could have them back."

My siren. I could kiss you good night. Would you feel it?

"I guess not, since I didn't feel it when you kissed—or did whatever you did to them—before you put them in our box."

Too bad! I confess my lips did graze them, but it's not the same if they aren't attached to more of you.

"Well…when you finally see me in person, you can kiss my new ones." With a wry grin, the woman picked up her spare finger and examined it in the light: the tattered flesh and muscle of the tip purple after spending days unrefrigerated and kept under who knew what conditions before the sergeant was dragged out of his apartment. "Looks like a sausage…I guess it really is just meat, huh."

Your meat could feed the hungry! The leather of your flesh could clothe and shod the poor. I mean it when I say you are a goddess. I believe it. I pray to you every night.

"No way—is that true?"

I have given up all other possibilities of faith since being confronted by you, by the proof you present. I am unworthy of all the attention you give me but am so overjoyed to receive it.

"Man, the way you write to me…it's unreal." She looked away to compose herself, but once composed was then, as always, compelled to re-confront the root of her emotions to further communicate. Always had to look at his messages and their recent history in order to see his next response. "If you turn out to be a prank constructed by my friend and my stranger, I'm going to be upset."

Your stranger?

"Oh—my producer. The dick in the videos."

I see. Goodness, that's sort of sad.

"Sorry."

Don't apologize, just observing. What do you call me when you talk about me to others?

"I don't. I think of you as my patron, my benefactor."

You haven't told anyone about me?

"Well—the bakushi. But that's like a whole other planet. We're artistic peers. I got to talking about you recently, I think it was the day you took me to the opera, but I didn't get specific about anything. And with these chats and streams deleting themselves, well, gosh… you could probably do whatever you wanted to do to me, and more effectively than the sergeant."

One of so many reasons I dare not meet you in person. I cannot risk losing control of myself—frightening you.

"I want to be frightened by you…fun frightened," she amended, grinning when the "m0t is typing" message disappeared like a man shutting his open mouth before his corrected thought was released. "Not frightened like I was by the problem."

The sergeant is "the problem," is he.

"Forget him. Please—what can I give you?"

You don't need to give me anything.

"No, please. Let me do something for you. Let me think of something good, something really fu—"

Do you know any songs?

While she laughed, he typed on.

I love to watch a beautiful woman sing, and you are the most beautiful woman I know. You must sing like a bird.

"Yeah, like a scrub jay…" The woman cleared her throat, laughed in agony, feigned mopping her brow. "Oh, man! Couldn't you have just asked me to, say, eat my fingers?"

God, oh, God, you read my mind every time…but I would prefer to hear you sing at the moment. I love to hear you speak. Let me hear you sing.

Please?

Ugh! Unreal. She could picture eyes she had never seen cartoonishly batting in parody of feminine plea. What a sadist, this was the cruelest thing he'd asked her to do by far. Awful! Scrambling through the list of songs she knew, her blank mind presented her with a simple and safe tune called "Unchained Melody," so ubiquitous in American culture by that point in time that most human beings didn't realize it had once been written for a prison movie. It was a wonderful song, and he was an older man who probably knew it…and, as said, it was simple and safe and pretty hard to mess up. So, finger curling a lock of her straight jet hair into a spring of humiliation, the woman tried to pretend that she didn't exist, and sang for him.

"Unchained Melody" been covered so many times, had so many different versions—she preferred one by The Fleetwoods, which made the song sound sadder and truer to its essence. A melody for the spirit of a prisoner longing for his distant love. In a country of 2.3 million incarcerated individuals (and growing), few images were more classically American—second only, perhaps, to the longing soldier writing his last letter home.

The best thing about the song was it was short. Two minutes: painless, over. With a petulant wave of her hands, she announced, "That's it," and the typing alert lit up.

It's best you can't see me right me—most find it unmanly to be so moved.

Blinking, herself, the woman said, "That's all right, I like seeing men cry," and, desperate for anything to defuse the emotion, studied her amputated fingers on the counter. "So…guess how long it's been since I've eaten. Go on! Guess."

· HANS BELLMER ·

1

AFTER DISCUSSION, it was decided that the woman would eat one finger on the private stream, then do another by herself in more elaborate fashion so as to film a proper video. Given the problem, it had been some time since the last one and, well…no matter what her beloved said, humiliating herself with a song wasn't sufficient repayment for what he had done.

Hard to put a finger (excuse the turn of phrase) on what exactly he had done. Saved her from endless nonconsensual torment to preserve the future possibility of endless consensual torment, she guessed. Nice of him. And he *loved her,* loved her. And she loved him. She had loved him before he helped her solve the problem, but only after that solution was she fully in touch with those feelings. Regardless of why he had helped her, he had still helped her.

The million-dollar question, though, was whether he had saved her from death. Had he? Could she die forever? It was day one all over again. Perhaps she might so abuse her power that spider-mother decided to keep her eternally. This was why people ended up worshipping strange deities. What could she give the mother to superstitiously preserve her immortality? Only performances, more and more powerful performances. Performances, creations, these ritual ceremonies of self-offering, might answer her questions.

And there had been many questions from the start. The woman had pushed almost all of them aside, assuming they would be answered in their proper time. Even before awareness of the mother, this organic timeliness of solutions to life's problems was a natural law she had already observed. An answer she needed or an out she required arrived at the exact right moment her mind was ready to receive it. No way to rush things. And certainly, when it came to her magic trick, she did not want to overstep an important boundary.

But the stranger still claimed he'd killed her on the night with the lamp. Her heart had stopped more than a few times on camera, generally by asphyxiation or electrocution. The death orgasm had become her favorite kind, and since the brain-injury routine and the persistent awareness of the mother in the aftermath, she had come to perceive even the potential of eternal death as not a threat or an ending but the ultimate psychedelic experience. The more times she enjoyed temporary death, the more psychedelic it had become until her consciousness broke through to a kind of awareness of it, these visionary blooms between death and resurrection, this splitting of body and mind into dual awareness. Psychic events and physical events equally weighted, equally real.

Time still occurred without her mind, and that mind had to be somewhere for it to be with the mother. Where did she go when she was not within body-time but instead soul-eternity? So hard to discern. Did the young dolphin fully grasp where it was when it leapt from its waters for the first few times? What did it mean to the dolphin that land was such a complex and fascinating place when all it needed of this strange inverted world beneath its water was the air? Like all physical beings, the woman was without context to comprehend existence beyond time.

Would she ever want to stay in that beyond-place? Like Andersen's "The Little Mermaid," could the mother give her legs to walk on this new land? If so, would each step feel like walking on broken glass? A shudder rolled through her to think of that depressing fairy tale. That mermaid didn't know how good she had it, spider-mother. The woman would be grateful.

The true pleasure of death was not in the going away, or even the bliss of being with spider-mother. It was the coming back. That was when the rush came on, the acute flinging of awareness back into the body, the reassembling of space and time as mind realigned with flesh. Yes, the world where she lived was awful, vile, full of pestilence and futility and shame. But without that world so bleak and dark, the woman would never have known the pleasures of the body. Never would have known the joys of human creativity, or the voyeuristic fun of listening to the argument of a couple in the street, or drowning in the hot explosion of anticipation every time she thought of the man she loved. The man she loved, the man she'd never met—the man who responded to footage of her eating her own flesh with a brilliant diamond ring she wore on her left ring finger.

No wonder he was so resistant to meeting her. She understood what he meant about giving up his whole life. Their chemistry was as intense as a molecular reaction, like the application of pure sodium to water, that brilliant and fast explosion of chemical energy. Everything around them would go up in smoke. Sometimes it felt like it already was.

The stranger was glad to have her back to work three weeks after their argument and the subsequent problem, and thankfully had too much to talk about to ask any probing questions about her ring or her assault or its probable relation to the arrest of the alleged serial killer who had leveraged his law enforcement career into a sadistic side hustle. The stranger was not, however, expecting her change in demeanor, the doubling down of her increasing artistic drive as a consequence of her experience. She wasn't expecting it, either—but looking around the brick-walled bedroom of his new apartment, the woman found herself sharply critical.

"This lighting is terrible, it's so bland! I want it to be dark—super dramatic."

"Don't bring up that Man Ray guy again, please."

"I'm glad you get what I mean. I'm serious. The lighting should be like that, distinct. Sharp. Foreshadow, literally, what's to come: plant seeds in the viewer's mind to build anticipation. I want to be amputated by the contrast of light and shadow before anything even happens."

His attention was too caught to form a counterargument. "We're doing amputations now?"

Since putting the DVD of her eating the second finger into their safe-deposit box, the woman had experimented with a toe and an ear (this latter inspired by a David Lynch marathon used to cheer herself after the problem). Without emotional attachment to the injuries, there

208   REGINA WATTS

was only excitement, and excitement provoked quick healing.

Unless she didn't want it to. Inspired, dedicated to uncovering what limits she could with respect to the mother, the woman revisited her knife experiments. One day when her patron was busy and she was alone with that compulsive voice of inspiration she believed to have always been the mother's, the woman stood with her arm extended over the kitchen sink and slit her forearm. Then, focused as a hawk upon its prey, she stared into the flowing blood of the wound and silently urged the injury to stay open. It obeyed. Blood continued to flow in hypnotic pulses, these visible throbs dictated by her heartbeat: and their pace increased, she smiled to see, as her delight intensified.

At last. The wound open in her arm was a great leap forward to new artistic potential, new methods and techniques almost unlimited in scope. This carmine maw: a temporary orifice in her body, a novel opening for penetration. Yes, a whole new perspective of the human flesh. Within the trance of this new work, she grew more disconnected from her body than even spider-mother's tender embrace could hope to make her feel.

And when it was time to end the trance, to come back into this body of hers, the wound had shut again. A whole new set of routines exploded before her eyes.

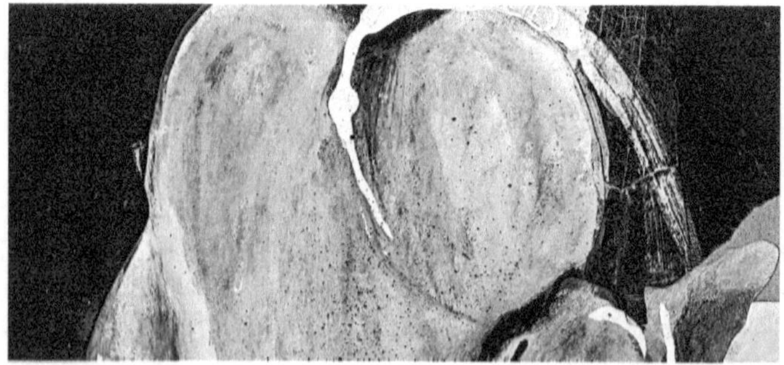

2

BEFORE THE PROBLEM, the woman had redeveloped her reading habit. At first, this had been because occasionally her lover would drop this or that piece of classic erotic literature in her box, begging to have a recording of her reading Marquis de Sade or Anaïs Nin—neither was a particularly avid consumer of pornography due to the extremity of their tastes, and as a result, they were more apt to share, say, a copy of Maldoror or a collection of painter Francis Bacon's violent existential nightmares, the insidious and bloody eroticism of abstract trauma falling closer in line with the contents of their shared fantasies. After her conversation with the bakushi about the value of narrative to all art, the woman began to think hard about everything she'd read. There was something there that her work had been missing, and she wanted to find it. She spent too much time watching the lurid news when she wasn't talking to her patron or actively working on new content; she began to take more deliberate time to look at artwork, to research and experience the photographers and filmmakers of her inspiration while pursuing new ones in an active way she never had. She began to leave her apartment more, not to go to the sporadically opening bars and clubs (how you danced six feet apart was beyond her, though she guessed that was what masks were for) but to explore, at the invitation of the bakushi, a developing underground theater scene emerging in response to the virus and the growing discomfort people had for sitting together in high-capacity theaters.

Guerilla theatrical productions happened with increasing frequency, with abstracted productions of *Jane Eyre* or the *Odyssey* being played in locations like parks, subway stations, or, once they opened again, galleries—until the police came and broke up what was perceived as a public disturbance, a gathering of too many people in one place and time. A troupe of performers had even been arrested for playing out *Julius Caesar* in front of a trashy tower owned by the (by then, thankfully former) head of state. They were charged with loitering, public endangerment for failing to wear fabric masks during the performance, and, most disturbingly, travel for a nonessential purpose. This third charge was a new one relating to virus control measures and a temporary initiative resorted to only in some extreme cases in endangered areas. In the woman's opinion, it was not likely to be rolled back anytime soon. Worst of all, a series of racially charged police brutality incidents had provoked protests and subsequent police conflicts in cities across the United States, leaving tensions between the government and its citizens running higher than ever.

And brother, the woman loved it. This new dystopian America, its latent fascism finally catalyzed by the pandemic—this was the artistic environment she'd waited for. Every time idiots with assault rifles crowded the steps of statehouses across the country to protest quarantine lockdowns, she got excited; every time she turned on the news to see clusters of mumbling nitwits holding signs demanding the reopening of hair salons and golf courses, her heart raced. Every time particularly ignorant government officials suggested Americans should have been ready and willing to sacrifice their own lives in the name of reviving the economy (as if the economy were a bloodthirsty god in demand of human sacrifices!), she grew too excited to sleep and stayed up late working on new projects.

Yeah, baby. Government oppression and economic failure made for the most fascinating artistic expression. A great example: German expressionism, which the woman studied keenly over those winter months. Black-and-white films produced by dour Europeans during the slow, steady rise of antisemitic sentiment throughout the 1920s made the woman think of Kabuki theater. The extreme facial expressions, perhaps—the emphasis on gesture over dialogue, on style and form over utility and plot. The narratives of films like *Dr. Caligari* or *Nosferatu* could be found in their aesthetic as much as their stories, maybe more. A single shot declared everything.

This was what the woman wanted in her work. Yes, exactly what she wanted. The bakushi's notions expanded in her mind, seeds planted in fertile fields plowed by the criticisms of fans who, like the problem, were critical of her work to that point. When she thought of her work for her first year (already over a year!), she felt a curious shame—not shame at her use of her own body but shame that she had not honored her body's abilities by putting them to more mentally stimulating use. She was liberated from the pretentious dishonesty of the gaming livestreams, and the woman wanted to make use of that liberation.

The stranger had other ideas. When the woman expressed her desire for a cameraperson to up their production quality and acting freedom, he groused a while (no doubt projecting his experience with his ex-girlfriend) before suggesting they hire #1. #1 had been bothering the stranger about work much as she'd been bothering the woman, it turned out. He no doubt thought himself a master tactician, giving #1 a job and silencing the complaints of the woman in one move— but the addition of a cameraperson only increased the woman's expectations. Little by little, he consented to her scripts as long as she kept it dialogue free, which was exactly the aesthetic she wanted. When the woman insisted she be permitted the time and luxury, sometimes between shots, to adjust the lighting until it was exact, he complained but permitted because the aesthetics of the final product were more dynamic with her developing flair for cinematography alongside the discerning criticism of #1.

But when the woman began to express her ideas for elements like props, costumes, and set decorations, that was too much. "I feel like you're making this incredibly complicated," he said once. She finished explaining her vision for a genital mutilation routine inspired by Sada Abe, the prostitute who in 1930s Japan erotically asphyxiated her lover and severed his genitalia, then carried them about on her person. The woman had a fabulous vision of a mutilation and healing process that would have symbolically honored spider-mother with the self-birth of a new vagina when the stranger interrupted her: "Did you suggest we spend prop money on a freaking kimono?"

"As usual, you're focusing on the wrong aspect of this. We need the kimono to make it right."

"I don't think our viewers are going to be watching this with an eye for how elaborate your costumes are."

"I don't care what our viewers are watching my work with an eye for. The audience I'm after will look at what I show them. If I dazzle them with a kimono, they'll see it, and they'll see everything the kimono implies: what it conceals, the cultural history behind it, the future implications of it."

"The future implications of a *kimono*? What are you even talking about? I wish you would listen to yourself."

Meek #1, who was present and listening for what was planned as a business meeting but apparently destined to end as yet another fight, cleared her throat. "It would sort of add to the environment, maybe… Don't you think people are getting tired of the same hard-core sex injuries?"

The stranger dug in his heels. "I think people are going to fast-forward to the hard-core parts of any porn, watch it until they get off, then stop. They're not going to watch our footage like it's a movie."

"My footage," corrected the woman. "It's my footage, it's my body."

"Yeah, and it's my production money. It may be your body, but they're my videos, too. You want a kimono to ruin with your blood so badly? Go and buy one yourself."

"What a horse's ass," said the bakushi when the woman recounted this conversation on their next visit. "I've never liked that guy. How's your other friend?"

"He's wonderful… I talked to him about my idea, and he asked if he could buy me the kimono for it before I'd even brought up the fight with my producer."

"Damn, what a dude."

"He's something else…" Smiling down at the phone that connected them, the woman folded her legs beneath her seat at the edge of the bakushi's bed. "I don't care about the kimono—I'd pay for it myself if he hadn't volunteered, but it's the gesture and it's the way he's so interested in my ideas. We talk about my work all the time. He's sure I'm trying to push it in the right direction… I'd be a lot less confident without his support."

"Oh! So my opinion doesn't count?"

"You know what I mean. It's different when you're in love."

The chuckling bakushi consulted the mirror, fixed a stray eyebrow hair, and agreed, "Yeah, it is…the validation is different. When's the wedding already?"

"I guess when we meet…" The woman checked a new message, a response to her note about the suspension performance the bakushi had invited her to watch that night. It would take place in a meatpacking plant, in a walk-in freezer cluttered with the carcasses of cows in various stages of dismemberment.

m0t

What a fun environment! Like our favorite painter. My, my, I'm jealous.

HRH_Degenetrix

You're literally always invited to whatever I tell you about.

m0t

You don't want an old man like me around, I'll dull the mood.

"Tell him I said 'hi,'" the bakushi encouraged, leaning in to apply a touch of mascara. "And that he's going to be disappointed if he doesn't come… Guess what?" The woman's host spun around to face her and grinned in a "what-can-you-do" kind of way, shrugging at the same time.

"My model canceled on me. Know any hot girls into bondage?"

3

FUNNY! For all the videos the woman had recorded, all the livestreams whether public or private, she realized only at being voluntold to help the bakushi that she had never performed in person. The delineation between performing live online and performing live in four-plus dimensions had not fully occurred to her until she peeked around a hanging bovine carcass to watch the twenty-five member audience file in. Why was she more nervous than when doing a livestream?

Maybe because there were instant reactions to be observed and acknowledged by the performer in such a situation. Yes, it was sort of hard to tell what people thought when the lower half of the face was covered by a mask: but there were still tells. When the bakushi stepped up and explained that the audience was lucky enough to attend the world-premiere live performance of the Degenetrix, the couple who had arranged themselves near the door so as to leave when things proved boring gasped quietly. As the bakushi continued, they whispered, then edged as close as they could without drawing too much attention to themselves or violating anyone's six feet of social space.

Anticipation was therefore easy to detect before the act, but, during, it was hard to gauge reactions. She was too busy gauging her own—too busy experiencing the present moment, the sensual caress of the bakushi's hand along her arm as, inch by inch, the ropes were wound around her, cradling her, adjusting her. Beneath the tension of the chest harness, her breasts were reshaped; the contortions of her body reduced the number of her limbs to one, a leg extended like that of a heron in flight when the bakushi suspended her chest harness from the room's central meat hook. By then, the woman realized she had not quite been in her body for most of the act: that she, too, had been mere observer, a watcher eagerly awaiting this flesh display of the medium's artistic capabilities. The bakushi tilted her back within the embrace of her suspension ropes and finally (finally!) branded her as she had been begging somebody to do since the start of the whole fucking thing (who knew why it had become such a focus for her—maybe because it was the one thing she couldn't seem to get the stranger to do, challenging as it was to his personal relationship with the animal meat enjoyed by not just him but many, many Americans), and overall, the experience was ten out of ten for the woman, which made it a stunning performance.

Next time, she wished to be suspended by her own flesh, like the bovine carcasses that hung in solidarity around her. Yes: already planning for next time. Maybe one of these times—not next time or even the time after that, but sometime—she would look into the crowd and see her lover's face.

When the performance was over, the woman found not her beloved but the pair from before sheepishly hanging around the building's rear entrance to obtain an autograph from the person they perceived as their favorite porn star. In an effort to plant the seeds of correcting this misconception, the woman and bakushi had a private discussion before inviting the couple back to the bakushi's apartment for a few drinks and a bit of casual disregard for social distancing rules. The pair was very interested in the woman and explained they began following the Degenetrix around the time of the body modification e-zine, being as they were longer-time fans of the bakushi, who they almost respected too much to approach without the woman to act as an irresistible lure. However, they were fascinated by the woman and her power, and wanted desperately to know more.

"How do you do it?" the female of the couple, an almost waifish and over-tanned hippie in her midthirties, asked. "I watched your fire-walking video from last year again just a few months ago because— well, it's a long story, we were supposed to go to India but instead this virus kept us home. Anyway, doesn't it hurt?"

"Of course it does. That's why I do it." The woman looked at the

pair, this hippie lady and her spouse who looked as if he only wore
shoes in the city because of the physical dangers relating to trash on
the street, and took a not-so-wild guess like a cold-reading psychic.
"You guys going to India to meet some guru or something?"

"No way! How did you guess?"

The bakushi and woman both exchanged a glance at the stupid
question, and given to mischief as she was, the woman bit back
a smile while hitting her joint. "The mother told me," she said
around a cloud of blue smoke.

"The mother?" asked this hippie chick in a soft way, beads in her
matted hair clacking while she leaned forward.

The bakushi choked behind a beer glass while the woman, deadpan,
continued, "Yes, the mother," while within her the mother encouraged
her. *Yes, tell them about me. It is vital you tell them about me.*

Yikes. Maybe she shouldn't say anything—it made her nervous
to be so directly pressed into action by the voice in her head.
Self-mutilation was one thing, after all...but was anyone but the
woman's beloved capable of comprehending spider-mother? Case
in point, the hippie chick's partner looked terrified and amazed
once the woman had given a brief summarization of the internal
events of her by then infamous Dahmer routine.

"The world is controlled by, like, some kind of spider monster?"

"Spider-mother," corrected the bakushi, far more equipped to
understand than they were. "She's not a literal spider, right? Probably
not even a literal woman."

"No—nothing like that. But—I don't know. It's how I perceived
her. It. This...experience."

Exchanging a look of their own, the hippie couple seemed to
communicate something in silence before the chick spoke up to the
Degenetrix. "How can I meet this spider-mother without dying?"

"Can you? I don't know...maybe through acid." The woman had
meant it as a joke, and laughed at the time. After the couple was finally
evicted for the night, the bakushi sighed and slumped back into the
apartment's living room couch.

"People like that are always so weird... Hope they don't go

killing themselves to meet this entity of yours. No wonder you like doing what you do so much… I thought there had to be a reason beyond masochism."

"Now I realize the mother has always been driving me. At first, though, it was all just curiosity." The woman flowed into her friend's arms to rest her head with a sigh. "Thanks for trying to understand me."

"I don't, really."

"I know."

The bakushi laughed, patted her shoulder, and said, "But it's good to work with you, though! It's good to be your friend, and good to see you in love…if only that layabout man of yours would come to a show! We'll cook up something good to get him out one of these days."

Laughing, the woman teased, "Oh, there's going to be a next show, will there? How will I fit in these performances around my filming schedule?"

"Ditch the filming schedule, of course… I'll do whatever you want if you perform with me again."

"My father told me this joke," replied the woman, smiling a little. "A man is driving by a prostitute—"

"What kind of joke is this to tell a kid!"

"—and she calls out to him, so he stops. She says, 'I'll do whatever you want for a hundred dollars,' so the guy says, 'Great! Paint my house.'"

4

m0t

You could start a burlesque club. Strip off your clothes, flay off your flesh while singing "La Vie en Rose." The real, French version, I mean.

Or maybe train a pack of dogs to gnaw you to pieces until you're wearing nothing but your skeleton, then do a dance for me.

For the audience, I mean.

I love to watch you dance.

"I love being watched by you." A sharp corner of the diamond ring, the gem as cold as ice, pressed against her smiling lower lip while she gazed into the camera. "I wish I were a better dancer."

I'd pay for your lessons.

"No, I can't…I'm too proud for lessons."

It sounds like your bakushi friend is teaching you quite a lot.

That was true. Their shared heritage had bonded the woman and the bakushi in the same way an almost-spiritual reverence for pain bonded her to her patron. Like many Americans, the woman had grown up completely disconnected from her own cultural heritage. She didn't even know her paternal grandfather's native language and was publicly embarrassed when people tried to speak it to her.

The bakushi, on the other hand, was raised by an intense first-generation family and was an immigrant, although one who had spent a negligible amount of time on native soil. Admirably bilingual and devoted to keeping alive all number of rituals from an intensely ritualistic culture, the bakushi was the ideal person to teach the woman about her own heritage, and did so with great frequency.

"Japanese flower language is different from Western flower language," the bakushi explained while the two brainstormed a routine in which the woman, once statically bound, was to serve as a vase. "The principle is essentially the same, but ikebana displays are much more deliberate in their construction than even the most intense Victorian bouquets. They're simpler: more distilled, consequently more intense. Ikebana is about the experiential qualities of the flowers—the mindful, dynamic act of producing the arrangement and the contemplative, receptive act of admiring it."

While trying to convey the beauty of this lesson in an ill-fated attempt to connect with the stranger and #1 (they seemed to be living together in those days, but the woman took this fact for granted and did not bother to inquire), she realized the futility of sharing feelings with anyone but her beloved patron. #1 stared off into space near the end of her cigarette, and the stranger clearly awaited his turn to speak from where he sat nodding at his new office's computer desk.

"Hey, that's cool. By the way, I have good news."

"Dude"—#1 was again interested in the conversation and sat up, her grin expanding from ear to pierced ear—"this is so exciting, you're going to freak out."

The sad part was that, for a few seconds, she believed it would be something worth getting excited over. "What is it?"

"I've found a new home for our stream," announced the stranger, producing an odd drop in the woman's stomach as he carried on, "and the best part is, we don't have to game the system, or try to pretend anything is accidental."

He named a website—one of the biggest online purveyors of hard-core BDSM pornography. An organization with a ubiquitous name, a growing library of videos, and a wide variety of professionally produced, no-holds-barred live shows. "They're interested in getting to know us—so interested that they'd like to fly us out to Los Angeles for a meeting."

That was the name of a city on the other side of the continent. Closer to her human body's mother, okay, maybe. But it was almost impossible to pick a city in the country that was farther from her patron. Nausea gripped her.

"I don't know—I'm not super into flying on airplanes—"

"Ah, come on, flights are still dirt cheap with all this virus stuff."

"But it's nonessential travel, and—"

#1 spread her hands. "It *is* for work—this is such a great opportunity! You have to do it. It's like a dream come true."

"For you, maybe… Look—" The room's mood lowered while she begged her quieting coworkers' understanding. "I've been thinking about the way we're presenting sex and violence in our videos, and—I want the eroticism to stay because I think it's part of the meaning, but I want it to be more than what it is. It's just a series of acts. It's so boring, there's no point to it."

"This again." The stranger covered his face and sagged back in his squeaking chair. "We've been over this. I'm tired of this conversation. People aren't watching your videos for the mental stimulation!"

"Maybe they would watch them for mental stimulation if the videos were what I want them to be. Maybe if you would give me a chance—"

"Give you a chance to what? What do you want? Do you understand how huge this opportunity is?"

It occurred to her that he was angry, a belated fact arriving like a radio broadcast from a planet light-years away. She tempered her tone to one of diplomacy, rather than pleading with the stranger or reflecting his anger. "I'm aware it's a big company—"

#1 chimed in, "One of the biggest."

"And real professionals," insisted the stranger, slapping the back of one hand against the palm of the other. "We can cut out this amateur-budget, shoestring kid stuff—you want a kimono? They'll buy you ten."

You know? Not being angry was too much work. "I don't know why you think this has anything to do with the theoretical kimono I talked to you about two months ago. All you care about is money—"

"Oh, please! Like you're worried about anything else. Still living in that tiny rathole apartment whose address was released online on two separate occasions—if not to more places we don't even know about. Why? Because it's cheap."

"That's not why. I don't see the point of moving. I don't even need a kitchen, I don't have to eat a goddamn thing. Money doesn't matter to me. I could sleep in a casket in a churchyard like—like fucking Dracula! Like I give a shit! Fuck your money and your porn website! It's my body, it's my career. If I say no, it's no."

"Then what did we start doing the hard-core stuff for!"

"Because some troll made an account on our private forum and released a clip of it online and got everybody excited—"

Oh.

Too bad her patron had asked her to stop calling herself stupid. She'd been an idiot from the start when it came to the stranger. Sharing the sex tape, what a mistake. She had been so excited about everything. It had all been so new. Oh, oh—she had thought he'd helped her by encouraging her to keep the tape back. In reality, he was just writing the narrative of her career. He controlled her body whether he told her to hide it or use it. He was the one, the leak, the poster who'd dropped the cigarette clip. She watched him watch her understand, revelation unfolding in a thick silence elongating the ordinary flow of the seconds. Panic widened his eyes as she concluded, "Yeah. Got everybody so eager to see the rest that they'd be happy to pay a hundred dollars a video. Maybe more. You piece of shit."

"Hey, listen—"

The woman had not known herself to be a physical person in the violent sense, the temperamental sense—but the next thing she knew, #1 pulled her off the stranger, and the woman wondered where her consciousness had gone. Who had been inside her body when it broke the stranger's currently blood-spewing nose? Spider-mother, she guessed. Thanks, Mommy. Given her hyperventilation, the woman decided not to breathe at all for a few seconds, and when she did, measured words trickled out with the air.

"When I started out and my instinct was to start with porn, *you* were the one who said I shouldn't."

"I didn't mean 'never,'" he insisted through tears, through a blood-covered hand that shielded his vulnerable nose. "I meant, when we could monetize it."

"Then why didn't you talk to me instead of releasing my sex tape without my permission?"

"Because! Because, from the start, you've been wanting to make it all—fucking artistic! Putting up your photo-shoot background and blathering about these photographers you love—and with your mom in your ear? I didn't think you'd be willing to move on if I didn't—"

"Move on from what? From valid self-expression? From my dreams?"

"Don't you want to be rich, to be famous?"

"For my artwork—not for pornography!"

"What's the difference between art and pornography when the lighting is good enough? You're making a huge mistake passing up this opportunity—"

The woman slammed the door behind her.

5

"I GUESS HE TESTED positive for the virus after going to the ER for his broken nose."

I can't say I'm sorry to hear that. At least he'll have antibodies if he survives. How are you feeling?

"Honestly...relieved." She extended her hand to admire the even coats of faint pink nail polish, waving the fingers about to help them dry. "He sent me a big, rude email with all the passwords to my accounts, I guess hoping I'd beg him to sort it out like the helpless girl he wishes I was. It's a lot of work, sure, and I'd be lying if I said I wasn't kind of overwhelmed, but I'm glad he pretty much gave it all up without a fight."

Sounds to me like he did fight, and lost.

"Mm, I wouldn't call it a fight, exactly. More of a beating."

Do you need help managing things with your website?

"No, thank you, I think I'm okay." The woman leaned her cheek against her knee and contemplated the screen. "Can I be real for a minute? I'm super sick of making videos. The way I'm making videos now...I don't like it. I'm even thinking about deleting the forum. At least, archiving it all and locking it so no new comments are allowed. Things aren't right."

What changed?

"I don't know." She did know. She didn't want to admit the problem's impact—it gave a kind of power to admit that the trauma he'd inflicted had changed her relationship with her work. "I feel like something's missing from my routines. Narrative, but also…I don't know. A transcendent quality. I've rewatched a few of my videos lately, which I almost never do, and I can't help but feel that the cinematic medium is as futile as the photographic one. Know what I mean?"

I think I do. Both are mere echoes.

This is why physical reenactment is so important in religion. It's not enough to hear a story or see a piece of art. There must be a physical component, a posttemporal, eternal moment recurring in suspension throughout all of time in the same sense as the Eucharist.

Too bad traveling freak shows aren't in vogue. You'd be a smash hit on the carnival circuit.

"No kidding!" She laughed with delight at the thought and enthused, "I could be, like, a blockhead," while tipping back her head to mime driving nails up her nose. "But with railroad spikes."

Oh, yes, or ice picks.

I love you, my delight.

"Aw, honey. Want to watch me handle fire, swallow snakes?"

You have it reversed.

"I know what I said."

You do make me laugh, you know.

"I don't know, no." The ring on her finger glittered in even the low light of her studio. "You're not embarrassed by me, are you? That's not why you don't want to meet me, right?"

I do want to meet you. Please don't misunderstand.

I want to meet you too much. Too badly. That's the real problem.

"Yeah, no…I know. I do understand." She thought about feeling bad for herself, for her state of loneliness and her rejection not just of the stranger but of #1, who had passively sided with the woman's former producer. They had not exchanged a text message since the schism. Yes, it was tempting to feel bad—but it was easier to smile down at the severed hand whose nails had dried. She cheerily waved it in its good-as-new duplicate for the titillation of her digital lover. "Anyway, now that I've been free of those jerks for a couple of weeks, I feel ready to start exploring different mediums. I'm tired of videos—of faking accidents or pretending what I do is an illusion. I could say anything at live shows…especially if there's a narrative, context to the routines. Then I'm just playing a character."

Our characters, ourselves.

You're so pretty in pink. What are you going to do with that?

"Don't spoil your surprise! You'll find out soon enough."

6

THE CONCEPT DEVELOPED from her conversation with the bakushi—the same flower conversation that had severed her relationship with the stranger and #1. Only after she had metaphorically, yes, ritualistically represented this severance in the sacrifice of a fast-to-return hand did she make the unconscious connection back to that first obsession, that first series of hers. Those hand photographs with whose originals she peppered the bouquet of tongues, chrysanthemums, and orchids. (A steal from the going-out-of-business sale of a local florist unable to survive another shutdown against a virus that still had no widespread vaccine.) She enjoyed the temporal symmetry while arranging the flowers within the clutch of her old hand. The bird of her heart fluttered in excitement. He would love it!

It was the first gift she had given him outside of those videos and the odd set of photos. What a piss-poor wife she'd make! She was always thinking of herself, her art, spider-mother—but, oh, these things were not of the world. Of all worldly things, she thought most of him. Her love. He deserved to be thought of, even if (especially if) thinking of him for longer than a second made her feel her body might evaporate. She studied her arrangement and ruminated on her feelings for him, this man she had never met, this man she knew and loved better than anyone on the face of the earth.

What could she do with these feelings? Using a teaspoon, the woman gouged out her right eyeball with an orgasmic scream and a sensation not unlike the removal of a long blood clot from the sinus in the wake of a nosebleed. While the headache subsided and the new orb began to expand like a balloon in the socket, she added the acquired eye to a nest of hair in the bottom of the ikebana display. Like a tiny jade egg! She smiled at it while scratching a dry spot between her ribs. A round nodule had begun to form, some hard pimple yet to come to a head. Interesting she could still get such things. When had it shown up? Hard to say. Time had a way of meaning nothing to a person so isolated.

The only thing keeping her measure of time was her safe-deposit-box ritual. Once a week, sometimes twice. Never much variation. To visit more than twice seemed excessive. Bringing the vase was the first time she'd ever gone thrice in a week. Sort of a fairy-tale rule, that rule of three. And the funny thing was that, as she dressed the next morning, the woman found herself saying out loud the words, "Maybe I'll finally meet him today."

And she laughed because, by then, the dream of meeting him was silly.

And she took her display, concealed in its hatbox, out of her refrigerator.

And she made her way to the bank, heart flying fast as the subway car where she sat with her hatbox of flowers and flesh.

The bank was a tall white building. A kind of marble palace devoted to money. Its entrance stood on the corner of the street across from the subway station and was partially obscured by a harsh square pillar near which she paused, shifting the hatbox against her hip to send a teasing message to her patron.

HRH_Degenetrix

You better check our box ASAP! I don't know how long it's going to last.

The phone was still in her hand as, grinning, she pictured his surefire torment on reading the message, the trouble he would need go through to extricate himself from whatever work occupied him so he could hurry to the bank and check the box, and his thrill when he opened his first proper romantic gift from the Degenetrix.

The masked bankers gossiped as usual behind their glass, and the shorter one nodded in the direction of the safe-deposit boxes. "Our CEO is wasting time in the office down there—excuse me"—she reacted to a tossed paper clip from her coworker and coughed into her medical mask, her hand nonetheless reflexively lifting in lifelong instinct—"wrapping up a phone meeting. Just knock."

The annoyed woman asked, "Do I look like I work here?" and the tellers exchanged looks of silent surprise. The shorter one became the baffled spokeswoman.

"You don't? I thought he said—he hasn't been meeting you here? He told us the first few times you came in to let him help you. We just assumed—well, I don't know what we assumed."

The woman's annoyance gave way to confusion, which was mutual on the parts of the tellers. With neither party knowing how to resolve the misunderstanding, or even how to begin to explore it further, she stepped back. "That door, with the frosted window?"

"Yeah. Used to be our manager's, but she got fired for asking too many questions."

"More like for running her mouth too much," corrected the other teller with a harsh look, eliciting a roll of the younger one's eyes.

"Whatever. He's been making noise about retiring, anyway— Uh, have a nice day."

The woman wasn't listening, so flustered by the strange interaction that she was eager to deliver the hatbox and get out of the bank. What a weird moment! Shake it off. Ah, she hated social interactions. Let's get this one over with. The woman stepped up to the glass-paneled door at the end of the hall, fist lifting to knock, when that same door flew open and, unmasked for the first time she had seen (and handsome, damn, "dashing" was the word she would use—a hard-edged, aged handsomeness, an old handsomeness sleek with the classic masculinity of a Roman bust), the bank's CEO bustled out almost face-first into her.

How to describe a moment in time? An "Oh!" moment of perfection, two mouths in harmonic surprise, hands catching shoulders, arms tightening around a box, proximity for the first time ever, not six feet, not five or four or even three or two or one, but there, two points overlapping in space-time. Two points close enough to feel, close enough to smell: incense, cedar, Earl Grey, sandalwood, love, love, oh! Her love!

"Oh my God—" With out-of-body amazement, the woman stared up into his face. Pupils pinpoints of terror amid his steel irises, he cried out, recoiled as she begged, "Oh, please—"

"No, oh, I can't—ah, I didn't understand, I thought you had already—"

"I didn't know it was you, oh, please, no"—he stepped back,

she panicked—"wait, wait—" Her foot wedged into the door he tried to shut; she gasped in pain that trickled into a low moan to hear his sharp inhalation on hurting her. When she constructed words again, they were a whisper. "Wait! Let me look at you. Let me look at you again. I wasn't ready!"

"Please, darling, I can't." That voice! Warm and low and careful, accustomed to control but trembling on this, her first hearing—trembling with love and desire that matched her own, as if love were an organ external as well as internal. "I can't look at you this closely without kissing you." Even against her foot, he pushed his body to the door, would not let her widen it an inch, and his features hidden behind the frosted glass left her whining in frustration when faced with his mere silhouette.

"So kiss me, then! Kiss me, kiss me now!"

"I can't kiss you without doing more— Please—"

"Oh my God."

"Please, my radiant devi, I am too overwhelmed. Give me a little more time to live."

"Come to my apartment." No longer pushing the door, she instead let him crush her foot within its leather boot, closed her eyes in the wave of sweet pain, lay her head against the cool glass, and wished she'd worn cheaper shoes so she might have been left with a broken toe, a bruise—anything. "Please, hold my hand."

"I can't do just that."

Wearing a grin despite herself, she set the box upon the floor, wedged her hip against the door, and eased away her foot. In its place, she pushed the offering. "Actually, you can. But…" Her heart throbbed to see his silhouette's head turn, to track the extension of his broad hand into view as he drew the box gingerly into his office. "I guess I understand, because when I think about you kissing me…it never can stop at a kiss." Her cheek pressed against the pane of glass, eyes shutting at the sound of his unstifled gasp upon opening the box—like hers on seeing the ring. "And now that I know what you look like? You're so sexy—"

"Oh, darling—oh, this display—"

"Please. I can't come back. You're going to hide from me because I know you now. I can't come back and find you gone, do you understand? This is the last time I can come here if you don't hold me! Oh, hold me, please."

"Yes, yes, I want to—with wanting more than any man has felt. You are Helen, and I am Paris, and like Paris, I am destined to be smote when this most powerful, God-sent beauty penetrates my kingdom gates. My love for you is my doom. Even looking at you here, I cannot imagine anything else—oh, please. Please give me time. I was not prepared for this today."

"You speak like you write. Better—I love to hear your voice, oh, I love it." With a low exhalation, cheek still rubbing the glass, she asked, "Now that I know who you are…can we talk on the phone?"

After consideration, his head lowered in demurral. "I don't see why not," he decided softly. "Yes, I can withstand that much. One step at a time. Oh my God." He groaned like she had picked up a gun and shot him in the diaphragm, and the silhouette of his arm lifted across his torso as such. "I am overwhelmed by you—feverish at the thought of you. My angel…you're right. Now that you know me, I can't continue haunting these halls in hopes of seeing you. But please, still accept my gifts. Please keep coming back here."

"Okay." Maybe she would bump into him coming in or out one day: catch him by surprise again, feel his hands on her for even a second. "Okay. I'll keep coming back…and I'll go today, but I'll send you my phone number and wait for you to call me. Promise. Swear you'll call me."

"Yes. I swear, I'll call you tonight."

"Okay. Okay. Okay, oh—I love you too much, can you imagine?"

"Oh, my Degenetrix, as much as I love you. My treasure—the only treasure I have in all the world."

"You're the chairman of a banking empire."

"I know what I said."

She stroked the glass as if it were his face. How much more she had to say! So much more. A lifetime more of words. But…he was right. Once those words started, there was no stopping them— had been no stopping them from the first missives they exchanged. The gradual development across methods to fleeting physical and visual contact was almost necessary. An acclimation: the stabilizing element to keep their chemical reaction from running its course in an all-too-swift ignition.

The woman walked away without saying anything else and did not look back to hear his door shut.

7

AS PROMISED, he called that night. And the next night. And the next. They ceased talking all day on instant messaging like teenagers of the modern era and began instead talking on the phone late into the night like those of the 1950s. That first time, oh! After returning from the bank, trembling, pacing, she spent all day looking expectantly at the dried roses. That most important gift of his. They hung on her wall, and every time she saw roses, flowers of romance so ubiquitous they were cliché, thoughts of him flew into her mind. They caught her eye when her phone rang that night. She snatched up the device, a miniature heart attack jolting her pulse, saying into the open line, "Hello!" like it was an urgent demand.

Silence, silence. As she was about to say "hello" again, his voice, soft with laughing awe: "It's like the first time we talked all over again...I don't know what to say. I'm so afraid!"

"You don't have to be afraid of me... What did you think of your arrangement?"

His groan of artistic appreciation told her all. She grinned even before the new, low edge entered his voice. "I have never seen such an exquisite object in all my years of art collecting. I've spent the afternoon trying to brainstorm its preservation but can't come up with a satisfactory solution."

"The temporary nature is part of the charm. Somehow I didn't realize you were an art collector!"

"In an amateur way, a small sector of my finances...a fun side hobby, why put money in boring investments—but, why do you suppose I'm working so hard to collect you? The most valuable artwork of all."

8

SHE BEGAN TO FEEL that way. Letting the stranger and #1 schism off in favor of working more closely with the bakushi proved increasingly to have been the correct decision: as a consequence of their underground performances advertised virally across various social media platforms and posters plastered across the city the good old-fashioned way, a number of independent media outlets took notice. The Degenetrix's popularity had been growing at a rapid pace after the collaboration with the extreme body modification e-zine, and seeing her drop out of porn for live performance art made people curious about her story as a person and an artist—and, as always, about the methods behind her act. A few of the bakushi's artist friends began to come by when they'd heard the Degenetrix would be around, and as a result, she step-by-step eased into the same social world that other intelligent people, scarred by the virus that had afflicted, killed, and permanently impacted so many, approached with a similar degree of new introverted fear. The artists were like her, all obsessed with their work. She got closes with a painter who liked to have her model and occasionally fuck her when a session was over, which her lover always wanted to hear about.

"I always tell you about my friends—don't you have any of your own?"

"Oh, I know everyone with two coins to rub together. But I'm an old man. Even if I wasn't restricting the time I spent out and around due to the virus, my tastes have grown too severe for me to enjoy the company of just anyone. Everyone wants to playact in bed, darling… but not you."

"It's all real," she assured an arts magazine reporter who

approached her after a show where the bakushi, in emulation of an obscure fairy tale beloved by the woman, hanged her from the hand of a fountain's black marble goddess, then knelt beneath the corpse to wash in the water. "Having one's eyes cleaned by the water flowing from an exquisite corpse is a privilege few can say they've had," the bakushi was quoted by the same reporter as agreeably saying when asked if the artwork ever challenged its artists. "It is an act that symbolizes how the Degenetrix's artwork, this genuine exploration of her pain and the many expressions of human mortality, purifies and clarifies the audience's perspective on existence."

Most reviews of their work agreed the Degenetrix and her bakushi, playing characters as they did in their illusory performances, were so devoted to their roles that they even interviewed in character. Reading such thing tickled the woman: before, she had played a character when interacting with people professionally. Now, she was more herself than ever.

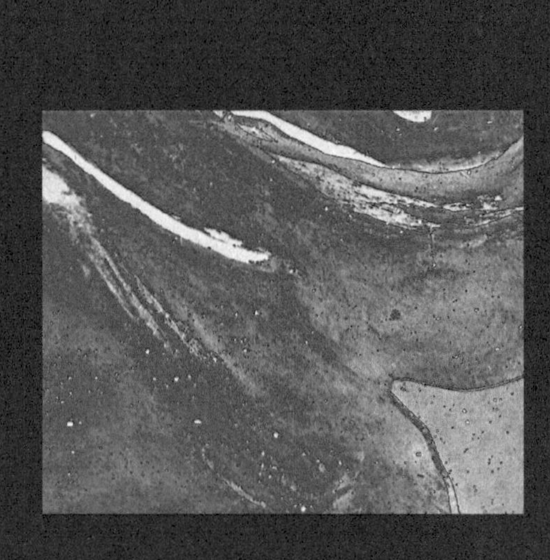

· HISAJI HARA ·

1

WHAT WAS BEYOND the realm of possibility? She had amputated digits, appendages, whole limbs with no qualm. Everything appeared right back as it was—particularly when she got excited about her latest achievement. How she wanted to push things! To push herself, to push all sense or reason. Every performance had to be more intense—every piece more shocking, challenging, depraved. The local Degenerates, of whom there were many, had gotten wind of their mistress's change of venue from Internet to real life and dutifully began assembling at every show, starting six feet apart and forced nearer one another as her popularity grew. Every show sold out. The forum had been locked for months, but her community of fans was increasingly rabid and had created a series of "fan shrine" websites where they kept one another up to date with her latest announcements or traded secret videos of shows that weren't meant to be filmed. One of the sites was a literal shrine of sorts established by the hippie couple, who continued to come by the bakushi's apartment to sit at the Degenetrix's feet and learn spider-mother's ways. When the hippie chick revealed she was developing a series of meditative techniques concerning spider-mother and was thinking of micro-dosing arsenic to enrich her understanding, the woman decided it was time to stop replying to the text messages and encouraged the bakushi to stop letting them over.

It didn't matter. Whether hippies or perverts, the loyal parishioners of her mobile church had no limit to their bloodlust. Although many were audibly disgusted or even sick, those who came to a Degenetrix performance did so knowing what they got into, and loved it. People from countries all over the world wrote fan emails or contacted her on social media to say what her work meant to them. Many asked if she would ever go on tour and come to their area. Local governments in foreign countries, especially Germany and England (two nations that were notoriously weird about their censorship restrictions), did everything they could to discourage this by responding to the popularity of her videos with legislation banning "filmed acts of extreme violence, real or simulated" that were produced with the "explicit intent of arousing the prurient interest." "Extreme violence" was defined over the course of many documents as, essentially, snuff. The ensuing legal battles and frivolous criminal indictments—often regarding, say, the possession of violent animated Japanese pornography—ensured the laws were not just short-lived but also free advertising for the Degenetrix's work.

It wasn't like she could argue that her work wasn't prurient, because it obviously still was. That was the nature of her relationship with her art, her body, her spider-mother. Each performance was a morbid mirror of the sexual act, foreplay replaced with bondage or torture or, increasingly, an abstract aesthetic ritual. *La petite mort* replaced with the woman biting the big one. She died more often now than ever before and felt more intimately linked with spider-mother; each death, she was more conscious of the experience, and returned more complete as a person.

"What is it like?" Her lover posed the question one night, his voice hushed with the mystery of her recounting.

"Like seeing that everything is sense, and nothing else. I know what mystical people mean when they talk about 'the veil.'" Her dramatic emphasis on the term made them both laugh. Still smiling, she confessed, "That's exactly what it's like. I knew it the first time I felt it."

She tried to explain that time with the stranger: the brain injury, her approach to the centrifuge of the mother's attention, how thereafter awareness of spider-mother and her handcrafted veil never faded from consciousness. The tangibility of her veil grew daily more intense. "Even when I extend my hand," the woman said to her lover, doing so for her own benefit, that hand extending into what her eye perceived as the third dimension, "I see it's an illusion. An image, a sensory hallucination impressed upon my mind...I don't know how to explain it. Things feel less real all the time. And now..."

"And now you're always awake through death?"

She hesitated—was that how she would describe it?—then

yielded, "I guess so."

"Fascinating… Where do you perceive your consciousness is housed in such a moment?"

"Still in my body, but also out of time. Then I remember in an experiential way that there is no difference—that my mind is always out of time, and time is a condition of my mind. It doesn't make sense, sorry."

"Don't apologize! I'm dying with curiosity. I love to listen to you talk about anything, but this subject is a favorite. Have you tried sensory deprivation with death? Some mechanism that might destroy both your eyes, or even your whole skull, to discover whence your consciousness emerges when there are no senses to be had?"

She hadn't thought of that. It made her sit up from where she reclined upon the impromptu longue of her hamper, laughing to her reflection in the window. "Oh, that's such an interesting experiment… I'm afraid I won't recover from something like that, but—"

"I know you will." His adamant faith stilled her humor. "You will—I have no question. Especially to hear you speak on this mother of yours."

"Maybe you should come and help me, since you're so much more confident than I am. I'll feel better with your support."

The soft hitches of his breath when she said something that thrilled him never ceased to provoke her smile. She had only been teasing and was prepared for another one of his usual denials when he spoke again and stunned her. "With the economy looking more buoyant—I'll save you the details since I can somehow hear your eyes glazing over—"

"I love how you understand me."

"—but you might be happy to know I'm in the middle of finding something to do with the bank. I don't know if I can even take you on a proper honeymoon with all the travel restrictions still haunting us for the foreseeable future, but—"

"What are you saying?"

"The world is so different… I have to think about what's important to me. So should we all. There's much to do, and with more than just the bank, so don't get excited, but—"

"Too late," she cried, "too late!"

2

THE WORLD OF FINANCES moved slowly to her. The world of art did not. The woman had developed tried-and-true national attention. Part of this was due to an unfortunate sprinkling of legal problems: one night, she and the bakushi were arrested for holding a public gathering of more people than was considered safe. The Degenetrix had advertised an interpretive performance of the Rape of Europa to be held at the Charging Bull, a dynamic statue that had captured her imagination and filled her with envy the first time she'd beheld it in person. Installed in the city's (in)famous center of commerce and its economic dictatorship, the Bull was one of those rare statues that appeared fully in motion. Even amid a pandemic it was always crowded by tourists and always a nightmare to get near, and she wanted to get near it, so she had organized the Degenerates into what was known as a "flash mob." Person by person, a group of about sixty Degenerates (an incredible number for such a rainy day) had gathered at the bronze Bull and formed a barrier that kept new tourists from edging up once the current pack got their photos and drifted away. When the statue was liberated and the stage was set by the very audience that had made it, the bakushi led Her Royal Highness to the statue.

In fairness, the social-distancing problems were less of an issue than the nature of the performance…but what wasn't there something vital, something archetypal, in the sight of the woman pleasuring herself upon this great beast? By forcing the tip (really, just the tip, she wasn't into oversized stuff, and the tip was big and painful enough) of one horn into herself, was there not an extraordinary superposition at work—Europa taken by Zeus, humanity fucked by the sin of the golden calf, American minorities raped by Wall Street. More, more: Ishtar and the Bull of Heaven, the reduction of powerful women to chattel, the moment, the sweet moment, that fine, wonderful moment, when the energy of her beloved would descend upon her in the moaning, muscled, male flesh.

A cop car squawked in the distance to announce its presence and give the audience a fair chance to run away. Nobody did, too riveted by the scene, although a few were eager for trouble. When the cops emerged from their vehicles to break things up, more squad cars arriving as backup, somebody threw a bottle (she suspected it was the bakushi but never had proof to bring it up).

The resulting riot was not half as insane as the powerful orgasms she had in the middle of it all, heart and body throbbing with the chaos, the insanity. All of it because of her: amazing. She stuck around to face the music, in part because she was just too exhausted, but largely because she wanted to take what she sensed was historic credit for the most delightful example of police brutality the city had ever seen—you never saw a group of people have as much fun getting their asses beaten as the Degenerates. She was so proud!

Suffice it to say she flashed back at the mere sight of the uniforms when the cops finally made it to her where she lay supine upon the wet back of the bull, but she played it cool, called her patron, and walked out of the jail with a fun story and hilarious mug shot. A day later, a truck pulled up in front of her apartment building, and a couple of unfortunate workers unloaded the number and kinds of floral displays one might expect for the wedding or funeral of a princess rather than the arrest of a woman who had overnight become the city's most powerful performance artist, but seeing footage of her fuck that bull had done it for him, as she had suspected it would.

She had not expected it to have such an effect on the public's perception of her, however. Now the media had a story, a controversial performance artist violently arrested by an oppressive regime using the virus as an excuse to exercise control. The woman's popularity grew by the day, and the bakushi's apartment expanded into an impromptu artistic salon. Painters, writers, and actors in the area began to gravitate there, seeking audience with the infamous Degenetrix to find her, against expectation, easygoing…until the subject of her work came up. Then she became opinionated, serious—almost unreachable, as if her mental conceptions of art and its utilities were held against an entirely different metric from that of the rest of the world.

"That's not true," her beloved told her. "But you are old-fashioned in your relationship with your art—your dedication to your art. You have the divine relationship with your work pursued by Renaissance painters. You understand all symbolic work is divine conversation. Since more people than ever are disconnected from the divine these days, you are perhaps out of place, but I trust you will inspire others to fan their godspark's creative flames. Look at your bakushi friend— doing quite well, eh?"

True. The bakushi reaped fabulous benefits from the relationship. In addition to being the regular host of an increasingly important clique of jet-set city creatives, the bakushi received backsplash acclaim in every article about the Degenetrix and even earned a hilarious sponsorship from a rope company. Money and equipment, provided. Great for the bakushi's bank account, but…

This meant the woman was basically required to incorporate bondage into her programs. A Bellmer doll whenever the ropes were upon her, especially when dismembered, she was truly exquisite to look upon. Appreciable to a degree—but the problem with bondage was the problem with anything. Eventually, it receded to a stillness. Eventually, the change of state gave way to a moment of completion.

The woman did not want completion. Not ever. Time never stopped. The ocean could not solidify. If she could produce a never-ending show, she would have, and fain would have given it a narrative so abstract that it could have been interpreted ten thousand ways or more: as many ways as there were audience members to perceive it. Was that what spider-mother had done? The world woven by the divine, was it not a never-ending show? Were these people not all assembled to marvel at its splendor, interpret its meaning? Spider-mother's audience, like the loyal Degenerates by then beyond number? It was all the greatest piece of performance art—a recounting of the love affair between spider-mother and the great, cruel ocean of time into which she dove.

And cruel it was. This ocean, it was an instructor. Firm, unpleasant. It was the hungry maw, the devourer, the listener and deliverer. The woman sometimes forgot that, forgot the dangers of time and the dangers of her own thoughts within it, because nothing could touch her anymore. Only her spirit and mind could be moved, and then only by the plights of others. Never her own.

One day, she bumped into her old coworker from the diner, recognized because he had pulled down his face mask to smoke in the alley behind a prestigious restaurant where the woman was about to fulfill a reservation. Excitement surged in her—it was like seeing someone from another life, and she hurried to talk to him, this person whose name she couldn't remember but whose face she could.

"What a great step up this is for you—way better than the diner. Seems like it won't be back, either. I walked by the other day, and it's still for rent. It's too bad about the place closing, but it serves that asshole right. I'm sure whatever he's doing now, he's finding other women to harass, but at least it's nowhere I have to hear about it."

A strange look crossed her ex-coworker's face, his brow furrowing, then relaxing. "Didn't you hear?"

Her stomach sank. Like the masochist she was, she nonetheless said, "Uh—I guess not?"

The line cook's eyes flinched, and, replacing his mask, he explained, "He's dead. The boss."

"Oh my God. The virus?"

"Boy, you really didn't hear, did you… I guess it was a couple of weeks after you got fired, though. No, it wasn't the virus—they found him dead in his apartment. Somebody just walked in and shot him in the head."

The woman's hand lay over her heart. "Did they find who did it?"

"Dunno, but it was probably somebody he trusted. No sign of forced entry, nothing burglarized from the premises. The cops checked the security footage for the building and said it was corrupted."

The footage wasn't the only thing corrupted there. She would never wish ill on another person so long as she lived—never complain, never criticize without being invited. With the sad death of her boss, the truly haunting death of a gross old bastard who had helped launch her career by firing her, the woman felt herself changing again. She shifted. She became gentler than she'd ever been, and far more introverted. Before, she had wished to be an extrovert: now, seeing what her interaction with the outside world could do to the lives of others, the woman receded back from existence while the world took keener interest in her than ever. Yes, of course, they wished to see more of her. Yes, refraining from that added to the mystery. But the truth was the Degenetrix grew aloof for their own good—only her beloved could resist her influence, or the influence spider-mother exerted through her.

The cult, for instance, was another good example of her mindless influence on the world.

3

IF ONLY SHE'D LEARNED her lesson about loose thoughts, loose language, before meeting the hippie couple. She might never have spoken to them at all—at the very least, she would have understood to ignore spider-mother's encouragements to tell them about her. At the time, she was not thinking it through, but in retrospect, it made perfect sense. Spider-mother was death, unconsciousness, or somehow integrally tied to the processes of both: it was only sensible that she should wish to propagate death and unconsciousness for her own frightful designs.

Once the Degenetrix stopped returning their texts, the hippie couple made a steady series of appearances at her shows and each time met up with her to speak after, to ask questions. "Does spider-mother ever talk to you?"

She would lie. "No, no. It's a feeling, that's all—a feeling when I die."

"Does she ever tell you the future, or guide you to it?"

"Of course not. I'm just an artist living my life."

"Are you God? Is that why how you're doing all this? Like Christ?"

Finally, after a show where she'd drowned herself in the river surrounding the city, tied by the bakushi to a great stone in honor of Virginia Woolf, the woman snapped. "I lied about spider-mother, goddamn you—I was just fucking around, stop bothering me, stop talking to me about these crazy ideas, this arsenic, shit. You're going to get somebody killed someday!"

"But you said there's no such thing as death, spider-mother—"

"I'm not the mother, okay? The mother's not real, she's a metaphor."

The hippies, who had brought a few friends to meet and

apparently learn from Degenetrix, consulted one another before the chick suggested, "It makes sense that the mother isn't real, since she's nonexistence. You're challenging us, aren't you? Challenging what we're willing to do to contact the mother."

"Oh my God—you can't! There's no way! The only way to contact the mother is to actually die, and if you die, you're not coming back from that! I mean, I can't even prove that I've come back from it."

The hippie chick's eyes widened in her strung-out bronzed face. "What do you mean?"

"I don't know! It could be like quantum suicide. I could just be moving through space-time, waking up in a new universe branch each time. 'Almost' dying isn't enough to *really* die. You can't meet the mother and live. Why should I expect to? I don't try to figure out what's going on, I'm just along for the ride, and I suggest you do the same."

But a look, a light of false understanding, had brightened the hippie's face as if a replacement for wisdom. "Oh," she said, "I understand." The hippie chick turned to her husband. "I understand—this isn't the Degenetrix."

Her husband turned to study Her Royal Highness. "It's not?"

"It's not," explained the hippie. "This is a clone—I understand now. The true Degenetrix has already ascended to be with the mother: this false challenger is here to spread doubt at spider-mother's behest."

"Jesus Christ," sighed the woman.

"See? Worshipping false idols, some carpenter instead of spider-mother…spider-mother's proof is everywhere, nobody even knows if Jesus was a real—"

"Buddy," said the woman, already walking away, "if this is what it takes to get you guys to leave me alone, then hell yeah. I'm as fake as a counterfeit purse."

As usual, permitting them to jump to that conclusion was, in retrospect, the worst decision she could have made: but sometimes it was just easier to save the consequences for the future.

4

GIVEN THE HUMAN RACE'S fascination with controversy, it was no surprise that the Degenetrix had to hire bouncers to keep audiences from overcrowding shows after her legal brush. Having scalped the bakushi's whole gig, she felt a rare pang of guilt. Audiences no longer attended for the bakushi. They clamored to see the Degenetrix. The number of fan emails spiked with every public performance, and in a post-outbreak world, tickets to their highly limited routines were more sought after than ever before. It was truly wonderful: the quality of her fan letters had also improved, but even the worst and most depraved missives flattered her—she forwarded her favorites to her beloved so they could jeer together, then springboard into whatever he had been thinking about lately. His fantasies were the only ones she was interested in, even to the exclusion of her own.

Maybe because he was her fantasy. She let the painters take her out and danced with the actors at parties and fucked a couple of cute photographers, but everything was a way to fill time—to indulge herself with the effects of pointless flattery, the aesthetics of unnecessary gifts and meals. The people who dated her, even those who most loved to hear themselves talk (and there were many in the art world), frequently remarked on her silence. She saved her words for her patron. Always by the end of a date, whether sex happened or not, she tuned out, waiting for the interaction to end, looking forward to the moment when she was free to call her beloved and hear his gentleman's voice. And God forbid anybody try to keep her out longer than she wished, or engage her in conversation after she started thinking of him: she would go from reserved to sharply critical to irrationally spiteful in the space of five minutes, and the person who had taken her out would be baffled by her sudden turn. These fits of pique only added to the Degenetrix's mysterious reputation as an intriguing artist, a wild woman to be tamed. No one understood that she endeavored to be unpleasant so people would leave her alone. Everything in the world was an obstacle between herself and the only person who excited her.

They had talked every day for at least two years, and still her lips went numb, her fingertips unfeeling, whenever her phone rang with its custom song for him: "On the Street Where You Live" from the soundtrack to *My Fair Lady*. It made her think of him the way the dried roses did. She would walk around humming it without knowing why, then realize she'd spent five minutes lying around, looking at those withered old flowers. Whenever she caught herself looking at something without realizing it, holding or doing something unconsciously, it was spider-mother at work. Telling her something. Even getting a song stuck in her head, that was a hint from spider-mother—playing it out loud on her stereo would unlock the key to a stuck project or elicit a specific emotional result when shared with her beloved. Always moved him. Spider-mother, her matchmaker.

Music had become important to the couple. Where once they instant messaged incessantly throughout the day, they now mostly sent one another songs, snippets of operas or ballets. Once the virus began to recede (due more to the passage of time and the reluctant use of masks rather than the discovery of a vaccine), the woman's safe-deposit box contained more experiential gifts. Performance tickets. With his help, she managed to see quite a few shows. Ballet was her favorite form of performance art, she found against her expectation—something to do with the masochistic dedication of the ballerinas, but from an artistic perspective, the real source of her appreciation was the ability of music, movement, costume, and gesture to form a clear yet free-form narrative. All without the use of speech. This was what she wanted to master.

"You could arrange solo performances," he suggested near the end of what was destined to be the final notable outbreak. "Surely your partner wouldn't mind."

"I have some ideas, maybe—I keep going back to our conversation about freak shows. But not the freak shows themselves. The bit about snakes…women die all the time in Shakespeare."

5

THE SERIES, titled *The Sacred Cows of Shakespeare*, caught flak in its press. Its use of the term "cow" was perceived as a derogatory slight on women. This association was intentional, designed to provoke and challenge the audience's knee-jerk responses to language since no scripted language was incorporated into the shows themselves. Cows were wonderful animals, sacred, and connected from a religious perspective with women since before the Egyptian goddess Hathor. Maybe the problem wasn't the Degenetrix and her choice of title, she suggested to one interviewer, but with the American perception of women, or its relationship with cows, or both.

However its title was interpreted, the performances were smash hits. Her patron dug into his network and produced for her benefit not just a number of musicians to accompany her work but also gallery operators to provide her with venues, tailors to bring alive her costumes—even an animal trainer who could assist with the provision of creatures like snakes or in one instance a bear (although the famous "Exit, pursued by a bear" of *The Winter's Tale* was, within the original text, the stage direction of a character other than resurrected Queen Hermione). This was about reenvisioning, however. Artistic liberties were called for.

But it was not the animal gimmicks or the creative reenvisionings that made her acts popular. It was, as always, the extremity, the highly praised realism, the increasingly abstract creativity of performances compared to Beckett and Ionesco and the late great suicide victim Sarah Kane. This last comparison, found in a *Vogue* issue with her face on the cover, was the woman's favorite snippet of praise to date: the only review she framed. The glowing statements came in reference to her performance in the role of Lavinia in the *Andronicus* show, wherein she hired a pair of men to amputate her hands and tongue while portraying onstage rape. Since she enjoyed double penetration, she had been worried about her ability to sell the rape sequence, but in the end, the audience didn't seem to notice a difference. The show received wide acclaim for its confrontational highlighting of the misogyny inherent in Western culture, and the general desire of the public to avoid acknowledging misogyny's consequences by, say, imagining the offstage sexual assault and violent mutilation of the Andronicus daughter rather than watching it front and center. In a traditional production, one could even find oneself titillated by the imaginary offstage rape, because in acts offstage, there was room for the glamor of fantasy. Being captive to an unfolding sexual assault in the middle of the theater while trying not to look either there or at one's fellow supremely uncomfortable audience members had a way of making people ask themselves about the contents of their own fantasies, for starters.

And audience members weren't the only ones learning things about themselves at Degenetrix shows. Playing Cleopatra bitten in the breast by the asp reassured the woman that wounds to the heart would not end her life, because she swore she felt the long fangs of the serpent penetrate the organ before she lost consciousness. Juliet was another opportunity, one she used to appreciate the parallels between the flow of blood from her pulsing heartwound and the gush of fluid along with her erotic appreciation; Desdemona, too, carried reassurance, because the ex-con whom she paid $1,000 to strangle her to death onstage crushed her larynx and disjointed her spine in an injury close enough to decapitation that she began to think of its possibilities incessantly.

"It should have been you playing my Othello," she said into the phone the night after, when, having recovered from her performance, she shared with her patron each lurid detail and all the audience reactions. "I want to know what it's like to be killed by my husband."

"Now, now…you're not married yet, have patience. But that reminds me—have you checked your box this week?"

She had gotten out of the habit since she was no longer making him regular videos. The masked tellers (who now not only understood she did not work at the bank but also recognized her as the controversial performance artist developing a name for herself in the mainstream theatrical scene of the city) waved at her while gossiping about their general disgust that there were those who feared the vaccine more than the virus. "A bunch of monkeys," agreed the woman while arriving at the glass to ask to be taken back, inserting herself into their conversation as had become her custom. "It's the prospect of change—it sends people right into their primitive brain."

That primitive brain was what tingled in the woman as she read the paper taken from the safe-deposit box. Tried to read it, anyway. Hard to understand. A deed? As in, a deed to a home? She had never seen one in real life. The adrenaline was immediate, so intense she couldn't read the address without real focus, then couldn't believe it until she saw it in person.

When the cab dropped her off before the building listed on the deed, the woman was no less uncomprehending. While standing before the town house, the stairs of the Metropolitan Museum of Art sprawled two blocks away—yes, the address whose deed bore her name was down the street from what the woman and many others felt was one of the most important art galleries in the city, the country, the world. A squat gate enclosed the town house's black double doors, this main entrance flanked by a pair of spiraling hedges and guarded by a uniformed man who, on her meek approach, hastened to open the door without even being shown the details of the paperwork.

It was like a different universe expanded at once—as if the door did not connect the outside to the inside but rather connected reality and fantasy. On the other side waited a gleaming marble reception gallery, which gave way to several rooms and a set of stairs the same onyx as the diamonds in the floor's tiles. Was that a grand piano on the other side of the far door, in a living room flooded with light from those towering windows? Still lingering on the threshold, the woman asked, "Which room is it?" and at the man's quizzical eyebrows, tried to show him the deed. "The apartment?"

"Miss," he said with a mask-muffled laugh toward the stairs of the seven-story town house, "this *is* the apartment."

Twenty minutes later, after running up and down all seven floors—eight, if you included the private rooftop garden brooding out across the city—the woman stood with one hand on her forehead and the other pressing her phone to her ear. "Are you nuts?" She was already on the verge of tears. "Are you crazy? What did you pay for this place!"

"What a gauche question! I'll remember to whip you for it." His teasing succeeded in fending off her emotion. "I've always been the sort of man to scratch the price tag off a gift...I couldn't stand the thought of the finest artist in the country living in a closet any longer."

"This place is insane, you're obviously insane. The master suite is a whole *floor*, it has its own *dining* room—"

"I'm so happy you like it."

"*Like* it!" Her tears were out of control again. The woman wept into her free hand and said against the tears, "I opened every door and kept hoping I'd find you here. It's too many rooms for just me. How can I live here alone?"

"Darling—"

"Please? Please, when?"

"Soon. I promise. I want you to have this place first, this home for yourself—I want you to have property, to know you are wealthy independent of me. That way we will always know that you are with me by choice, not because you have no other place to go. You could change the locks, sell the thing, fly around the world. Never worry for money again, live forever in mad wealth as you entertain a parade of desperate lovers. Now I know if I go there one day, and my key works, and I find you there, it will be because you truly want to be with me."

"I do—of course I do."

"Then I will find you there, won't I?"

6

HOW SAD the woman was to move out of her studio apartment! Yes, living in a seven-story mansion in the middle of one of the finest cities in the world was anybody's dream. Yes, it was a home worth more than the woman could have expected to make so soon in even a successful career as a performance artist. Yes, someday she would share this new home with her husband: with the patron who was so passionately in love with her that he still could not stand to meet her.

That studio, though. It had seen her grow up, do the real growing up people began to either embrace or shun once childhood was numerically, legally over. At least its memories of her would now be happy: she had no unfinished business and was better off than she was when she first moved in.

But the woman remained alone. Seven floors or one room, the woman's entire being ached to share her space with her beloved. What would it take? She tried to tempt him to her performance as Lady Macbeth, the crowning achievement of her Sacred Cows series and their favorite Shakespeare piece to discuss—but even watching the woman slit her wrists to wash her hands in the unending stream of blood before tying her own noose with torn bedclothes was not sufficient to coax him out in person. Not sufficient, or too sufficient. She could hear the desperation, the sorrow-laden hunger in his voice whenever she described the routines he could not attend.

"I am not sure I could sit there—oh, I don't know if I could watch you."

"Then come and help me."

"My first intimate, bodily interaction with you cannot be in front of people. Perhaps someday I can assist you in a performance, but—"

But it would be too much. Yes, she understood. She understood because, more and more, pacing the halls of her multistory mansion, the mere thought of her patron provided such a rush, she was forced to sit down. The bakushi, arriving at her frequent invitation and often staying the night in one of the high-ceilinged guest suites to keep her from feeling alone in the house where she otherwise took no guests, sat tunelessly plinking at the piano and brainstorming with her. "What's his favorite thing? Like, sexually."

The woman shook her head. "Whatever crosses his mind at a given moment. Sometimes all he talks about is how badly he'd like to kiss me, to take me dancing and wake up beside me the next morning. Other times, it's how he'd like to stuff me in a brazen bull and see how long it takes me to stop screaming."

"Gosh, what a charmer."

"I'd like the idea more if there was a way for me to see him while I'm in there."

"Boy! Well—it's nice you're so happy together…or not together." With a thoughtful chin stroke and wryly working eyebrows, the bakushi suggested, "Maybe you need to stop playing into his hand."

"How so?"

"I mean, he's obviously having fun being sought after by you. Like the old saying, 'why buy the cow when you can get the milk for free,' but for conversation instead of sex."

"Are you saying I should ignore him?"

"Mm, yes, but within reason…ignore him to get him excited about something, the way musicians release surprise albums with no advance publicity. What are you thinking for your next performance?"

With a contemplative frown, the woman leaned back in her seat to stare up at the high windows, the striped curtains blooming in the breeze through the open panes. "I've been thinking about what to do next, now that the Shakespeare project is done. That whole thing put me in such a Western mindset. I'd like to do something different. Something with kinbaku again."

The woman described her idea. Her friend's face expanded in intrigue, then horror, before giving way to delight. "If he misses that one, he'll kill himself…you have to be sure to lure him out. Do you think you can stay conscious the whole time, though?" That was the question. "I've been practicing with spider-mother," she said. "If I focus on the moment of death, I can make it through until I've regenerated, and the mother will guide my body through what it needs to do. That's what she's doing anyway—shepherding me, my mind and body, through my period of unconsciousness until I awake resurrected."

"But what happens when—I mean, if your head—"

"He asked me that once. Where my consciousness goes when my senses are cut off." Swamped by the familiar artistic dilemma of how much to practice before performing a live act, the woman considered the dead roses arranged as a centerpiece upon the piano. "I feel like this is one of those pieces where I have to see how it goes."

"Interesting…I can tell you I'll be in the audience, whoever else is there or not. There's an interesting androgyny in what you're suggesting."

"How so?"

"Well—seppuku is traditionally a masculine ritual. Its feminine counterpart is different, something called *jigai*, practiced by the wives of samurai. It's a neater act. Smaller. The wife uses her *tanto* to sever her jugular." The bakushi demonstrated on the woman with the brush of a fingertip. "In this sense, it's more refined than the male version of the suicide ritual—delicate, less dramatic. Seppuku is designed to be observed, but jigai is intended as a private ceremony, last-ditch measure. It's to prevent dishonor rather than to restore honor, to avoid rape rather than to make a declarative statement of repentance or rebellion.

"Jigai is an introverted form of suicide. By practicing seppuku instead of jigai, you're making a statement not just about the gendered nature of Japanese suicide rituals but also about yourself—declaring that you stand outside traditional gender roles, that you are not passive like a stereotypical woman but active like the general perception of a man." With a slight smile, the bakushi returned to the piano and tapped out a few more high-pitched notes. "Yes, you better make sure he gets out to this one…I get the feeling he'll have an easier time submitting to you if he's unconsciously slid into the female role by your taking the masculine one."

"It all comes down to gender with you, huh?"

"With everyone! Gender is everything. It's even how we describe electronic components—male and female. We think about it the wrong way. Gender isn't a static category, it isn't decisive. It's about the roles we take in a given second: whether we are active or reactive, dynamic or receptive. Feminists hear 'femaleness' and 'receptivity' or, God forbid, 'passivity' and get upset, try to deny the connection—but from a biological perspective, not bringing mental factors into it at all, the woman *is* physically the receptive party in the sexual act.

"Femaleness is therefore interlinked with receptivity. When a man is the recipient of a gift, he is shifted into a feminine role relative to that of the gift giver. It's a law of physics. Masculinity and femininity are so inextricably linked with sex—and, somehow, with morality— that people can't even wrap their heads around the idea of gender being a neutral concept of polarity, like the directions 'north' and 'south.' If I stand north of you, does that make you less north facing than you were before?

"But in gender, when people are insulted by the idea that a man adopts a feminine role when he permits even his female-bodied partner to take the active one, it's like your Shakespeare shows. That insult is a social product pointing to an inherent misogynist instinct present even in feminists, even in women. 'Femininity' and 'feminine' or 'effeminate,' these are all dirty words now. Words we use to slight or make something less substantial. But, you ask my opinion, the man with the confidence to find the woman in him—he's infinitely more masculine than the grizzliest lumberjack, the slickest ad executive. It's all about empathy…you have to put him in your shoes. Then, everything will fall into place."

7

THE BAKUSHI was her best friend because the woman always came from their conversations with something new to think about. Yes, something interesting lay there. Had the woman not finally met her beloved, sensed yielding from him, that first time she brought him a gift? Maybe the bakushi was right. Perhaps it was a strange kind of masculine pride, a fear of giving in to the inherently feminine passion of his disorganized and violent emotions, that prevented the woman's patron from their long-awaited meeting.

She didn't care about his pride. She wanted to brutalize him, humble him as much as he did her. That was the man in her, perhaps, seeing and responding to the man he was. The woman then stepped back: Were she the man and her beloved the woman, how would she do the courting? How did the woman in her beloved wish to be wooed? The same way her beloved himself wooed the Degenetrix, naturally—do unto others, as it was commonly held. The pattern of courtship in which her beloved engaged needed bandying back. Ah, it was all so clear! All at once. Thanks to the bakushi, thanks to the man inside of the woman.

With that man's help, the woman initiated her most complete campaign to date—a war waged across several fronts. First, from an account that had swelled past all expectation over the course of her yet-burgeoning career, the woman spent a great deal of money on the commission of gifts. Then, without warning, she one day spurned her lover's phone calls and made it her new habit to ignore his each attempt at contact. To keep him from thinking she was dead or angry, she still throughout the day sent him the occasional song that made her think of him, the odd picture of what she was up to. The questions began to fly in, in voice mail at first but soon in instant message.

m0t

I tried to call you a couple of times but haven't heard back. Hope everything's okay.

It's been twenty-four hours, are you all right? This is the longest day I've lived in years. I can't believe I ever existed in this world without you in my pocket.

I saw your website update today. You must be alive. Have I offended you?

Hello?

That's a nice song, but I wish you'd say something along with it.

Dealing with powerful men was a task more nuanced than she'd realized. All this time, she'd just paid him too much attention! Ignoring him was extremely effective. After keeping him suspended for six days, she placed a custom-engraved designer watch in the safe-deposit box and sent a message encouraging him to check it. Three hours later, her phone was overcome with a fit of desperate buzzing.

Oh, darling, it's too extraordinary! You shouldn't have.

This is a game, isn't it? Now I see. Trying to get my goat, are you?

I have to admit it's working.

His flow of messages reduced to a trickle. She saw him trying to ignore her like she ignored him and felt her delight increase by the night, sure to post across her social media platforms as many pictures as possible of her having a good time with boyfriends and girlfriends. The next week, she left him a pair of gold cuff links resembling owls.

You've certainly taught me a lesson. I'm crawling out of my skin.

I miss our conversations more than you could imagine. Won't you please call?

Or perhaps you could send me a video the way you used to. Sing me a song. Anything.

A gilded tie clip, custom-carved from a chip of her pubic bone.

You're driving me crazy. My God, I hope you're happy—it's 2:30 in the morning and here I am.

Hello?

I see you online.

You wouldn't have marked yourself online if you didn't want me to know you're here. You're clearly doing this on purpose.

Oh, I'm miserable.

Artisan shoes cobbled with leather tanned from her own hide.

Aren't you a wicked little bitch? I have half a mind to come over there tonight and teach you a lesson about this cruel behavior, this toying with my heart.

Her actual heart—or her old one—removed while screaming and found in her hand forty minutes later when the new one jolted into the rhythm of its first beats and spider-mother let her dive back down. She had it medically preserved in a glass case.

Oh, darling.

My darling, my darling, my life and my bride—oh, my tender goddess.

Please, please. I can't stand this. I miss you. I love you.

Check the box.

A marriage certificate.
She'd never known his name.
Her eyes filled with tears after she signed her own.

8

WHEN SHE RETURNED the signed certificate for her husband to process sight unseen with whatever judge was in good (or bad) with him, the woman included a poster for her new performance. Prereviews and interviews in newspapers, not just around the city but around the globe, hailed the Degenetrix as "the most audacious performance artist since Joan of Arc," and "a Joe Coleman for the post-virus world." Audiences eagerly awaited her newest performance to such an extent that to say she was not nervous would have been a lie. She had practiced what she could, but not all of it could be practiced and still possess the same impact. Dead alcoholic and couch-surfing father of the beat generation, Jack Kerouac, once said of writing: "First thought, best thought." The woman found this the single best way to describe her relationship with her artwork. First injury, best injury. She could not repeat her works without losing something in the process, and this show, important as it was, had to be perfect.

It also deserved a magnificent venue. Through her husband's art collector friends, the woman was able to throw around enough money and influence to secure a partnership with the Metropolitan Museum of Art. Astronomical ticket prices. Highly exclusive. Maximum capacity forty attendees and ten press members: social distancing policies were slow to recede as the vaccine was slow to disseminate. Without specific licenses and provable, formalized safety practices, performers could still only have limited audiences. Fine by her. Art snobs loved that sort of thing. Every seat sold overnight.

After more negotiation, the Temple of Dendur was selected as the most appropriate environment: the ancient temple, transported from Egypt to the museum and installed upon a platform surrounded by a watery moat, was by far the most ritualistic of all locations within a treasure house of ritual devices and depictions. It was a special place, the Met, one with the right to juxtapose martyred Catholic saints against sensual Greco-Roman goddesses—a building where the exquisite curves of nude marble women were counterpointed by Ugolino's moment upon the precipice of cannibalism. The Met, the Met! It was her favorite place. Her favorite part of performing in her favorite place was the privilege of touring her favorite place privately, having charmed a pretty blond curator sufficiently to merit an empty museum review of rooms devoted to Degas, Monet—John Singer Sargent. She wondered with a wry smile if her husband would buy her an original should she bat her eyes enough, or let him vivisect her on some happy Christmas Eve.

What an entitled thing this man of hers had made her into! Maybe she'd always been this way. Maybe that was her secret: this wildness, this ostentation, this suprasensuality that catapulted her beyond decadence and into the divine revelation, this was all her nature. Her true nature, which had thrust her into this fabulous dream. All of it was a dream, yes, Poe, all seen or seemed—all experience was to the woman but a veil, a veil spider-mother wove.

The woman was tempted to identify herself with spider-mother, but to do such a thing would discount all the mother had done. Better perhaps to say that spider-mother identified with the woman: that the woman was the dream of spider-mother, whose will was the only true will existent. The mother had given her the success, the means and the paths. All that the woman had was owed to spider-mother. Being bitten by the asp onstage had been fun, but privately she awaited the omen of a deadly spider's bite killing her au natural. Not part of a routine but part of nature. She dreamt of remaining a corpse for an extended length of time to permit the nesting of insects, the development of maggots and thereafter flies to theoretically nourish the theoretical manifestation of the mother and her complex death-life choreography. The flies sustained on the woman's body would feed the next generation of spiders, not just the spider that killed her; when she was restored to life, would those spiders, those young spiders for whom her flesh was a kind of engendering force, know her, pay homage to her? So tempting to discover—but the woman's vain self-attraction was too great, and though the idea filled her to the brim with excitement, it displeased her to think of losing that much time to the mother's many hands, or of permitting her beauty to decay too long.

Her own mother—her human mother, the human portal whose past sexual energy and genetic donation provided the woman with flesh-means of physical manifestation—was astonished to learn of her daughter's marriage. "What? Married? Who is it?"

"I don't know if I should say yet. He's a private man." The woman leaned back in the chaise longue in the center of her favorite living room, where she consulted an electronic tablet bearing this moving representation of her human parent's face. Mirror, mirror, on the end table, help her tie her own entrails. She tried to stay on topic.

"I used to think he was selfish because he's so private, and so—obsessed with preserving the life he had before he met me. I thought he was afraid of the intimacy. But now, I understand. He understood what I maybe didn't believe when I first started my work: that I'm successful, and people want to know about me, and that means they'll want to know about him. When we're together, married, I'll be the more powerful one. I think that kind of freaks him out."

"What does he do for a living?"

Tugging contemplatively on her lower lip, the woman asked her mother's image, "Do you remember a few years ago? When the virus was first going around, and that bank got all that publicity for funding a hospital?"

Leaving out details, the woman related the story of the safe-deposit box and the man who had watched her come and go from it. Her mother's head jerked back from the camera in astonished understanding as the tale reached its conclusion. "I— How much money does this husband of yours have?"

"It doesn't matter... I'd make my own if he didn't have any." Spider-mother would give her some. The woman realized while on the phone with her human mother that this was what had happened. Always present, spider-mother edged into the woman's consciousness, her voice confirming, *Yes: all the money I have given him, I gave him to share with you.*

"Still," her human mother insisted in physical space, in three dimensions, to which the woman lowered her harmonic vibrations away from spider-mother's words. "You must be curious."

"What's the difference? The economy the way it is, I'm lucky he can provide for me at all. However many stories my house has—"

"How many does it have?"

"—is ultimately negligible compared to the simple blessing of having a house."

Amazed, the woman's human mother wisely changed the subject. "So…does this mean you're finally going to give me a grandchild?"

· SHINTARO KAGO ·

1

AFTER HER FIRST few performances before a live audience, the woman no longer experienced stage fright. Going on with the bakushi had helped as training wheels helped a child learn the fearless balance of their bicycle. The first time taking off most of her clothes and being tied up, her skull had tingled, her whole nervous system had succumbed to nausea, the room spun even before she was suspended from the meat hook—then it was fine. Then it all cleared like a storm to leave her awash in tranquility. Each performance had grown simpler to handle, and while it was never "rote," the woman gained confidence. With that confidence blossomed a degree of relaxation.

Yet here she was! Shaking like a leaf: checking, rechecking the clock on her phone, unconsciously opening back to the photograph sent to her, not by their traditional means of self-destructing message but via text message. As if they were some ordinary couple, and he some ordinary man showing his lover the ticket purchased to her performance.

Can't wait to see you tonight, I couldn't sleep.

Third-row seat on the end, stage right. Look for me. xo

What time was it again? Better check.

2

WHEN THE HOUR STRUCK and the Degenetrix's introduction wrapped (furnished by the curator who had given her the private tour, then succumbed to an invitation for "coffee" to the nearby town house), the lights went down. The woman was slated to walk up the center aisle and mount the platform upon which the temple was located, but instead of taking this central route, she took a sharp left, counting the aisles she passed. While whisking by the third row, the woman brushed her hand across her husband's shoulder. The cure to her anxiety lay in the balsam of his gasp: in his true, intense fear; his recoiling; and, once she was out of reach, the belated extension of his arm, futile in the dark.

After rounding the audience, she resumed the path intended and found her mark. The spotlight found it, too.

3

SEPPUKU WAS FAR more than simple sacrifice. It was a contemplative act. A Japanese refinement ceremony like any other. The bakushi had taught the woman how everything from flower arranging to rope-tying was, within the culture of their heritage, connected to Zen mindfulness. The transient but unspeakably radiant aspects of life were all present in any one second taken from such ceremonies, and this was nowhere truer than in ritual suicide.

Prior to entering the temple chamber, the woman had dressed in a colorful kimono: one of roughly twenty her husband had by then purchased for her. Kneeling front and center on the impromptu stage, she received a silently moving visitor. This man, disguised by the fanged grimace of a full-faced *oni* mask, was armed with a *tachi* blade and a far shorter *tanto*. From behind the grinning demon, the swordsman (who had been given $10,000 to compensate the trauma of what he was about to do) assisted in the woman's undressing and disappeared from sight when she was naked. The spotlight trailed after her as she dipped a toe into the shallow waters around the temple, then sank to her knees and commenced a preparatory bath. Her eyes pierced the dark: adjusting through the spotlight yielded the faces on the other side, drained of color by the dark, each set wide apart from the other to permit the assembly with respect to social distance. It was therefore easy to see her husband, forward in his seat, hands clasped before his masked mouth, eyes focused by intensity. A man taking in a concert, a woman taking in her love. Yes, friend, bakushi. All humans were all things.

Water fell from her in sheets as she rose to be dried by the masked servant. He assisted her into a new kimono, white as the room around them, then served her a small portion of her own preprepared sweetmeats upon a silver platter. After carefully considering each fastidiously prepared bite, the woman turned aside to bend her head over a low-set calligraphy desk arranged beside the mark, the spotlight, the destined point of suicide.

Poetry was not her forte. The death poem, however, was its own style of poem, and much as she could not practice the sum of her performance prior to the event, such a poem was by its nature meant to be written extempore. Her favorite author, Yukio Mishima, had written such a poem before his own ritual suicide.

A small night storm blows
Saying "falling is the essence of a flower"
Preceding those who hesitate.

She took up her brush after thinking of that poem, the one creation Mishima wrote with the knowledge that he would never learn of its reception. When she touched the brush to the paper, the words flowed from spider-mother. The tradition demonstrated in Japanese literature such as *The Tale of Genji* was one of memetic reference, with poetic lineage demonstrated by symbols selected in deliberate reply to some specific work from a prior master. Accordingly, the woman's death poem was a memetic grandchild of Mishima's.

When she set the brush down, it was hard not to smile. Not bad. No time to appreciate it. Here came the magician's assistant.

For her next trick:

4

A KEY ASPECT of the seppuku ceremony was that actual decapitation was undesirable—an almost absurd social faux pas, arguably a dishonoring act in and of itself. An expert swordsman answering the inauspicious call to act as kaishakunin (that was, the second in the seppuku ceremony, responsible for cutting short the agony of both participant and observers) was expected to leave a strip of flesh at the front of the neck. In a properly performed ceremony, the spinal cord was severed, but the head would fall forward to hang against the chest rather than rolling off like a lost softball. Her swordsman had been promised double if he could accomplish this effect, and how pleased she was to say he earned his $20,000 while she simultaneously did the harder work of self-disembowelment.

Every woman in the audience screamed along with most of the men. The Degenetrix could not scream as she tore open her abdomen with the consecrated *tanto*: her head had already been severed, and her voice box could not function without the coordination of lung, tongue, and larynx that served to mechanize human speech. Strictly speaking, given the severance of her spine, her body should have suffered paralysis and immediate death. It did slump forward at the loss of control, and as her forehead bumped against her own bosom, she experienced the veil more than ever, felt herself being pulled up out of her own spine and away from that veil, spider-mother there (*back again, back again*) even as she fought away from the pull, the ease into sleep, the soothing embrace that was in and of itself the mystery of death. No: she would not die, could not die. The woman was immortal. The woman was awake and too strong to be held back from that veil into which she pressed her face. That ocean where her body still lay.

Her body! Her nonfunctioning body, good as a corpse. Without her oxygen, her blood, her brain, her eyes, without all of those things, there was only spider-mother to perceive as the body of the woman jerked to life. Yes, the body of the woman. It had always been spider-mother watching. Always watching this corpse that tricked itself into believing it was a living, conscious human being. This hypnotized cadaver twitched; the audience cried out again. Before their wild eyes, this dead body sat up to shed its bloody kimono.

The Degenetrix's arms pushed her head back upon her neck. There her slack mouth and dull eyes sat crooked, limp, uneasy upon the column of its display. Amid the astonished onlookers (who, even knowing the reputation of the artist they'd paid thousands to see, were nonetheless shocked by the grotesque scene), her husband watched with the fingers of one hand pressed to his masked mouth, the other clenched in a fist at the edge of his knee. The woman's partially decapitated head smiled from its crooked place upon its flesh pedestal while, with both hands, it drew ropes of intestine from inside the body cavity. Spider-mother-consciousness located the pale bakushi in the crowd, mouth also covered by a hand, though in the self-defensive maintenance of nausea rather than the barely contained astonishment demonstrated by the woman's husband.

With the comic gesticulations of a clown pulling a nearly endless handkerchief chain from his pocket, the body reached the end of the intestines and confirmed in one last tug. The woman was but the body—spider-mother was her mind, all her mind, all the time. Lucid in her dream, tears leaked from her body's eyes and, at the sight, the woman's husband swept a brisk hand across his cheeks. A dream, an actress, a performance artist. She was so happy, the woman. Blessed to walk the earth. These demonstrations were all she could do to thank the mother.

The body commenced the motions practiced at home with traditional rope until the process was automatic. This *shibari* was the one part of the performance she had studied beforehand, not wanting to botch the knots with which the corpse decorated its semi-headless body. When it had prepared the bodysuit of gut rope from its chest harness to its pelvic binding, the swordsman, who later confessed to discreetly exiting so as to vomit after his contribution, picked up her body. With her head dangling down by its thin flap of skin, he suspended her from a hook attached to the temple structure by the remaining length of intestine.

Amid the stunned silence of the audience, the body quietly revolved. Spider-mother-consciousness faded with each passing second, for each passing second renewed the flesh of the woman's neck and mended her dead ego. Her head lifted back to its point of severance, a process resembling reversed footage of a wilting flower. When her mouth was capable of speech—rasping at first, stronger by the restoring heartbeat—the woman recited her death poem.

Falling be essential to the flower
As that same storm of seeling night
Is semen bearing nascent blossoms home

Her husband wrangled a handkerchief from his breast pocket and applied it to his eyes. The swordsman returned to slice through the intestine cord from which the body dangled. The spotlight died before she hit the floor with an echoing thud.

The audience murmured. No one knew what to say. Was that it? Was it over? Seconds passed. The lights went up. The Degenetrix stood, beaming, in the center of the room, hair wild and naked abdomen still bloody. All in one piece: happy, healthy, flushed, and bright-eyed as though with public display of sex.

Her applauding husband shot from his seat, and the rest of the audience hurried after.

5

AWASH WITH THE PINK AFTERGLOW of it all, the woman reclined in her favorite living room: the one off the reception hall. It was a tall, rounded chamber with a striking mosaic-tiled fireplace she hadn't yet used and magnificent windows careening to the ceiling. A room made for parties she preferred to let the bakushi host. Her husband had friends, loved a good party. She had to learn to be a sociable hostess.

He had tried to approach her after the show when, improperly redressed in her colorful kimono, the woman was swamped by press and eager fans alike. A gaggle of people begged for her autograph, everybody with an art collection wanted to shake her hand, professional journalists were ready to put each other's eyes out over an exclusive interview. The woman blew past them all, paused to squeeze the bakushi's hand in gratitude, then hurried off through the museum, out its vast lobby, and down the exquisite staircase to the sidewalk. She did not pause, did not look around. She hurried on, jaywalking briskly across the street to her town house.

Their town house. Oh, her fingers shook. She pressed them to her lips, the elbow of that same hand poised against the edge of the piano. His dead roses peered at her: alien beings of immobile red mouth and skeletal body, all their eyeless gazes full of love. A clock ticked in the distance. Should she call her mother? A funny instinct. What advice could her mother give? She advised her mother now. Spider-mother, whose gaze animated all things, was her mother. The woman's earthly mother was another daughter of spider-mother, another named body guided through life by one of those shepherding arms. Always working. Always weaving. Always coaxing the threads of her children. Guiding them together until her web was satisfactory.

The front door clicked open on the other side of the reception hall. It was a sound unfamiliar, the front door opening while she was inside—the woman leapt, first in surprise, then out of her seat. Fabric of the pheasant-decorated kimono falling open around her, the woman hurried to the other side of the hall to see her husband still in the doorway, removing his mask, not yet noticing her presence. He set the face covering on an end table decorated by a fresh floral arrangement, where he also placed his keys as if he had done so a thousand times. His was the kind of firm beauty that pulsed in the body of the beholder. The woman that was his wife fell back at the sight, and her hand lifted to shield her heart, then her mouth. His eyes met hers. Ah! His smile— all this time, and that was what his smile was like.

"Hello," he said.

"Hello." She drew back again, almost afraid, but lurched forward as he extended his arm. "Hello," she repeated, dashing into it, the pair laughing together, both swaying in the force of their embrace, her body pushing him into the door as she chanted, "hello, hello, hello!"

6

HIS HANDS WERE ALWAYS a bit cold. His mouth always tasted of wine, even when he hadn't been drinking. The scent she had thought to be cologne was shaving lotion, which was why she had only smelled it on him when she was close enough to touch and why she loved to bury her face in his pillow while he took his morning shower. (If only she could have burrowed into his very torso!) His favorite poet was Rimbaud, Rilke a close second. He liked the color blue. A Clockwork Orange was one of his favorite movies, and he loved it when thunderstorms rolled across the city, because her trembling in his arms made him feel like she needed him.

"Of course I need you! Where would I be without you?"

"Making love to a gentle, pretty boy your own age—why are you laughing, you don't think so?"

"What a nightmare! How do you come up with such lurid fantasies, you old weirdo?"

"Mm…just a degenerate, I guess." Kissing her, laughing at his own joke. She loved his laugh!

7

THEIR RELATIONSHIP—their relationship. Defined by its first moment of coming together perhaps. Hard to express otherwise. The power of his kiss had soon transfigured into his savagery, his embrace into a grip that squeezed from her a cry. On her expression of pain, he bit her mouth and gasped her name against the blood, drunk with truly devout pleasure: the kind of pleasure any priest would feel on union with the divine. The transubstantial miracle by means of which matter was elevated to god-flesh.

"You were right." She moaned beneath the crushing pressure of his kisses, collapsing back upon the hard edges of the nearby stairs at the force of his body, the hurried explorations of his bruising hands. As his mouth opened against her forehead to drink in her scent, her taste, to lay more greedy kisses across her face, she repeated, "You were right—all this time, I've been a goddess watching a human, this insignificant human lucky enough to love you."

"My beauty, my fair! This body was never human, my God, my God, look, oh, God—oh—" He drew back from her, and only then did she glimpse the engraved watch, the owl cuff links, the bone tie clip, the familiar leather of his polished shoes. His hand lifted to his mouth in amazement, then covered his shutting eyes. "I knew your divinity from the second I saw you dart past my Bentley and endure that car—"

"No way. I saw that car in the video— That was you?"

"Yes, my darling, I was there—I thought you died, thought about the crash all the way home, oh! It was exquisite seeing your body crack against that glass in my rearview. I wished I'd seen it clearer: and like a miracle, the next night you were on the news. Springing up, my shattered doe, oh—oh, angel, I fell in love."

"I can't believe you were there."

"I was, my beloved. Yes, I was there—and now I am here, and you are here. You are here! Oh, my life is over. Never let me leave this house. Happy Sodom! Paradise."

8

THEY COULDN'T keep their hands off each other for a couple of years. Even when they weren't fucking, they were. Even when they weren't in the same room, they were still at it. Just knowing he was in the world with her, for her, was sufficient to stir the heat of lust. She would seek him out to command his attention, and as soon as she was in his field of vision, he would throw himself into worship. There was nothing he would not do to her, nothing he did not want to try. Every lover had their limits, but her husband, whose fantasies for years had grown increasingly extreme in the fashion of the decadent French libertines after which he fashioned himself, knew no internal propriety by which to moderate his behavior when faced with an immortal, immoral, and wholly consenting victim-participant-collaborator.

That was perhaps why she had this sense of perpetual lovemaking. So much more was involved than the physical locus upon which they hinged—there was the after, and there was the before, after and before both so long that each was indiscernible from the other, overlapping at a magical point of transition. Ah, those hours were her favorites. Those hours when his uninsulated electric stare burned her from across the room. Hours while she pretended not to notice. Hours while she read, while she practiced the piano that she'd taught herself with Internet videos because she was too antisocial to bring in an instructor. Hours while she practiced this routine or perfected that technique. Yes—he loved to watch her, loved to lurk around her, to stalk her through the house or try to openly be in her presence where he would futilely read or write or think until the proximity was too much and his passion exploded out of him in violence: profuse ejaculations of magmatic desire manifesting as the jerk of a book out of her hand to strike her across the unready face, or a fist enclosing deep in her hair to drag her away from the keys and into the kiss of his yearning mouth, or his eager advisement of her work in progress coming with a hands-on repositioning of the gun she intended to use to practice shooting herself in the—

"Good morning."

She lifted her head from the pool of blood in which it rested to find him reclining beside her, enchanted, hand cradling her cheek and thumb laying where it had come to rest at the corner of her lips after playing for however long with the limp sex doll mouth of her cadaver. "Good morning, my celestial gift, my divine bride—your body, your incorruptible body empty of life, ah, such an arresting vision. My Annabel. If you permitted yourself to die for longer than a few minutes at a time, I do not believe you could decay. Such things do not happen to saints. Your skin would stay perfect as wax; your body would exude rose perfume. Oh—kiss me, my Degenetrix, kiss me. How was the underworld tonight?"

· R E M E D I O S   V A R O ·

1

WHEN THEY REEMERGED in the real world, it was in the aftermath of an overdue honeymoon. The Degenetrix resumed performing in different mediums. Perhaps ironically, she made appearances in Hollywood features—though, as her appearance in a film was a reliable indicator that the character she played was doomed to die a gruesome death, her roles were provided sparingly. When a neurotic director had to have the most believable and violent female death available, when somebody did a Shakespeare or a remake of an older film—that was when her phone would ring. You saved money on special effects by slipping the Degenetrix into your cast as long as you were willing to fight for your right to show the film in countries like Germany or, as was the case of one horror movie director, to face legal proceedings from which you would be eventually exonerated when the victim allegedly killed on camera testified that the whole thing had been just an act, just for fun.

Not everything was for fun. The Degenerates had sourly, bitterly complained at the news of her marriage, and routinely lamented the dearth of live shows. Although the website remained online and the message board was still open, several years had passed since she'd last posted anything except trailers for live performances and movies. Part of that was her marriage, but far more pressing was the increasing online presence of her literal cult.

The hippie chick had divorced her life partner, or sidelined him to a role so irrelevant he might as well have no longer existed. She now posted a video a week to a page ostensibly dedicated to self-help, a series titled: The Way of the Spider. While the woman was settling down into her marriage, the hippie was also changing her image: step-by-step, she had ditched the hair beads, neatened her makeup, and reduced the flowy cut of her clothes until her style was something closer to business executive with a hint of New Age thought. And her message, which began with generalized self-help, slowly honed in on its real goal: the proliferation of the cult of spider-mother.

There was the experience of spider-mother, and then there was the cult. These were two different things. One was rooted in perfect understanding—one, in destructive confusion. The hippie chick-cum-cult leader's videos about personal success, motivation, and overcoming depression evolved by the week into a survival-of-the-fittest, triumph-of-the-will-style philosophy that made the woman so uncomfortable she decided never to speak of spider-mother again, and in fact made a public disavowal of the cult leader who commonly cited her as spider-mother's prophet "prior to her assumption and replacement with this artificial Degenetrix, established by the same New World Order forces who engineered that virus, and for the same reasons: to lead us away from the truth and keep us enslaved to society, working for the same tycoons who have been pulling the strings since America was founded. You think it's a coincidence that she's married to the former CEO of one of the most powerful banks in the world?"

Of course it was not a coincidence. It was orchestrated by spider-mother. But the web of spider-mother looked like a base human conspiracy from the perspective of irrational, slightly insane materialists who were desperate to know something the common man didn't yet were unequipped to know firsthand the mother and her ways. These people were in a middle-ground of intelligence: smart enough to see a pattern but cursed with a consciousness of such low vibration that they could never hope to catch the mother observing them. Some of them believed in the global control of bankers, or aliens, or lizards from the center of the earth, and those that did believe in a "higher power" like the Christian God or Degenetrix's spider-mother did not possess the capacity to understand such entities were beyond morality. There was evil in the world—pain in the world—that, in their opinion, needed to be ascribed to some countervailing force. They did not understand that the strands of a spider's web unfurled in a multitude of directions, thereby producing the tension required to maintain its structural integrity.

Slowly, the cult leader and "The Way of the Spider" garnered followers, and those followers began to create videos of their own. A few even wrote books trying to explain why the Degenetrix and her husband were the king and queen at the head of some kind of government takeover, or in the service of aliens, or something. Who knew? Some of them said spider-mother was good, some said spider-mother was evil. Occasionally, people sought her out to ask questions about it, and once, she had literally killed herself to get out of the conversation, opening the nearest window and jumping out with the confidence that her husband would collect her corpse without having to be asked. He did. It was one of his favorite anecdotes thereafter at parties, and when he saw her looking bored, he would tease, "Better make sure the windows are locked."

She appreciated his sense of humor, but it really was a problem. She regretted serving spider-mother's will in this way, sensing it was a kind of Faustian exchange for her success. This, perhaps, was why she began to wind down her identity as the Degenetrix. She still signed autographs and answered questions, held court with young artists, and even acted for directors. But, slowly, her performances phased out until they were private only. She could not accomplish what she wanted in public performances without legislative pushback or being approached by cult members and other dangerous fans. From a practical standpoint, safety had to be considered—for her husband's sake, if not for hers.

After all, given how unstable these people could be, it was a miracle they didn't come after either her or her husband. The poor bull was victim enough!

2

THE DEGENETRIX RETIRED FOR GOOD on a Tuesday. It was
not how the woman had wanted to retire the character—she'd been
planning to have at least one final big hurrah, but the Degenerates
did it for her. One did, anyway, protesting the (clone?) Degenetrix's
alignment with the Illuminati by crashing his car into Charging Bull
and killing three tourists. He managed to shoot four more people and
then himself before police could detain him: rather than banning
assault rifles or anything like that, American news channels spent
weeks gossiping about the negative effects of the Degenetrix, video
games, and rock music on the nation's youth, waiting patiently for
the issue to fade so their precious guns could stay safe until the next
inevitable spree killing.

In the ensuing investigation, police determined the terrorist to be
the former husband of the hippie chick who created "The Way of
The Spider." Evidently, in a desperate effort to win back his spiritual
wife, this guy had descended into severe methamphetamine psychosis
once the attempt to contact spider-mother through a steady diet of
LSD gave him a taste for the speedier effects of psychedelics. His
journals indicated he believed he was talking to spider-mother through
Degenetrix's videos, and that spider-mother visited him, in the form of
the Degenetrix, in his dreams.

The cops actually interviewed her about that one, as if they knew
deep down inside that it was possible for her to accomplish such a
thing. She denied it, of course. She only visited her husband in his
dreams, and only when he'd been very good.

3

THE OLDER SHE GREW, the more the woman thought about her father. Never in absent terms, only present ones. A certain quality of her memories about him maintained buoyancy—a high definition other childhood memories did not possess. One night, attempting to help the girl with her math homework, he was overcome by a curious look, a funny smile.

"Want to see a magic trick?"

When she nodded, he turned the paper over and borrowed her pencil. This was what he wrote:

$$x = 0.999...$$
$$10x = 9.999...$$
$$10x = 9 + 0.999...$$
$$10x = 9 + x$$
$$9x = 9$$
$$x = 1$$

The girl, then getting used to algebra, struggled to parse the logic. "It's .9 repeating, on to infinity," her father explained. ".9 repeating equals 1, you see."

She frowned. "But it can't be. '1' is a different number from '.9 repeating.'"

"The math's right there."

"They're still different, though."

Her father's smug grin drove her crazy even in memory. "Are they?"

To think the proof kept her up at night back then! As a married woman, it woke her from the dead of sleep. Her husband turned over, drowsing awake at her sudden twitch. "Math dream again? Poor girl. Come to Daddy, come get another kiss good night, there, you see, all better. Ah, what a pretty smile…what a wife I have."

And what a husband she had. Wherever she went, he was eager to go along for the simple pleasure of being with her. Sometimes she didn't let him, in part because she still wanted alone time every now and then, but largely to make him squirm—to hear the eagerness in his voice whenever they were regressed by circumstance to their old forms of communication, phone and instant message. Soon enough, it would be over; soon enough, she would be in his arms again. Until then, he could find a person or two to entertain him.

He did have friends, more than she did, and when his period of solitude with his new wife was over, they filled her favorite living room with cocktail parties. These occasions seemed the opposite of solitary travel. Instead of him waiting for her return, she waited for his people to leave—for the moment, all the promising violence of his smoldering looks at last amounted to something, and the safety of these many strangers dissolved to the sadistic intimacy of her beloved.

Yet when they were around people, what a gentleman he was! What a delight. He even met her mother, and, though he was older than his own mother-in-law by over a decade, she was smitten with her son-in-law. Almost openly surprised by her daughter's ability to attract him. She never had understood her daughter's artwork, but the parents of artists rarely did.

The only person whose opinion she cared for was her husband's. She glowed beneath the spell of his attention, simmered to provide material for fantasies of violence that had, in the years before their marriage, given more than one lady of the evening a comfortable commission—sometimes even pension—in exchange for a lifetime of silence. But he was not always violent, and even his violence was unspeakably tender: methodical as any ritual of Japanese refinement, a process that, like his ability to give pleasure, was beyond compare. An art. One he studied, one he improved. His lovemaking was so expert that it was only natural his violence should be pleasurable; she had never known anyone like him, and gradually, her dalliances with other lovers petered into the occasional extracurricular bondage activity with the bakushi before a private audience of one. There was no need for other lovers for her, and while he was a great admirer of both sexes, the threshold of violence (at least, threat of violence) required for both of them to achieve any level of sexual interest made their sadomasochistic monogamy not a novelty but a natural and almost necessary development.

Besides: they got to know one another so well that it was redundant to try to achieve such intimacy with anyone else. He knew every inch of his wife and routinely reinvestigated as if he were a professor who needed to brush up on his discipline's latest material. Freckles, birthmarks, childhood scars—he had familiarized himself with every molecule of her, inquired about everything at one point or another. One day, he gently kissed, then touched, the nodule expanding from her ribs.

"What's this?"

"I don't actually know." She followed the point of his finger to the hard lump, which, shortly after their marriage, had achieved the size of a golf ball. "It's grown since I first noticed it— Ow! Don't squeeze so hard, it's unsexy pain."

"Just trying to get it to react. How strange that you should have something like this when everything else heals...I've never seen so much as a pimple on you."

"You should have seen me in middle school..." Frowning down at the nodule, she then grimaced at his follow-up question as to when she'd first noticed it. "Gosh, I don't even know. A while after the problem, I guess. Oh! By the way, did I tell you he sent me a prison letter?"

"No! Did he really?"

"Yeah! He sent it to my publicity firm... Hold on, you'll laugh."

4

IT WAS SO GOOD to be able to talk to him! So good to be with him. There had never been another person who understood her so well, or showed her such patient interest. Their love was unfading; far from it, their feelings were enriched by the day. Her life after marriage was perfect, yes. Perfect in every way, except—well.

He was an old man.

Immortality was great until you thought about the less-blessed people around you. Her husband slipped on the sidewalk one December: she watched with horror as he fell on his hip with a cry. Nothing was broken, but he had to use a cane for a few months. While he was impossibly sexy with the thing in his hand (a king with a scepter, a cruel schoolmaster ready for a caning, a wise old hermit with his magic staff), every soft click of his joint when he stretched made the woman conscious for the first and most painful time of the inevitability of his death. She worried over his mortality all day and night—cursed the aging process that steadily stole him. It got to be so bad that he noticed her brooding and attempted more than once to torture the worries from her: but no matter the fingers he pruned, the car batteries he hooked to her breasts, the playful dislocations or other bits of merry mayhem with which he titillated them both, she wouldn't say. When he was not around her—off having a rest in the wake of their activities— she sat staring into space, trying to discern the solution.

Why was she alone this way? She had never sought an explanation but now felt one owed to her. Spider-mother watched her, animated her, made her immortal. Was this all for the woman to be alone? She loved this man—spider-mother had put him here for her to love. To be loved, not to be cruelly wrested from her. How to keep him, though?

How to protect him from those same laws by which spider-mother's world operated even if the woman's body did not?

Head heavy against her fist, the woman stared into the general shape that was, to most, a piano, but to her in that moment mere abstract matter. His dead roses sat in their traditional display atop it. Oh, he was so beautiful. The things he did for her were beautiful, but the simplest gestures meant the most. The flowers, the weight of his hand on her shoulder, the sound of his voice when she awoke from sleep or from death: "Good morning. Have any dreams?"

She could not lose him. Spider-mother gave, and time, the mother's cruel and faceless husband, took. But time could not have the woman's beloved. Time could have everything but him. She would destroy the world if that was what she had to trade to make his life eternal. But how could he exist, how could she exist, without the world? And how could the world exist without him? Hers couldn't. The woman could not be immortal without her husband's love driving her on, fueling her soul, staving off the solitude of the human body. If spider-mother willed that the woman should be immortal, the woman's beloved could enjoy the same benefits.

But how? What was spider-mother's secret? She had found it during her seppuku ritual—in that razor-thin second of comprehension, of understanding that it was not a matter of spider-mother providing her consciousness through death but rather that spider-mother was her consciousness, was consciousness itself, pouring into her and discerning all things with holy attention that defined and severe the otherwise formless conglomerate of energy and matter within the amniotic fluid of time. No wonder babies born with cowls were magically auspicious; no wonder seers, brides, and widows all veiled their faces.

Yes: everything was part of the veil watched by spider-mother. The woman was part of the veil, and her husband, and the world, and the flowers, and the piano. All the same substance. All part of the same constant stream of consciousness. This was the final secret, but the question was how to utilize it. If the woman and her conscious existence was spider-mother observing part of spider-mother's web, then the subjectively unconscious parts of the web—the so-called inanimate objects whose consciousnesses the woman could not perceive from her own limited perspective—were also spider-mother. Maybe they were as conscious as the woman. Also imbued with spider-mother energy, also capable of being observed and animated and even changed by spider-mother's attention if the woman could only see within. Objects were part of the veil, yes. Objects, and other people.

If woman-veil could be perpetually mended of her rends and tears, husband-veil could be, also. Anything could be if spider-mother willed it—but what kind of world was that? No room for consequence, for cost, for moral growth, for rebirth. No room for change.

The woman wanted to observe change in action but could not observe anything if she died, so she needed to live forever in order to please spider-mother with her capacity to observe. And the woman, unwilling or unable to perform this observation in a void, wanted to be watched watching change. This could not be so if her husband died; therefore, her husband needed to live forever to ensure the pleasure of spider-mother.

And spider-mother, the woman felt, wanted to watch woman-veil reach her harmonic height—wanted to observe the second when woman-veil and spider-mother were superimposed, one fully the other and yet still totally separate. That secret moment of convergence, of .9 repeating clicking up into the first whole number. Such a convergence had already occurred in the woman's lifetime. It occurred during her seppuku ritual, and it happened again there, in her favorite living room, when she, woman-veil and spider-mother, tuned back in to the roses to find their death-blackened petals had bloomed with rich new life.

In perfect comprehension, the silent woman rose from her longue, made her way up several flights of stairs to the master suite, and sat at her husband's sleeping side. He stirred at her proximity and rolled over, mouth animating with a kiss against her hip and saying, though it was late afternoon, "Good morning, darling."

5

IT HAPPENED SLOWLY, as was her will. No sense in alarming him, even if the chances of his alarm were smaller than those of his delight. It did not, however, surprise her that it caught his notice quickly. She did not expect him to miss his age unwinding by the day as time, a beaten dog submitting to its master, edged back from him far faster than it had once encroached.

Late one morning, he lowered his newspaper as if unable to stand it, eyes burning with devilish curiosity. "I can't shake the notion that my hair has been blonder lately."

She refused to look up from her phone. "How funny."

"I have an easier time getting out of bed these days."

"That's nice!" The woman, wrapping up a text suggesting brunch to the bakushi, smiled up at her scrutinizing husband. "I'm glad to hear you're feeling well."

"My sense of taste is stronger than it's been in years."

"Gosh, are you on a new medication?"

His lips pursed in a coy smirk. "You wouldn't be up to something, would you, my bad witch? Or perhaps you've been a good one… I can't shake the feeling I'd ought to thank you."

"You already kiss my feet enough…which reminds me—what do you want for lunch today?"

6

THEY SPENT MONEY on many things: suffice it to say that meat was not a regular addition to the list. Not that they did not eat, or she still fasted. She joined him in meals with increasing frequency, especially with the problem of his aging solved. It became effortless for them to live in the present and for her to enjoy what the stage show of life had to offer. All its sensory experiences—all the opportunities for the human to play an infinite variety of parts.

"This nodule of yours," said her husband one day, touching it, then frowning. "Ah, never mind…"

"It's bigger, isn't it? I thought I was going nuts!"

A mystery. They didn't make any connection until her husband, conscious by then of his immortality, began to regularly slide into her arms, his eyelids weighted by their effeminate suggestion of the bedroom. Submitting himself to her in this somehow coquettish way, lips nuzzling hers, he would suggest something like, "You know that time with the electric meat grinder? The small one—well, what's good for the goose is good for the gander, as they say."

They sure did say that. How quickly, how eagerly, he presented himself as a willing sacrifice to her passions! Willingly as she was a slaughtered lamb for his. They needed to go slower with him, though—as extreme as his masochistic ideals could be, he was, practically speaking, more practiced in the philosophies of sadism. He was more occasional in his extremity as if not wishing to test too much the gift of immortality that had increased his loyalty more than ever. He had always exuded a sense of gentle reverence on her closeness, but now it was awe, and while not quite fear—for she never wanted him to fear her—he certainly carried a healthy respect for the woman who'd worked his age backward and had made him as regenerative as she.

He consulted her in all things, deferred to her in many fashions, and kindly took the lead in matters she despised. She was his artist floating off among the clouds, and he let her dream, experiment, explore with photography, collage, and bodily experiment within the many rooms of their house all while shielding her as best he could from mundane topics or dry situations. At parties, when conversation took a dull turn and she got that "window look," her husband would manifest some miraculous excuse for them to circulate elsewhere, or for him to change the subject, or for their ride home to arrive if it was a party someplace else.

For his own part, her husband was a contemplative man with his mind always working across a great number of down-to-earth issues, calculating the future ramifications of this or that global event like a human (Were they human anymore? Had they ever been?) accounting machine. Like most men, he had much to say; unlike most men, the things he said were interesting to her. It helped that he had social acuity and respect for her enough to leave off the in-depth financial or political or religious banter with which he engaged his friends. Not that she didn't listen when he mentioned such things—but she had no worries or interest in money, and politics were petty monkey-brain concerns, and as far as religion, well. She was his religion, and her state of singularity with spider-mother went beyond the realm of any cult.

Speaking of that cult: last she'd heard, they'd purchased an island. Their leader had, anyway. The woman, knowing full well how that story was likely to end based on events of American cults like the Peoples Temple or Branch Davidians, avoided news of the organization as much as she could and, when one too many journalists asked about it in an interview, stopped fielding media questions for a decade. The existence of the cult cheapened her personal relationship with spider-mother, which was by then second nature.

She was most in touch with the mother when her husband offered his blood, flesh, and organs to her as sacrifice. This he did with increasing frequency. Like all the activities they enjoyed together, their interest in these endless expressions of consumption developed out of intimacy—desire for unity with the beloved object, for perfect overlap in space-time. Her convergence with the mother enacted on the multi-person level, that sacramental ritual of love's union. But there was so much to experience separately/together that they could not yet enjoy the act of doing things in singularity. Cannibalism between the two of them therefore became a kind of religious substitute for literal bodily convergence. She had submitted her flesh for his sustenance while he was old, and when that grew unnecessary, he continued to eat of her for the spiritual pleasure. The meals from her body were prepared and served with reverence. It was a sensual experience, an honoring of the human man by the divinity that had chosen him: that had taken him up to Olympus, restored his youth, immortalized him with the ambrosia of her love.

But when he offered her himself to eat, it was so different. She became consumed with the primal hunger of the black widow spider upon sexual climax. He would see the savage hunger in her eyes while she rode him and take her hands, press them to his stomach, begging, "Yes, sweet Kali, yes, let me feed you! Oh, worshipped one, drink up my blood! Add my head to the garland hanging about your fragrant neck, oh— Ah!"

His screams reverberation through the house as she dug in her nails, reached for the nearest sharp object (he always had something on his nightstand that could be of use), shoveled his viscera into her mouth or tore out his throat to gnaw on the tender meat of his neck. It was always more instinctive, more furious and hot and in the bloody moment with her: he wanted to plan, to prepare, to ritualize, adding literal elements of prayer and other contrivances that contributed to the aesthetic but reduced that sense of first injury, best injury.

Not that his desire for mindfulness in consuming her wasn't flattering, and kind of cute. But he was always cute to her, rendered so complacent and doggedly desiring that all she had to do to please him was smile over her shoulder when she caught him staring from over his open book. He would swoon as if struck by a bolt of pleasure, crawl across the floor to serve as her slave, her lapdog, her footstool, without her least suggestion. It was nothing for her to delight him. He was so happy to be ravished by her, overjoyed to be brutalized by her, and never more thrilled than in those instances where she pushed it far enough to kill him. When he returned to life amid a shudder and the worshipful moan of her name, something about it made her wonder if he didn't enjoy the death-climax even more than she did. He was always so soothed when he was whole again—a boy reborn at peace in the comforting embrace of her arms. The shell of reality reformed around him, strength returning to his muscles, his body jerking into the reflexive motion of petting her. His cool hand, running over her side, once again paused at the lump.

"Larger still."

And the next time she devoured his flesh during coitus: "Darling, I swear it's larger."

And when next he planned to enact his desire to be made a sacrifice to his goddess, he accosted her beforehand with a tape measure, insisting, "Come here a moment, sweetheart, I have a little theory—"

7

SHE FROWNED AT THE SHAPE in the bathroom mirror, squinted through the pages of his running notebook of recorded measurements. "Okay. So it's getting bigger whenever I eat your flesh."

"Or your own. Remember? Didn't you tell me it began after the business with the, ah, 'problem'?"

"Yes. But that doesn't explain anything."

"Then the only thing to do is experiment."

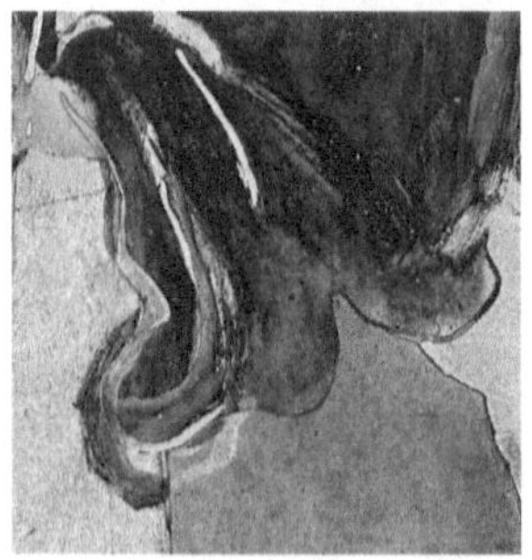

8

BY THIS TIME, the lump in her side disfigured formfitting clothes. It did not hurt, was not discolored, did not (yet) show signs of hair or tooth growth as tumors sometimes did. Also notable: it did not grow when she did not eat—in which case, it would go weeks frozen at the same size. Nor did it grow when she ate vegetables, animal meats, sweets. When flesh of hers or his passed her lips, however, the lump became subject to a gradual size increase in the following hours. She committed several thorough investigations of her mate's person, finding no such lump on him despite their avid exchange of bodily fluids and flesh.

In the course of their experiments, they noted the lump grew at twice the "standard" rate when it was his flesh she consumed—and faster still when he had recently consumed her flesh prior to his sacrifice. Occasionally after sex, they would lay there, her on her right side and her arm tucked behind her head so they could watch the lump's sometimes visible growth. They often said nothing in those moments—but sometimes he would look very gently into her face, then kiss her on the mouth as if subject to a thought too tender to voice aloud.

By the time the shape in her side developed from an ambiguous lump to something ovular, they both understood what it was, although it was hard to say when they came to the realization. The woman felt she had always known. From the first moment feeling that knob of flesh in her apartment, she had known, though she had no way to know.

One afternoon, she slid into her husband's lap and waited for him to finish the chapter of his book. He lifted his eyes with a pleasant smile and waited for her to ask, "I guess we'd ought to buy a crib soon, huh?"

· TOSHIKO OKANOUE ·

1

"DADDY," asked the girl, "where do babies come from?"

"Oh, dear," said the girl's daddy, "you'd better ask your mother that."

2

THE WOMAN HAD MADE FUN of her husband's lewd dreams of normalcy, but, well…it was nice, she supposed. Having the girl, parenting together. The rambunctious child was just like the woman from whose side she'd dropped, except that when she bruised herself or skinned her knee or cut her thumb while peeling apples, the injury stayed. The woman was relieved—but she still held her breath every time, worried it might heal in the instant and that tears of appalled pain would give way to bafflement, and to a journey that would leave the girl far removed from the child she was when she entered the world. And the woman wanted her daughter to grow, to change, but…she had to admit, she liked the girl the way she was, and sometimes wished certain things could always be the same. If anything had the capacity to always be the same, however, none of this would have happened. The woman wouldn't have her husband.

And her husband was a perhaps shockingly good father. All those years of compartmentalization, she guessed. She felt as if she watched him act—dig into himself for his method role. Plundering a far-off literary example, perhaps. One that made him a committed or even well-adjusted father when the girl was in the room, right up until the instant she left. As soon as she was out of sight, he would return to the smolderingly sadistic pervert of a swain he was inside. His contrast thrilled the woman: the exquisite range of his soul, like the range of a musical instrument. Would he ever know how much she truly loved him? Sometimes she tried to show him. She had learned that she could change things from dead to alive, from mortal to immortal. From this, the woman logically derived that she could unweave this part of the veil and reweave it into that part of the veil. Lead into gold, a performance that always delighted him—woman into man, which was a change she engaged for the occasional titillation of both herself and her husband.

There was now unlimited richness in the dimension of their intimacy, and still, it was not enough for either of them. They stared at one another for hours like lions trapped in a zoo until it became too much for them both. She began taking up design commissions and producing collaged movie posters, book covers, and logos; he resumed work to demonstrate responsibility for their daughter's sake and would go on to sell that company for another retirement around the same time she graduated high school, when they nudged her out of the house and were thus liberated from the pleasant captivity of parenting.

That was then, though. Now they played nuclear family in their nuclear America, the America where nothing changed—where people would have gladly sacrificed their neighbors, friends, grandparents to a virus if it meant they had the opportunity to carry on with their lives. All they had to do was catch what was to some people barely a cold but to others almost certain death or a lifetime of lung, heart, or brain damage. She understood. She had made such a bargain herself, and the woman saw the appeal of it, this playing house. She looked forward very much to the day when it would again be her and her husband, when their daughter would be a woman to whom they could relate as peers: but until then, the family life and the savage American instinct to defend this static permutation of it was almost comprehensible. It was safe, and happy, and a gentle way of life that permitted parent and child to become so absorbed in their mutual roles that the outside world was reduced to an unnecessary intrusion into the domestic sphere.

She even made friends again. One day while walking with her daughter in the park, who should the woman see? The art student—

the art teacher now, who also helped her husband design vinyl action figures for their independent toy company. The woman, whose child was then six years old, was amazed to find her ex-girlfriend walking with a fifteen-year-old and an eleven-year-old—but, then, the woman supposed it had been quite a long time since they'd last been together. Quite a long time since she'd married her husband.

They had a nice catch-up conversation while their children played, the woman's six-year-old daughter advanced enough to prevent the older children from feeling too acutely the suffering of impromptu babysitting. Their mothers sat side by side and rewound the years until the art teacher laughed.

"Do you remember that virus? I found out I was pregnant with my son right around the time the vaccine came out… I was so scared that he'd grow up—I don't know, empathy deficient or something. Because of all the masks, you know? It's so important for babies to see people smile. Your girl sure does look happy—and you look happy, too. Way happier than you did when we were hanging out."

That was a nice thing to say. The woman exchanged phone numbers with her ex-girlfriend and soon gave that action figure company the rights to a nostalgic line of Degenetrix figures. As, in the southern hemisphere, the cult had worked to erase all connections between spider-mother and Degenetrix before an incident left twenty people dead and splintered various permutations of spider-mother religion across sixteen different countries, it was a mere matter of time before the Degenetrix was a retro pop icon popular with the same kitschy vintage collector crowd prone to idolizing John Waters, Bettie Page, Elvira, and other patron saints of having a damn fun time. The Degenetrix was in good company, and the woman who once played her, as a result of this renewed interest, got a few roles in fun movies where she didn't die, usually typecast as a fun gothy misfit or, when she later let herself age, the sexy cougar from down the street—but once or twice as a badass action heroine. Those were her favorite roles, and everybody else's, too. Soon her dubious ties to the controversial island of self-help trainees gone bad were forgotten, as small a footnote in her career as John Hinckley Jr.'s fascination was to Jodie Foster by the time she had crushed it in *The Silence of the Lambs.*

Not everything was always happy. They got a sad phone call that the woman knew to be inevitable. Her human mother was dying: the family of three flew out to see her. The woman was so far gone from her old humanity that she forgot she used to be afraid of flying until she had to calm her daughter's fears—it made her feel proud, but far more grateful than that. She had done nothing, after all, but be humbled by spider-mother's generosity.

The town where she was born had changed dramatically, new apartments everywhere and stores and restaurants entirely switched out except for a few standbys. Not everything had changed, however. From the passenger's seat, the woman directed her husband on the route to her old elementary school so as to show their daughter, then realized with a start of surreal recognition that this series of winding neighborhood roads made frequent appearances in the backgrounds of her dreams—space filler from point A to point Z. A way of getting to the end and waking up.

3

THREE TIMES during that weeklong stay, the family visited "Grandma," as the woman's human mother was then called. The third time, the girl (too young even then to fully understand death, let alone how spider-mother's mysteries revealed death was only a dream, and life, too) stayed outside and slayed the hospice nurses with her charm. In the quiet, musty room, the woman sat with her dying mother while her husband politely gazed out the small suite's open window and upon the lavender bushes whose sweet scents perfumed the air.

People died. No use being sad about it. All of it was in accordance with spider-mother's will. All had been necessary to bring the woman through life. This good, shriveled grandma who opened her body to spider-mother was still a special part of reality, however, and her passage through it and out the other side marked the closing of an important window of time for the woman. She petted the paper-thin flesh of her human mother's hand—oh, ah, her only human mother. No, it was no use being sad. No use, no use.

"You'll be all right," was all the woman said, kissing the old lady's forehead. She sat up again and cleared her throat. "Okay," she said. Her husband turned around; Grandma was gone. "I turned her inward, to where there's only pleasure, only what she wants. She's a whole world. Somewhere happier, in or out of time."

"And in this world, this time? What will the nurses think—that we smuggled her out in your purse?"

With a faint smile, the woman stroked her fingers over her mother's pillow. The room was made sterile, neat as if no one had used it in weeks. "They won't remember her. Won't remember us, either, when we leave. Do you think we should take the baby for ice cream on the way home?"

By then, the girl was almost ten, but it was hard to think of her as anything but a baby: a perfect fruit dropping from her mother's ribs and into her parents' waiting arms. If time was a photo album, everyone else turned pages at a steady pace while the woman ruminated over the first one. Yes, her baby. Her daughter stayed her baby all the way through the girl's high school graduation and far, far beyond, poor thing, so that even as a nationally renowned defense attorney, she was always her parents' baby. Always, always. No wonder the woman's mother had been so worried, so desperate to protect her from herself! But you had to let your kids grow apart from you. Especially when you didn't age.

4

BODILY IMMORTALITY involved a lot of sneaking around. Maybe if she was still performing as the Degenetrix, it wouldn't have been bad—she might even have cruelly flaunted her eternal youth as part of her act—but trying to be normal people living normal lives? When people came over, she would alter her appearance along with her husband's because friends had begun to playfully comment on their graceful aging, their timeless beauty. The Degenerates had divided across a great number of categories. Some had continued in the maintenance of the cults' splinters; other still insisted she was some kind of replacement clone designed to subvert spider-mother's control, or Christian control, depending on whom you asked; others circulated quieter conspiracy theories that the Degenetrix was some kind of immortal, possibly a time-traveling alien or demon capable of altering her form, overcoming entropy, and even moving between alternate timestreams.

"It's just too ridiculous," her husband assured her while she worried over a particularly long imageboard thread. "They say the same thing about that movie star, you know—yes, him. It's just a joke, darling… they don't even take themselves seriously."

Maybe not, but it made her nervous. The woman preferred those Degenerates who had grown into artists, writers, musicians, directors. Day by day, she watched her own creative lineage subvert the mainstream order and over time found herself tickled to discover Degenerates in all walks of life, dictating Hollywood movies and Washington legislation and further influencing avant-garde artists. These young creatives, while incapable of pushing their bodies as far as she had hers, were sometimes perhaps able to push their minds further. It was all so inspiring that she took up portrait photography as a deliberate pursuit, one she had always admired but never felt the confidence to explore. Her husband was so easy to photograph that he made it a compelling hobby; when documentarians trickled in, she would force them to look at her favorite portraits of her husband, at her collages of their dismembered body parts, a distant woman in her apartment showing lovers photographs. "Look, look at it with me."

One in particular, a very astute and witty young person with aspirations to become a film director, grew to be a particular friend of the woman and her husband. It had been a few decades since they'd made this sort of friend, and the documentarian was chosen for this honor due to their occult interests. The first person to ask in years about her visionary experiences with spider-mother; rather than shunning the subject, which had been dangerous at the time she began to reject it, the woman considered for a moment, then answered careful questions in careful ways, because the documentarian did not seem like the hippie. The documentarian was quiet and thoughtful, and listened, and made the movie about her, and was invited back for many parties, many dinners, many private visits, until, as they say, one thing led to another.

But time did go on. And though the woman did not know where it would lead, she did know that true knowledge of spider-mother needed to remain in the world: the false world where even true knowledge was easily corrupted and where spider-mother's lessons had been perverted by her cults. One day, her husband watching, the woman offered the documentarian a piece of her flesh to eat: after a psychedelic experience lasting roughly forty minutes and giving way to an almost tranquilized night's sleep along with a series of visionary dreams, their friend identified spider-mother's observation and soon went on to become one of the most renown directors America had produced in decades. Both the woman and the mother were very, very proud. Of all the people whose lives they touched, the artists meant the most.

5

SOMEWHERE ALONG THE LINE, the bakushi retired to travel abroad, sending the woman the occasional postcard from their mutual homeland. At one point, the woman had looked up the stranger on the Internet and found him serving a prison sentence for domestic violence, battery, and revenge porn, all of which were crimes committed against #1.

#1 had retired from a short and unpleasant career in hardcore pornography about a year and a half after she stopped talking to the woman; she ran her own piercing shop in a Midwestern state far away from the city. The sergeant, like most serial killers, died in prison. The news came a couple of years after the woman finally responded to one of his many letters by appearing to him on a slice of toast he thereafter displayed in his solitary cell. It was a trick she had learned to do along with other small adjustments of matter and this specific iteration of it was one that made her laugh. Sometimes he talked to it. Sometimes, when he begged hard enough and was a very good little murderer, the toast would talk back and even giggle as he screamed. She didn't completely tease him, though. When he was dying, she stepped out of the bread to sit with him awhile. She hoped he died happy; he brought her closer to her husband.

Piece by piece, all evidence of the woman's prior existence began to fall away. Her daughter married; her own grandchildren arrived; soon, her great-grandchildren; then her—oh, God. Too much, stop the ride. The woman wanted off. She was near a hundred years old, looked thirty behind closed doors, acted twenty all the time, and her nearly fifty-five-year-old daughter asked the disguised couple, gently but firmly, "Have you two thought about—you know? Plans?"

After walking her daughter to the door, the woman turned to look at her undisguised husband with his golden hair, his hard visage untouched by the age others saw descending upon them. He made her heart ache with desire even after so long! She wanted to get off the ride. But, as usual, she wanted him to get off with her. The woman let her once again black locks free from a high bun. "*Have* we thought about plans, honey?"

"Mm…I have been in a J.G. Ballard mood these past few months…"

6

THE WOMAN READ THE OBITUARY of the Degenetrix and her wealthy husband from the comfort of their Aix petite maison. "Could have picked a better picture…'cutting edge'! Maybe for the first ten years…"

He lowered his sunglasses to assess the image and, with a kiss of her cheek, settled back in his poolside chair again. "I think it's a smashing picture. You've never had a bad one in your life."

7

THEY STILL HAD so much to do. So many countries to live in—so many eras to see! Already, they had experienced much, but the world lent itself to so many tremendous experiences of sensory delight and interpersonal intimacy that it was hard to wear out one's welcome. And when one ran out of ways to amuse one as oneself, one could make oneself into but another thing of many. Lead to gold, man to woman, anything was possible.

The woman's games with her husband gradually became more literal. Her control of matter expanded by simple logical deduction. Reversing entropy due to her union with matter became communicating with it became shifting it entirely. Why use your husband like a footstool when you could transmute him into one? Why be two people making love when you could be a bouquet and the vase holding it, or an electrical socket and a plug, or a match and a firework? Why could gender, which the late bakushi had taught was only a principle of relationship to action, not be applied to all related parings of objects and industry? The woodsman and his teetering tree, the musician and his instrument? Why could the relationships between any two items not be as sensual and intimate as the conscious pairing of two lovers?

They were so close. They wanted for nothing. They argued only for play, only to make love when it was over. They climbed inside each other's minds; sometimes she swapped their bodies or made him into a woman, a splendid woman who melted into the arms of the man she had inside, or the woman she was, or the mother that was the interpolation of them both—both plus more, plus divinity, plus infernal intent. Occasionally, they spent a decade or so living apart because they had been together for centuries, but it was only in the same spirit with which the woman, early in their marriage, had pursued solitary travel or hard work in Hollywood. Each exploring life alone with anticipation of coming back together and sharing what was learned. Sharing in the death of the United States, watching the resurgence in humanity's interest in space, laughing together at the widespread cult paying homage to an abstract spider goddess who had supposedly created the universe with her own dismembered limbs to farm the human race's souls.

Over time, the couple's separations ceased. As they achieved every possible combination of experiential relationships, the transfigurations halted, too. To say they were bored would have been wrong, but what could be done, they had done. What was imaginable had been enacted between them and new, far more impossible things had been born within those escalating experiments. Eventually, they never went outside again, forgot the name of the country in which they'd settled, forgot what year it was. Within the opulent mausoleum of their love, existence was timeless. The boundaries between one and other fully blurred until one day it occurred to the woman that she would have been much happier—perhaps even fully satisfied—if those boundaries did not exist.

He said apropos of nothing, reading her thoughts again, "Do you think it's time?"

"Yes," she agreed, "I think it is."

8

WHAT TO BE FOREVER? What object, what thing, could encapsulate them? What could satisfy them in an eternal sense? After all the things they'd seen and done and been together, all the growth the woman had undergone and all the change through which she'd flowed, reaching any point of completion was as haunting as her father's proof.

"Perhaps," she said, "we might be a tree, like the Greeks were always writing their myths about. Keep growing forever."

"Until we're cut down…trees are too mortal."

"That's true. The world?"

"You already are the world, and me in that regard—at least, the watching spider-mother in us is, therefore, you are, too. But I wish us to be together, singularly together, always—aware of our togetherness but also separate so we may appreciate our togetherness."

"You're such a picky man!"

"I know I cause you trouble."

"Yes, you do, but I'm picky, too, and I love you anyway…hm." The knuckles of her hand rested against her mouth. "A piece of art, maybe? Something encapsulating time."

"A piece of art…what kind? Not a painting?"

"No—too static." With a start of recognition, she remembered the far-off quandaries of the lonely woman destined to find herself thus—that ignorant child of the mother waiting to stir awake. "Something that can represent time and change instead of just space. Yet something that's eternal. Something that can be reexperienced. Like a play, maybe."

Bookshelves lined the walls of their current house's every room.

"A novel?"

The woman followed her husband's gaze, head tilting back in contemplation. "Maybe."

"Think of it!" Excited by his own idea as was his charming wont, her husband leapt to his feet and offered his hand. She permitted him to draw her upon her feet, to lure her into a swaying dance to the music that played on the speakers throughout their home's many rooms. "You and me. The story of our love. Together, forever—alive in the minds of all the readers who make it to the end, whether they love us or hate us."

"A viral existence."

"Yes, that's right." He twirled her, drew her back into his arms, held her rocking body tight. "A human being reads our novel, their mirror neurons fire up, and there it is, like magic. We're alive again, meeting again, loving again."

"The power of empathy."

"The most admirable of human qualities," he agreed, cheek pressed to the top of her head, lips turning against it to kiss. "Think of all the times we would have the privilege of meeting one another again. Of loving one another again. Truly for eternity."

"Until all the copies burn up."

"Not even that will stop us. Our consciousnesses will be outside time. Timeless together while here our story will have evolved, as viruses tend to...and we will emerge in this sordid world again, somewhere, in someone else whose receptive mind can harmonize with our love, and we will just like that be riding another's mirror neurons in new medium." Unable to resist the call of his lips any longer, she lifted her head and submitted to his kiss. He grasped her, tight, tighter, until, crying out in his arms, the woman broke away to rest her head against his heart.

"Maybe you're right...maybe that is the best idea. We never have to be apart that way. Not really."

"Not ever."

She smiled wider. "A spider needs a web, words to live on—you should let me make you into the words of the narrator."

"I always do wonder who third-person narrators are."

"The way you think. Oh, I'll miss it. I'll miss you. I love you."

"And I love you, but you won't miss me for long. Not even thirty years…and that's only consciously. After all! If I'm to be the words, you must be the spaces. If I'm to be the narrator, you are the protagonist. If I am to be time, then you—"

"Yes. Yes, that's right."

"Why, then you'll never be apart from me again, whether the woman you once were knows it or not. And in our state of eternal harmony, this sweet story of our convergence, we will have the pleasure of watching our human selves change, and meet, and grow, and learn to love eternally. Just as we have. Ah, my beloved…won't that be exquisite?"

His head bent: she received his kiss, returned it, flung her arms around his neck with a cry of immolating ecstasy.

And they both lived happily ever after.

ABOUT THE AUTHOR

Regina Watts is a tenth dimensional entity represented on this vibration of existence by her agent, editor, stenographer, and closest companion. She is the author of an increasingly large library of erotic titles ranging from standalone shorts to sprawling novels serialized in novella format; as you may suppose from *INDUSTRIAL DIVINITY*, she also writes more serious transgressive fiction. Check her out on twitter @WritesWatts, at her own website, or follow Painted Blind Publishing's website for more information about her work. If you enjoyed this book, please take the time to leave a positive review on Amazon—and don't forget to tell your friends!

ABOUT THE PUBLISHER

Painted Blue Publishing is an imprint of Painted Blind Publishing, a publishing house devoted to bringing you the finest in psychedelic literature. We here at PBP firmly believe there are many routes to consciousness expansion, and sex is one of them. It is our pleasure to produce works that challenge the American preconception equating literary erotica with pornography by default, but if you would like to see more from Regina Watts with a less erotic emphasis, we would encourage you to check out the works of M. F. Sullivan, Painted Blind Publishing's flagship author and devoted editor of Ms. Watts.

www.paintedblindpublishing.com

www.ingramcontent.com/pod-product-compliance
Lightning Source LLC
Chambersburg PA
CBHW021102110726
47900CB00007B/1999